The Probability of Us

BROOKE NOEL

For the women who aren't aspiring to be humble.
Be loud. Be bold. Be strong.

Content Warnings

Loss of a Parent (In the Past, Off-Page)
Alcoholic Parent
Attempted Sexual Assault
Frequent Language
Open Door Romance

One

There are plenty of bars in Hartford that are more popular —and much nicer—than The Dizzy Acorn. But ever since we stumbled across this cramped, hole-in-the-wall bar eight years ago, we haven't gone anywhere else.

From the outside, you wouldn't know this place was here. The skinny, brick building has windows on either side of a red door that give off townhouse vibes, and there's only a small sign beside the door with their logo—an acorn, with wisps of air curling around it, as if it was spinning, and the name in small block letters below it. It's on a quiet street, almost as if it wants to stay hidden, but most of the patrons have been coming here for years, just as we have.

I smile as I open the door and I'm hit with a wave of sound and humidity. It's a small room, and the décor only makes it feel more haphazard. The brick walls are covered with antique photos and rusty memorabilia that are barely visible in the warm, dim lighting. There are too many tables squeezed into the left two-thirds of the room, and since I made it here later than I'd originally planned, all of the free space between them and the bar on the right side of the room is packed with people waiting for tonight's entertainment to start.

There's a small open space at the back of the room that houses karaoke on Monday, trivia on Thursday, and on Friday—like tonight—a local want-to-be DJ. He's still setting up in the corner, and after catching a quick glimpse, I don't have high hopes for tonight's music. Any other night of the week, the space ends up used as a dancefloor that Ali loves dragging us onto.

I make my way through the crowd, pushing past groups of people shouting in order to hear each other, and hoards of people crowding the bar trying to catch the attention of one of the three bartenders who never appear stressed no matter how packed this place gets. One of them notices me in the crowd where I'm currently boxed in by a big group looking for more drinks and shoots me a sympathetic smile before turning to help the next guest. The workers here all know our group by now. If not by name, then because of how loud we can get.

"Excuse me," I yell, as I finally find space to push through the crowd. But instead of continuing, I freeze. My eyes catch on the small chalkboard hanging beside the bar and I gulp.

The Dizzy Acorn Trivia Ranking

I generally avoid looking at that part of the bar for this very reason—to avoid this very feeling. The top five rankings change frequently—the smeared chalk behind the names makes them harder to read each time they change. But the name in first place is still as clear as ever, and still hurts me even after all this time.

The Summers

I quickly avert my eyes and after a deep breath I keep moving, leaving all thoughts of him behind.

"Analise." Will sees me first and smiles, then three other faces turn my way, and I can't help my grin.

"Sorry I'm late," I say as I plop down in the empty chair, flustered from the throng of people. Ali slides me an ice-cold beer and I shoot her a grateful expression, taking an immediate sip and letting out a sigh that makes everyone chuckle.

"If you'd have just stayed at Triniti with us, you would've been on time," Sterling prods, lifting his hand to flick my slicked-back bun. I came here right from work, so I'm still in a plum pantsuit while everyone else had time to change into casual clothes.

Across the table, Ali and Trent's eyes go wide and they freeze, waiting for my reaction. Even Will looks hesitant behind Sterling and it makes me feel as pathetic as ever.

Will and Sterling have been together for two years now.

He left six years ago.

Will shouldn't know anything about him or what happened. Saying the name of the company we all met at shouldn't still trigger me.

So, I place a small smile on my face and pretend it doesn't.

I ignore their reactions, and instead say, "And I miss you guys every day."

I met Ali, Sterling, and Trent eight years ago. We were all in the Actuarial Department at Triniti Insurance—it was my first job out of college and Ali invited me out to lunch on my first day with her, Trent, and Sterling. We've been friends ever since.

But with *him*, it was different.

He became part of our group because of me. He was four years older than me, just beating out Trent as the oldest in our group, but quickly we all became inseparable. After he left, working at Triniti just wasn't the same. Staring at his desk all day sent me spiraling into a dark place, and everyone agreed leaving was the best thing for me. And since Hartford is the insurance capital of the U.S., it wasn't hard to find a new actuarial job.

It ended up being for the best since I was introduced to the concept of value-based care at that new job, and without it I'd never have ended up where I am now—Chief Actuary and Vice President of Transcend Consulting. Our firm specializes in the strategy and implementation of value-based care contracts which aim to improve patient outcomes, quality of care, and reduce costs by tying provider payments to the outcome of their patients, instead of just paying for the quantity of visits. I love the work I do—being at the forefront of innovation in the health insurance space makes me feel like I'm making a difference.

"You learn anything new about the company that's acquiring yours?" Ali asks, and my smile falls into a frown. I finish my beer and shoot Trent a grateful look when he offers to brave the crowd and grab another round for the table. "What's it called again?"

"Vi . . ." Sterling starts, but his voice trails off. "It definitely starts with a V."

"Vitality Health," I grumble.

I was shocked when Clara, the founder and president of Transcend, announced we were being acquired by a health-tech startup looking to center their strategy around value-based care contracts. Considering I manage most of the financial work for the company, and am responsible for strategy, it makes me nervous not having been a part of this deal. Clara is brilliant but has a tendency to make decisions based on emotions and skip over details—that's my specialty. It's why we make such a good team.

I met Clara through a friend of a friend in the business. Value-based care was still relatively new to the insurance world, and everyone was trying to figure out how to implement it effectively. When I left Triniti, I ended up in a role that developed the value-based care programs for that company and learned quickly. I believe in the work, and I'm good at it. Coming up with new strategies or how to implement them was something that I could do, and do well, and Clara wanted to ask me a few questions as she considered starting a consulting firm. We worked well together, and I knew that to make a larger impact, we needed to centralize these programs, so I took a job with her, and we started working out the logistics of a primary care model before moving onto other specialties.

The first few years were a grind. We not only had to

convince people that we could do it better and achieve better savings—but then had to prove it. It started as just a small team cranking out these designs and reporting, but as we met and surpassed our goals, more companies wanted to hire our services, or join our existing programs. We quickly became known as the best value-based care consulting company, and we grew like crazy. I take so much pride in what we created—it's beyond what either of us imagined and I'm worried this deal could change that.

"See, I knew it—started with a V," Sterling says, turning to beam at Will who pats his hand and kisses his cheek. Sterling met Will two years ago when we were bar hopping because The Dizzy Acorn was closed. They got engaged earlier this year and are planning a November wedding.

"Brilliant as always, my love," Will says, but rolls his eyes at me when Sterling's not looking. I start to laugh but cover it with a cough when Sterling looks over. He narrows his eyes and glances between us.

I clear my throat and keep talking before either of us gets in trouble. "But no, I haven't learned anything new about them." Even though a meeting about the merger is what made me late today. "Their executives are coming down for the next two weeks to help facilitate the transition, and since we don't have a C-suite of executives, Clara pulled me in to help show their CFO around while they're here."

"Is he at least cute?" Ali asks, brows raising, and I laugh.

"The only thing I know is his name is Mitch."

Trent returns with more beers and we each grab ours. We've been doing this long enough to know what everyone's favorite is. Blue Moon for me, Stella Artois for Ali, Guinness for Will, and Sterling and Trent are still making their way through the ever-changing list of IPAs.

"That has potential." She raises her beer toward me before taking a sip and I shake my head with a laugh before sipping my own.

"What's new with you guys?" I ask, directing the attention away from me. Talking about this deal sours my mood.

I listen to everyone's updates with a smile on my face, trying to avoid thinking about work, but without much luck. Sterling and Trent still work in the same actuarial department where we all met, but Ali switched over to finance after a few years. She switched before she and Trent *finally* got together, and it's good she did because Triniti is extremely strict about dating within the department. I learned that the hard way . . .

It's not until Sterling says, "Rob got fired," that I completely forget about everything else. The words are so unexpected that I almost spit out my drink and end up in a coughing fit when it goes down the wrong pipe.

Everyone watches me with worry, but my eyes are still wide with shock, and as soon as I can speak again, I say, "No fucking way." It comes out scratchy and hoarse and makes me cough all over again.

Trent nods, affirming the story and a smile grows on my face. With how many bullets Rob has dodged over his career, I'm surprised Triniti finally gave him the boot.

It's about time.

"What'd he do this time? Try to take credit for a man's work?" I snort, mostly joking.

But when I look between Trent and Sterling, who have both pressed their lips together, I realize it's not a joke at all. My mouth pops open when Trent finally says, "Basically, yeah."

Some of my smugness is gone, replaced with anger. "Right. Because when he did it to me, he just got moved to a different project and ended up getting promoted a few months later. But God forbid he steals a *man's* ideas. *That's* completely unacceptable."

"Oh, trust me," Sterling says, "everyone who's been here since it happened to you said the same thing."

Trent nods again and I do my best not to think about the man who stood up for me eight years ago when it happened. But after seeing the trivia board earlier, he's already fresh in my mind.

"It turns out the analyst whose ideas he stole is the nephew of the CEO, and that's the only reason he actually got fired for it," Trent adds, as Ali and I both say, "What?!" and Will leans back and sips his drink like he's watching a soap opera.

"I haven't heard that part," Ali says, wide-eyed.

"Rumors about it have been going around all day," Sterling says. "But it didn't get confirmed until we were heading out."

"What goes around, comes around," I mumble, and at that Ali raises her bottle.

"To that piece of shit finally getting what he deserves," she says, and we all clink glasses and laugh.

The music abruptly stops—somehow making it seem louder in here—the chatter bouncing around the room, signaling that the DJ is about to start. The entire crowd gets quieter in response, but when his set begins, my earlier assumption proves to be right. The music is not good, at all, making us all groan in response.

It's late enough that the bar is clearing out and the DJ is tearing down his set-up. The bar's usual playlist is blasting through the speakers again and we're all relieved to hear the mainstream pop music.

That may have been the worst set we've ever heard, and we've sat through some *rough* sets. It was so bad we considered leaving halfway through, but this is our spot, so instead, we turned it into a drinking game where we'd drink whenever it somehow got worse.

I haven't drank this much in a *long time*.

I'm talking to Sterling and Will, slightly slurring my words, when the next song starts playing over the speakers. With more people starting to leave the bar for the night, it's one of the first songs we can hear clearly.

"Oh no," Trent breathes. I assume he didn't want me to hear that, but I do, just as I realize what song is playing and I freeze.

"What is it?" Ali asks him, but her face blanches just as tears spring to my eyes. I'm not sober anymore and "Cruel Summer" by Taylor Swift steals all the breath from my chest. I can't ignore it anymore. I can't push him out of my head.

"Summer," I whisper, and it breaks the dam holding back my emotions. "I was *his* Summer."

I'm too drunk to care that I've sucked all the fun out of the air.

I can't breathe, and something has to fill my lungs.

"Why'd he leave me?" My lips tremble as tears start to roll down my cheeks. "Why didn't he ask me to go with him?"

Ali sighs sympathetically at me, but mumbles to Trent, "It's been a while since she's been drunk enough to bring him up. I thought we might've been past it."

They're all looking at me like those were rhetorical questions, but I want to know the answers. Not knowing is what's holding me back from moving on, because it still doesn't make sense to me, six years later.

"I thought he was going to propose," I cry, all the pain in my chest exploding with the words. It's been tearing me apart, over and over, since that day—like a volcano that starts spewing lava again just when you think it might be dormant. "But instead, he left. Who does that?"

"Oh, honey." Sterling puts his arm around me and I lean into him. I feel more like a child right now than someone about to turn thirty, but I let him comfort me until my tears slow.

"I'm a catch, right?" I look up at his deep-brown skin and bleached, buzzed hair, eyes-wide, desperate. "You'd marry me, wouldn't you, Sterling?"

My body shakes with his when he chuckles, and he reaches

out to grab my hand and raise it to his lips. "If Will hadn't asked me first, I'd be all yours."

He winks and I smile into his chest as my eyes flash up to Will, who's laughing warmly at the interaction. Sterling couldn't have found a better partner, or addition to our group.

"Thank you," I murmur.

Now that we're quiet, I can hear Ali and Trent's conversation as they talk amongst themselves.

"Maybe we should set her up with your one friend from college, babe," Ali says to Trent.

"You really want to set her up with someone when she still cries like he left yesterday?" he replies. "It's been, what, six years? I don't know if she's ever going to get over it at this point."

"She only cries over him when she's drunk," Ali says, and it's technically true. But just because I've stopped crying over it, doesn't mean I don't still think about it, about him. I've become desensitized to the pain his memory causes, but that doesn't mean the pain isn't there.

Maybe Trent's right, maybe I'll never get over it.

I don't want to hear what they're going to say next, so I cut in. "I can hear you, you know."

Ali gives me a sad, pitying smile. "Usually, when you get like this, you don't remember it the next day."

Again, not true. I *wish* I could forget, but I just pretend I don't remember because it's easier than having to talk about it with them sober and have them realize just how in love I still am with the guy that shattered my heart to pieces.

"Well, if that's the case, has he posted anything new on social media?" I ask. Ali doesn't like to tell me about it, but I know she keeps tabs on him for me. I refuse to download those apps just to stalk my ex, even though I almost have a thousand times.

She sighs, and because she thinks I won't remember, she tells me, "He mentioned something about flying this weekend, but no mention of where he's going."

The knot in my stomach loosens fractionally—it wasn't about another girl.

That's the update I'm dreading hearing.

As the song fades out, I force myself to stop talking about him and pretend my drunken brain has focused on a new topic, but really, it's just replaying every memory we have in this place. There's one that's playing more frequently than the rest and it's slowly fracturing every other thought I'm having. A few feet away from where we're sitting is where he kissed me for the first time and I don't think I'll forget that night for as long as I live.

After closing the bar down, we say goodbye to Trent and Ali who head to their new apartment on the West side of town, and Sterling and Will drop me off at my building on their way home —we both live in the Northern boroughs.

"Call us if you need anything," Sterling says before I walk into the small lobby. I smile gratefully at them and wave before heading straight to the elevator. Once I get in my room, I slip into one of the T-shirts in my middle drawer and pray that darkness is the only thing that finds me in my sleep.

But he's waiting for me, with his squinty-eyes and sunshine smile, just as he always is.

$$\mathcal{T}wo$$

AUGUST CURRENT DAY (MONDAY)

"Shit," I murmur as the Tupperware container full of blondies almost gets knocked out of my hand when I suddenly stop in front of Lola's Flower Shop. The two blue tulips I keep in the little white vase in my office started to wilt on Friday. I really should pick up new ones, but I'm already running late and have my hands full with these baked goods.

After Friday's fiasco, I didn't wake up until midday on Saturday. And even then, I didn't get out of bed until late afternoon. It was one of those weekends that doesn't happen as often as it used to when he first left, but still happens more than it should. My mind wouldn't shut up, dredging up every memory, starting with when we first met. Normally, I keep those memories locked away—buried deep. But the waves of emotions Friday night eroded their hiding place and exposed them again.

Late Saturday night, when I couldn't sleep, I resorted to making my comfort dessert—his favorite. I love blondies too, but they'll always be *his*.

It's been a while since I felt compelled to make them, and it feels like a step back, but everyone at the office loves them so I just pretend I baked for them.

I make a mental note to stop by the flower shop tomorrow morning as I rush to make the next crosswalk. The executives from Vitality will be arriving just after lunch and Clara texted me, letting me know there's a lot to go over before they do. Luckily, I can make quality coffee in the office because there's no time to stop at Kallia for a latte either. I splurged on an espresso maker last Christmas and still end up buying coffee most days, but it's nice to have it for days like this one.

The modern-looking, glass building glows in the morning sun, like a beacon, as I round the corner. I almost drop the blondies again trying to open the door, and nod at the security guard at the front desk as I head toward the elevator. Clara wanted to rent out a higher floor originally, but my fear of heights vetoed that idea so we ended up on the third floor.

The workspace embraces an open atmosphere. High-walled cubicles like all of my old jobs sported, have been traded out for long tables with multiple workstations. The offices are grouped in the middle of the floor—a blessing to me, because even the third floor makes my stomach queasy if I have to stare out a window all day. But as I weave across the floor, I feel many eyes following the blondies, and I make another mental note to lock my office door anytime I leave. I learned quickly that if I don't, they'll all be gone before lunch. The process also tends to go smoother when I'm there to moderate.

My baking quickly became a hit here, and word spreads fast whenever I bring a new treat in. Things have been hectic lately, so it's been a few weeks since I last baked. The war-ready look in the eyes of the people I pass makes me think it's only made the cravings worse.

I drop my bag in the cubby next to my desk, setting the blondies on the coffee cart next to my espresso machine, in front of the vase of flowers that needs replacing. I start the espresso machine and move around the room, gathering what I need for this meeting in the meantime.

People immediately file into the room and grab at the blondies. I cut everyone off at one slice and use the excuse that we need to save some for the guests coming later so they don't disappear in the first fifteen minutes. There are some grumblings at that rule—most people like to grab an extra to have with lunch—but everyone adheres to my guidelines.

As soon as the espresso is done, I add oat milk and a few pumps of mocha syrup, then gather my belongings, usher people out of the room, lock the office door, and head off to the meeting—hoping to get a few more answers than I currently have.

"All right, everyone understands the schedule?" Clara eyes the three of us after explaining the plan for the next two weeks. She looks stressed and exhausted, and the day has barely begun. I nod, along with Jason, our director of Partner Relations.

Serge, our Director of Implementation, asks, "So, what exactly is our role in this?"

Clara sighs, and I don't blame her. She's covered this in emails and multiple meetings over the past week, but Serge is the kind of person who's brilliant at his job but cares little for anything else. "I've paired each of you with one of their executives that best matches the line of work you do. I'm paired with the CEO, Peter. Analise is with the CFO, Mitch. Jason is with the CMO, Mackenzie. And you, Serge, are with the COO, Ben. What that means is you are that person's main point of contact during their stay here. You will show them around the office, answer their questions, and give them suggestions for what to do in town if they need them, etc. You are the main representative for our company to your partner, so represent us well."

I study the schedule again and notice there's supposed to be a group dinner tonight. "Do we have anything planned for dinner tonight yet?" Clara's eyes go wide at my question, so I'm assuming she completely forgot about the dinner. "I know of a great Italian place in Buena Park with a beautiful view of the city. We'll need people to drive there, but it'd be a great introduction to the city."

And it's been a while since I've been there. Just because it used to be *our* place, doesn't mean *I* can't still go. I won't let him ruin all my favorite things in this city.

But even as I think it, my chest gets tight.

"That sounds great. Please, book it. Thanks, Analise."

I nod, and after a reminder that we'll be meeting back in the main conference room at noon, Clara dismisses us. Jason tries to catch my attention, but I leave the room and move as fast as I can, ignoring the way his eyes drop to my ass as I stand, hoping he won't follow. I don't want to deal with him right now. I don't want to deal with him ever really, but there's only so much I can do about that.

When I get back to my office, I call *Il Piacere*. The woman who answers has a kind, light voice—a bright voice—and my smile falters. All I can see is a montage of the dates we shared there, of the brightness in his eyes as we talked and laughed a million different times. Eventually, my thoughts drift to the picture frame sitting on my shelf at home. The one I've never been able to get rid of no matter how much it hurts me to look at it now. Is it a good idea to go here tonight when memories of him haven't subsided yet?

"Hello?" the woman says when I don't answer her first greeting.

I shake my head. No more thoughts of him. It's time to stop letting him in.

"Hi," I finally say. "I'd like to make a reservation for eight people tonight, at six, if possible."

"You said eight people?"

"Yes, and out on the back patio if we could." The view overlooking the city is so beautiful. I think back to the first time I ate there. I don't know what made me more speechless that night—the view, or the fact that I was on a first date with *him*. I close my eyes and take a deep breath. I broke my own rule not ten seconds after I made it.

"We can make that work. What's the name for the reservation?"

"Analise Summers."

"Great, we look forward to serving you tonight."

Just as I'm hanging up, Jason comes stomping into my office without knocking and I internally groan as his eyes drop to my chest before he looks up at my face. His smile is big—it's always just a bit too big.

"Can I grab one of these?" he asks, beelining over to the half-empty container of blondies.

Be nice or he might go bother one of the other girls, I remind myself when I want to tell him where he can shove it. It's become a game of perfectly treading the line of keeping his attention on me without showing interest in him. He hasn't crossed any lines yet, but the way he so carefully places himself around me and the other girls makes me believe he'd have no problems crossing that line if given the opportunity.

I nod and smile, sickly sweet and forced as hell. "As long as there's enough left in case the Vitality execs want any."

He pauses before taking a bite, as if considering if it's safe to eat, and a muscle in my cheek twitches. I *wish* I poisoned the piece he chose. It'd make my life so much better if I didn't have to deal with him five days a week. He sniffs it and I fight an eye roll, then he shrugs and shoves half of the piece into his mouth. My face starts to twist into disgust as he chews with his mouth open, but I try to stop it from falling into totally horrified territory, although I am—totally horrified.

"Delicious as always," he says, while still chewing and I cringe as he flashes a thumbs-up.

"Thanks." I try to sound cheery, but I dread it every time

Jason comes to my office . . . because he doesn't ever leave. I honestly don't know how he gets anything done because he will waste hours in my office if I don't find a way to kick him out. A large part of me truly believes this is his passive aggressive way of trying to force me to go out with him. Like if he just doesn't go away, I'll cave and say "sure." What he doesn't realize is that the longer he sticks around the less I want to be near him.

"Did you go to The Dizzy Acorn this weekend?" he asks, and I regret the day I let it slip that I often hang out there. As if five days around him isn't enough, he constantly shows up and tries to ruin my weekends too. "I was there on Saturday but didn't see you."

"I have some work to get done before the execs come," I hint, ignoring his comment, but there's enough of an edge in my voice that he looks over at me and his face drops.

"Right, I guess that's my cue." He grabs another blondie, and I don't say anything because it might stop him from leaving. "See you later."

I let out a sigh of relief when he's gone and get to work. The Vitality execs sent over a strategic plan for our business post-acquisition, and a few points stuck out to me that I want to look into before they get here, particularly their salary projections—it's much too low for the amount of people we have now. And they're not showing any consulting fee projections in revenue, which is the core of what we do here.

Are they planning on absorbing us into their business and getting rid of the foundation of our company?

"Analise."

I look up to see Clara at the door, looking expectantly at me.

"Come on. They'll be here any minute."

My eyes widen when I check the clock in the bottom right corner of the computer screen. *How has that much time passed?* I save the files I was working on, close my computer, and lock my office again as I leave.

On the walk to the main conference room I ask, "Did you

take a look at the financial projections they sent over? It looks off to me."

"I can't stress about anything else right now," she says under her breath, walking so fast I have to speed walk to keep up. "If you find something substantial that needs to be addressed, please let me know, but otherwise, can you handle this?"

"Yes, of course." That was the plan anyways. "I just wanted to let you know. We should be paying close attention to anything they say regarding strategy."

She opens the glass door for us, and we take our seats on one side of the table. Jason and Serge take the seats around us—Jason chooses my side and scoots his chair closer to mine. I fight an eye-roll and shift closer to Clara. I'm not sure what it is—just general worry, the concerns about the financial documents, or something else entirely—but there's a seed of dread that has taken root in my stomach and is beginning to flourish. By the time Stacy, our administrative assistant, rounds the corner with the group in tow, I'm convinced that something is seriously wrong with me. I've never felt this way before.

Clara stands to greet them, and the rest of us follow her lead.

As the group gets closer to the conference room, I catch a glimpse of familiar, honey-colored hair and I don't have to see his face to know.

The source of my dread isn't something, it's someone. It's *him*.

He radiates light—his sunny disposition appears to glow. When he looks up and our eyes lock through the glass door, my legs stop working. I drop back into my seat, and I can't move. My arms are frozen, white knuckles gripping the edge of the table. I'm struggling to catch a breath through the onslaught of emotions and memories that feel like a thousand punches to my gut. And when his eyes skim past me as if he doesn't recognize me, my stomach twists. I think I'm going to be sick.

Clara gives me a strange look and whispers, "You okay?"

"Yeah, all good." I force deep breaths into my lungs and

slowly rise back up, keeping my hands on the table to steady me. Jason puts his hand on my arm and I pull away. My mind is pure chaos, and I'm not sure I keep it from my eyes, but I force my rose-colored lips into a smile to greet our guests.

His eyes run across everyone as he enters the room, and when they get to me they freeze for an extra second before looking away. No emotions play across his face. The corners of my mouth drop into something that can only barely pass as a smile.

What is he doing here? And does he really not recognize me?

We go through the introductions by pairing. First is Clara and Peter, their CEO. Jason and Serge are paired with Mackenzie, the CMO, who goes by "Mac," and Ben, their COO. When there's only me and him left, I realize what happened.

Clara was wrong.

The CFO's name isn't Mitch, it's Warren Mitchell.

And as he shakes my hand with no flicker of recognition running across his face, I think these next two weeks might just kill me.

Three

MAY 8 YEARS AGO

I look down as I stand twelve stories above ground.

From under my feet, the sidewalk stares back, taunting me with visions of what my sprawled out, jagged body will look like if the pane of glass beneath me decides to give out. My breath quickens, and I swear I hear the splintering sound of glass. I jump back onto the worn, navy-blue carpet as a shudder travels from the tips of my freshly manicured toes to the ends of my freshly cut hair that falls in soft, brown waves to my shoulders.

I wanted to look nice on my first day of work, but now I regret the extra blush I put on because it'll only exaggerate the flush on my cheeks from my fear. I've been preparing myself mentally to work on the twelfth floor. The day of my interview, I spent ten minutes in the bathroom trying to calm my breathing, so I didn't seem like a crazy person, but the room they put me in had a wall of windows. I tried to focus on the questions they asked me, but a few minutes in, the interviewer asked what was wrong.

They were kind about it, and switched sides with me, so I did the rest of the interview from behind their desk, the windows at my back. It's partly why I decided to accept the offer here—even though the other company's office was only on the second floor of their building.

But it seems weeks of trying to prepare for this wasn't enough.

My focus narrows to a loose strand of carpet as I try to convince my body that I'm on solid ground. Slowly, the fuzziness in my head and swaying feeling start to fade. But just as my heart rate slows down to a normal rate, the image of my mangled body flashes in my head again. My eyes snap shut and my hands clench into fists. I focus on taking slow, deep breaths, over and over, until the movement of my chest is all I can feel.

"Not a fan of heights, I take it."

I jump at the words, then quickly jump back again when I realize I landed closer to the foot-wide pane of glass at the edge of the floor.

"They're not my favorite." I smile nervously at Alison, who's been tasked with giving me a tour of our department's floor. "Why, exactly, is this floor a foot wider than the rest of the building?"

She shrugs and I hope one day I'll be as unaffected by it as she is. "I don't think anyone knows. It could've been a mistake when they built it"—*Mistake?!* That word does nothing to help my fear—"or the architect was going for an inverted tiering effect. A handful of random floors have the same thing."

And of course, I got stuck on one that did.

Alison's eyes soften as if she understands what I'm thinking, and her smile turns sympathetic. "Don't worry, your desk doesn't have a view of the windows. Come on, let's get you settled in."

I nod and follow her, watching the people who are now my coworkers as they carry on with their day. I conclude that a bunch of them are in the same meeting after seeing the same PowerPoint slide on a fifth person's screen—the numbers and figures, meaningless to me. Others work silently, but in one cubicle, two girls sit side by side, chatting away. There's a spreadsheet open on the computer, but it appears they're gossiping instead of working. One of them glances up at me as I pass by and I quickly avert my eyes.

I wipe my sweaty palms on the new, black business trousers I'm wearing and try to keep a smile on my face even though all I feel is intimidation. This place is a well-oiled machine, and I don't even know where I'm supposed to sit.

"This one's you," she says as we approach a group of four cubicles in the back corner of the floor. "The back two are still empty so it should be pretty quiet over here." She gestures to the front left desk of the group.

Compared to the desk across from mine—that's full of basketball posters, a few pictures, and a mini basketball hoop hanging off the back wall of the cube with a container of mini, foam basketballs—my desk looks dull and lifeless with everything in the same beige color. I'm already trying to mentally design my cube, and make a shopping list for what to pick up after my first paycheck comes in.

"I'll give you some time to settle in. Your station should be set up already, but you'll have to follow the directions on the paper there to log in and set up your computer. I sit right over there." She points to a group of desks halfway across the room. "If you have any questions just stop on by."

"Thank you." I'm too overwhelmed to say much else right now so I take a deep breath. Does everyone feel this underprepared on their first day of work? I hope it's not only me.

"Hey, Alison?" I say as she's starting to walk away. I wasn't going to ask, but panic got the best of me because I didn't bring any food with me.

"You can call me Ali." She smiles back at me with such kindness I know I'd like to be her friend.

"Ali," I repeat, a smile on my face. "What do people usually do for lunch around here?"

Her eyes light up like she's realizing she meant to bring this up herself. "I usually have lunch with two others from the department. You're welcome to join us if you'd like."

"I'd love that." My stomach settles fractionally now that I know I won't be alone *all* day.

"Perfect, we'll come grab you around twelve-thirty."

After Ali leaves, I sit down and rummage through the three drawers in the filing cabinet under my desk and the small overhead cabinet in the corner, cataloging what supplies I have and what I still need. I only find a half-gone pad of sticky notes, a small notebook, some paper clips, and a pen that doesn't write. Underwhelmed with what I find, I turn to the computer and start working through my step-by-step manual.

I manage to log into the computer and am working on setting up some of the applications when footsteps grow closer and soft noises of papers shuffling and a laptop getting set down come from the cubicle beside me. I quickly drop my hand from my face and try to sit normally, but it's not quick enough.

"Come here often?" a male voice says, and I can hear the smile behind the words.

When I look over, he's leaning against the opening of the cubicle across from mine—his cubicle—with an amused grin on his face and an eyebrow quirked in curiosity. My cheeks heat, thinking about how my face had just been pinched in concentration, lips pursed and twisted into a frown. Not to mention, my head had been resting on my index and middle fingers causing my cheek to bulge out the sides. This easily tops the list of worst first impressions.

He has to be about six feet tall, and even in a long-sleeved button-up I can see the sinewy muscles in his arms that are currently crossed across his chest. His honey-colored hair appears as if he'd just run his hands through it in stress and forgot to smooth it back out. Freckles spot his face, as if a painter speckled them on with no prior intention, but they all landed in perfect chaos across his nose and cheeks, and his butterscotch eyes shine brighter than the sun outside the windows I thankfully can't see from my desk—I was relieved to find that Ali was correct about that statement.

The humorous tinge to his smile and playful look in his eyes clues me in that he's purposefully being ironic by using a pickup line I've only ever heard in a bar, in an office setting, so I play along with a shrug. "I'm new to town and this place came highly recommended, so I thought I'd check it out."

His face lights up with delight and a hint of surprise, and I forget to breathe for a second. "And what do you think so far?"

"It's a little too far off the ground for my tastes, but the people are great so far." I smile when he chuckles, the sound coating me like liquid sunshine—warm and bright. "But ask me again in a few weeks, my mind might change by then."

"About the height or the people?"

The corner of my mouth quirks up. "What about you? Is this a favorite spot of yours?"

"It is now," he says, smiling so big his cheeks scrunch up, causing his eyes to get all squinty. He steps closer and reaches out his hand. "Warren Mitchell."

"Analise Summers." I take his hand and try to ignore the flutter in my chest, but his smile is contagious. "Looks like I'll be your new neighbor."

Four

AUGUST CURRENT DAY (MONDAY)

"And this is my office," I say as I finish the tour of the floor. Clara had suggested we each walk our respective executive around while she and Peter meet in the conference room. I unlock my door and he silently follows me in, not having said a word the entire time. "If you ever forget where to go, or need something, feel free to stop by. I think we'll have the four of you set up in the conference room we started in, but you're welcome to hang out here while Clara and Peter finish up their meeting."

He just stands there, feet away from me, staring. Those eyes that I used to know better than anything are drowning me—I can't look away. I'm being sucked in and it's suffocating. My lower lip begins to tremble. I don't know how to look at someone who once looked at me with love but is now devoid of any emotion without crying. I turn away, eyes closing and hoping this is all just some bad dream, or a cruel joke. This is *really* fucking cruel.

"Would you like some coffee while we wait?" I don't wait for his answer to begin making two cups, because even after all this time, I never stopped buying the syrup he likes.

My hands shake as I make the drinks, and I can feel him watching. When I'm almost done, a warm presence steps up behind me and I gasp when fingertips graze against my arm. I spill some of the coffee and drop the stirrer in the cup. My hands move to the edge of the cart to steady myself.

"Analise," he whispers, inches from my ear. My eyes close. The way he says it makes it obvious he knows exactly who I am. A stuttering cry of a breath comes out of me as I think of all the times he touched me like that in the bed we shared.

His voice used to do something to me. The way he'd say my name was a holy experience. I always thought if he ever came back, anger would be my leading emotion, but my body reacts as if he never left. Maybe it's how much I've been thinking of him the past few days, or how I never got the closure I needed to move on, or the things I've come to learn since he left, but I want to reach out and hug him instead of wanting to punch him.

I take a deep breath. "So, you *do* remember me?" My voice is nowhere near steady.

"You think I could forget you that easily?" he replies, his voice pained. "Do you still not know how unforgettable you are?"

The initial hit of relief I felt fades away with those words. Anger might not have been the first emotion I felt when I saw him, but it's all I feel now.

How can he say that after being gone for so long?

"It seemed pretty easy for you for the last six and a half years," I let slip with enough bitterness that I can feel him flinch.

"I never forgot you," he says, softly.

His words and his closeness are too much for me. I turn, hand him his coffee and move to my seat so there's a desk between us. Something solid to keep the distance.

"It's okay, we don't have to have this conversation," I say, more so because I'm scared of what he might say—why he left. I motion for him to sit in the chair on the other side of the desk. "I'm under no delusions that you came back for me, it's just business. We're both professionals here; we can manage to work together for the next two weeks, then you'll go back to D.C., and I'll stay here, and it'll be as if it never happened."

"If that's what you want." The corners of his mouth turn down and his eyes have lost their usual glow.

I almost laugh. What *I* want? *Now* he cares what I want?

What I wanted didn't matter to him back then. He didn't even ask me what I wanted back then. Because what I wanted was to be where he was, to go where he went, but he obviously didn't want me.

I gesture for him to sit again. He starts to move but his eyes catch on something, focusing back on the coffee bar and light comes back to his face.

"Blondies?" he asks, walking over to grab one. He searches for the biggest piece, the one I always left for him because I could never cut the slices evenly. Part of me hopes that Jason took that piece earlier, but another part of me hopes it's there waiting for him because it was always only his. "It's almost like you knew I was coming."

I huff out a laugh. "Because me quite literally getting knocked on my ass by the tidal wave of shock that hit me when you walked around that corner wasn't indication enough of my knowledge on the matter." I forgot how easy this was, how easy *we* were. Slipping back into this banter with him feels like slipping into a favorite sweater. It overwhelms me with a comfort I haven't found since the day he left. "But you . . . *you* were the picture of unaffected indifference," I continue and his face scrunches up as he takes a seat. "You obviously weren't surprised at all."

"Well, I did receive an agenda on Friday that named my point of contact for the next two weeks," he says and my cheeks warm because I knew that was sent out, but at the time, I didn't know it was him on the receiving end. "I choked on my coffee, which, might I note, wasn't half as good as the one you just made me, when I saw your name beside mine."

I stare at him with an incredulous look on my face.

"I'm serious," he pleads, still able to read me like a book. "After I choked, I ended up spitting it out all over my monitor and keyboard. To make matters worse, Peter walked into my office as it was spraying out of my mouth. Ask him, he'll corroborate my story."

I'm holding back laughter, but my ever-inconvenient imagination produces, what I assume is, a perfect reenactment of the event and I burst out laughing. "All right, all right, I believe you. That does sound like you."

His mouth pops open and he grabs a small piece of the blondie in front of him and throws it at me. I'm already laughing but I manage to catch it and toss it into my mouth.

His liquid-sunshine laugh joins mine, and for a moment I forget the past six and a half years happened—he never left and we're just two lovers laughing together. It's easy. It's fun. It's *right*.

But the past six and a half years *did* happen. He left, and while I understand why he did, there's still so much I don't understand about what happened to us. The weight of those questions sits on my lungs and steals my breath; my smile fades and it gets hard to breathe again. I drop my hands into my lap and squeeze my leg just above the knee, trying to distract myself from the pain stabbing through my chest with no luck.

Warren's face drops and he leans forward as if he's about to comfort me, then hesitates, thinking better of it, and leans back in his chair. Pain is etched across his face—not in a way that most would see, but to someone that's memorized every millimeter of his skin and knows every expression in his repertoire, it's as clear as a sunny, summer day.

"I tried to look you up, to double check if it was you," he says softly and I look up, getting trapped in those butterscotch eyes that never fail to make me melt. "But I see you're still determined to stay off social media."

"You looked me up?" I hate how much hope there is in my voice. How much hope I feel.

His cheeks turn rosy. "Many times. I kept hoping you'd appear, but you never did." He looks down. "So, I had to resort to obsessively stalking Ali's accounts to catch anytime she'd post a picture with you in it."

My mouth drops open, but he glances up and continues talking before I can say anything. "Since you refuse to even download any of those apps, I'm assuming you haven't looked me up."

Something about the way he says it has my heart twisting. There's disappointment in his voice and I want to dispel it, so I skip the banter and jump right to the truth. "I have Ali keep tabs on you and give me reports."

My lips snap together—I can't believe I actually admitted that to him. *Why* would I tell him that?

I shouldn't want to dispel his disappointment. I shouldn't be feeling bad for him.

Heat rushes to my cheeks and I'm sure it shows itself as deep red embarrassment. I have to look away. Luckily, I look at the door and catch Jasmine, one of the newest employees on my team, walking away, assuming I'm in a meeting. I get her attention and wave her in.

"Oh, blondies this week." Her eyes light up when she sees the treats. "I've been waiting for you to bake these again."

Warren's eyes light up in curiosity and he looks over as she grabs a square, but his eyes snag on a different feature of the coffee cart this time—the flowers. The corners of his mouth tug down when he spots the two blue tulips that are wilting in the little white vase. I really wish I stopped at Lola's this morning.

Better yet, I wish I didn't buy them at all. Old habits sure do die hard.

"Did you need me for anything?" I smile at Jasmine, wanting to focus on anything but all the ways I've already given away how much I still think about him.

"I just wanted to let you know that I got that code working we were discussing on Friday." She smiles with pride. "You were right, it was an issue in the join statement between the claims table and the membership table. I'm just going to validate it one more time and I'll have the final analysis sent to you by the end of the day."

"I look forward to seeing it. Thanks, Jasmine."

She smiles and practically skips away. When I turn back to Warren his eyebrows are raised. I press my lips together and ask, "What?"

"She worships you."

I blink a few times, shocked by the words. "What are you talking about? She's just doing her job."

"Oh, come on. I used to work with you, I know what you're like. You're a brilliant teacher, and even before you were a manager, people would come to you for help first. Trust me when I say that girl thinks you walk on water, and I'd bet the rest of your team feels the same way." His smile is reminiscent and mine wobbles between happy and sad. "They're lucky to have you."

I settle for rolling my eyes, but a flutter ignites in my chest at the way he's talking about me. "You're grossly over exaggerating."

"Fine, don't believe me." He shrugs and takes another bite of the blondie. It looks like he has to actively stop himself from making a noise at the taste. "I'm only telling the truth, though."

I try to hold back the smile that only he can pull out of me, but when I catch a glimpse of his bright smile, mine shines through too.

This is bad, this is *really* bad. I can lie to myself as much as I want, but I've been talking to him for all of fifteen minutes and that pull is back. He was once the sun, *my* summer sun, and I'm already caught back in his gravitational pull.

I jump when my phone dings with a new text, already forgetting where I am and what I'm doing here. My lips pull into a frown at the message on my screen—confirmation of the reservations for tonight. This is about to get interesting, that's for sure.

"Something wrong?" he asks before I've even looked at him.

"Not exactly," I say, but look up hesitantly. "Before I knew you were coming, I made reservations at Il Piacere for the group." His eyes widen and his breath catches. I take that as a bad sign. "I can cancel and find somewhere else if it'll be too weird."

"No, keep it," he chokes out, swallowing and blinking until his eyes aren't glassy. "I've missed that place."

My chest constricts at the emotions behind those words and all I can do is nod.

It's a welcome reprieve when he has to go to the conference room. My mind is racing, my thoughts are all over the place. Is this real life? It can't be. What are the chances that he works for the company that's buying mine?

But really, what *are* the chances?

$$Five$$

A shiver runs through me when he steps beside me. As everyone takes in the view from the top of the hill where the restaurant sits for the first time with awe, we both take a deep breath. It's different being back here with him, being here feels right again. The surrounding park is where he asked me out for the first time, and this restaurant was our first date—it was our spot.

"How did you find this place?" Jason asks, standing on my other side, so close that his hand brushes against my thigh and I subtly step closer to Warren just to get further away from him. "I had no clue this was even here."

Small, conspiratorial smiles bloom on both Warren's and my lips as I answer. "A friend showed it to me."

Thankfully our table is called, and I don't have to answer any more questions. But as we take our seats, I quickly realize there's nothing to be thankful for. I don't think I could be in a more uncomfortable spot if I tried. I'm sitting between Warren and Peter, with Jason directly across from me. And since Warren and I are in the middle of the table, we're squished together tightly.

Our arms keep brushing and it's threatening to make me lose my shit in front of everyone.

Polite conversation flows until everyone has a menu, then it's obvious everyone's hungry because it gets eerily quiet.

Warren leans toward me and whispers, "Did they get rid of the lobster tortellini?"

I laugh softly at the panic in his voice. "They removed it from the menu, but they still stock all the ingredients so it can still be ordered. Like a secret menu item."

"Oh, thank god, I've been dreaming of that dish since I moved."

Since you left me, I want to correct.

A flash of pain runs through me, but I smile. "You always did say it ruined all other pasta for you."

He laughs, loud enough to draw attention to us, and Serge, who is sitting on Warren's other side—who we didn't realize could hear us the entire time—says, "Do you two know each other?"

Jason's head snaps over to us. His eyes lock onto Warren and narrow, sizing him up like he's suddenly been revealed as an enemy. *Fuck me.* Figures we couldn't even make it twelve hours without everyone figuring out we knew each other. Not that it was a secret, but it was a hectic day and there wasn't a good time to bring it up.

"Yeah, I used to live here in Hartford," Warren says.

"We both worked at Triniti for a few years together," I add quickly and notice that Peter has a smile on his face. If Serge heard us, Peter must've been able to as well, but he doesn't look surprised. Maybe Warren wasn't lying when he said Peter walked in as he spit out his drink on his computer, and maybe he told him . . . What *did* he tell him?

That he knows me? That we used to date? That we used to live together? That, to me, he's the one that got away, and I wonder daily what life would be like if he hadn't left?

Although, Warren doesn't know the last part so he probably wouldn't have said that.

"Why didn't you tell us you knew him?" Clara asks, and I laugh.

"Because *you* told me his name was Mitch, not Warren Mitchell so I didn't know it was him until they walked through the door."

She smiles sheepishly, as if just now noticing she told me the wrong name. "Sorry, I misheard on the call."

Everyone laughs at that, and the topic fades away into new ones. I let out a silent sigh of relief that we moved on, but Jason doesn't stop watching us all night.

As everyone begins to pile back into the two cars we took to the restaurant, I hang back. "I think I'm just going to walk home."

It's been too long since I've walked through the park, and it's prettiest at night, with twinkling lights scattered in the trees and the view of the city becoming a beautiful sea of lights. Even though it's an extremely long walk, it's worth it.

Jason's face turns to stone. "It's not safe to walk home alone this late."

I almost laugh at the irony. I'd feel safer walking home alone than being alone with him.

"I'll walk with you." Warren moves to stand next to me and I smile. I was hoping he'd volunteer to come. We should talk outside of a work environment—sooner rather than later.

Jason's face contorts into rage and his voice comes out gruff and aggressive. "I'll come too."

I roll my eyes and hope that I'm far enough from the street-lamp that the shadows hide it. "You drove, Jason. You have to take them back."

I begin to wonder if this was subconsciously my plan the

whole time, because something pushed me to make sure Jason was the second driver today. I even pulled the "I want to ride in your Tesla, it's so cool" card. That's what sealed the deal. Little does he know that I spent the whole ride focused on Warren, who was in the backseat with me, instead of on his precious Tesla.

After grunting and grumbling, Jason finally gets in the car, and everyone drives away. Warren falls into step beside me and muscle memory has us turning down the path to the bench—*our* bench—without a word.

"I've missed this place," he whispers when we're overlooking the city from our favorite spot.

"Like a sea of stars," I whisper back and see the corners of his mouth curl up from the corner of my eye.

"Exactly."

The brush of his hand against mine is as soft as his voice, but it hits me like a bus—head-on, going sixty miles per hour. All the breath leaves me, and I stumble a step away from him. This is too much—him being here, how quickly it feels normal, how much I still want him, how angry I still am. But for some reason the words that bubble up and blurt out of me are, "Are you seeing anyone?"

He chuckles uncomfortably. "I see your small talk hasn't improved."

The amount of panic that washes over me is embarrassing. "Is that a no?" I squeak, feeling foolish for asking, but knowing it'll drive me mad to not know.

"Analise . . ." His voice is small. "Is this really a good idea?"

"Please." I'm breathing heavier. "If I don't ask now, it'll be on my mind all night. I just need to know, so I can stop wondering."

He eyes me a moment longer before saying, "No, I'm not seeing anyone," and I let out a silent sigh of relief.

"Okay," I whisper to myself, nodding.

Why do I care so much?

Scratch that, I know the answer to that one. The better question is: Why did I let him *see* that I care so much? Why did I bring this up?

It gets quiet between us again and we turn to go.

After a few steps he stops walking and hesitates. "Are *you*?"

I don't know what makes me say it—if it's being here where he first asked me out, where we had so many date nights—where our fall out began—but I tell the truth. "No, it seems I never quite got over the man who broke my heart six and a half years ago."

He looks up at me, shock and then pain flashes across his face. I look down, a sad smile on my face.

"Ana—"

"I'm sorry," I cut him off, not sure I can handle hearing my name from his lips again when all I can think of is all the times he whispered that name against my own skin. "We don't have to talk about this—we *shouldn't* talk about this. You're only here for two weeks. You're leaving again. We broke up. We—"

"Analise." He cuts off my rambling of why this isn't a good idea. Or at least the reasons I'm trying to convince myself that this isn't a good idea.

"Stop," I practically scream, on the verge of tears. "You need to stop saying my name like that."

"Like what?" He's taken aback, completely unaware of what he's doing, and it only makes it hurt more.

"Like you did back then," I say as the first tears fall down my cheeks. "Like it's a plea. Like it's a promise. Like it's a prayer. Like I'm your salvation."

"I—" He shakes his head like he can't comprehend my words, but his eyes tell me that he feels them. They reflect a deeper truth that he might not have discovered yet. "I don't know what to say to that."

"You don't have to say anything." I suck in deep breaths until I have better control of my emotions. "You're here. We have to work together these next weeks. We can keep it professional."

I don't know who I'm trying to convince, him or me. Maybe the more I say it, the more likely it is to be true.

He still looks like he's fighting an internal battle where both sides are taking severe casualties, but he follows when I start walking again.

"So, tell me everything about D.C. How do you like it there?" I break the silence after we walk halfway back without speaking.

"It's amazing. It's beautiful." His face lights up in a way it never has when talking about Hartford. "In the spring, the cherry blossom trees bloom and it's unlike anything you've ever seen. There's this path along the Tidal Basin that passes the Jefferson Memorial, and the cherry blossoms form a canopy over the trail. You would love it. It's breathtaking."

"Seems like you have a new favorite season," I say, softly.

He shrugs, one corner of his mouth pulling down into a frown. "Well, summer hasn't been the same since I left."

My body gets stiff. Each step feels foreign, like I no longer remember how to act like a normal person. Like his words have short-circuited my brain and stolen my ability to function . . . and my will to keep things professional between us.

Why is he saying things like that? *He* left *me*. He walked away from us and never gave us a chance to make things work.

What is happening?

"What happened to the company you originally went to work for out there?" I ask, desperate to shift the conversation to anything else. And because I'm curious. Vitality wasn't a name I recognized, and I never heard that he changed jobs.

He glances over at me for a moment before answering. "I'm sure you remember that they had this incredible vision for the company, and that's what sold me on them. But a few years in, things weren't quite working out as planned and the company kept changing directions just to stay afloat. It wasn't the same, and I didn't believe in the direction it went." He looks sad as he talks, and I remember how bright his smile was whenever he talked about it back then. "Peter was actually my boss there—it's how we met. We both had the same vision for what we wanted to achieve, so we took a risk and tried to do it ourselves. It took us over a year to develop the business plans and get funding, but here we are."

"And that vision is value-based care?"

"That vision is creating a system that puts the members at the center. That makes sure people get the right care, at the right time, for the right price. And when we saw the impact Transcend has been able to make on the markets it's in with value-based care, it was a no-brainer to reach out and see if we could team up." He stops walking with a laugh and turns to look at me. He runs his hand through his hair, leaving it only slightly messed up, but in a way that makes him look so much more attractive. "Why does this feel more like an interrogation than a conversation?"

"Because it is." I cross my arms across my chest and turn to face him, trying to keep my boss bitch face on and not get distracted by thinking about running my hands through his hair. "I wasn't involved in the negotiations or discussions for this deal, so I'm trying to figure out what your intentions are here."

A smile pulls at his lips and he drops his voice. "Your dad asked me that too, the first time I met him."

All of the air in the world disappears with the words. It feels like someone just took a knife and plunged it into my stomach. I'm gasping for air, clinging onto reality with a shaky grip.

He doesn't know.

I mean why would he? I never reached out, even though it would've been easier to run back to the arms I always felt safest in when my life flipped upside down. Instead, I dealt with it on my own, because I'm not the kind of girl who's going to beg someone to stay in my life if they choose to leave. I had assumed that someone would've told him over the years though. It's a stark reminder that even though I had my friends, I didn't have him.

Hands landing on my shoulders ground me and I look up to

find wide eyes full of worry staring back at me. I step back out of his reach and take a deep breath.

"Just so you know." I jump back to the previous conversation without explanation. "I don't care that I know you. I'm going to do what's best for my people and the company I've spent five years building into something I'm so fucking proud of."

He narrows his eyes that are still full of concern, but eventually just sighs. "I wouldn't expect anything less." A small, sad smile rests on his face as he looks me in the eyes and adds, "I guess you finally found your thing in this business that you're passionate about."

I blink, flashbacks of that Labor Day, when we walked around the city, talking about our lives and why we chose this profession before we ended up on the hill in Buena Park where he finally asked me out, cutting in and out of my vision. He remembers that? I just nod, unable to speak and unsure what I'd even say if I could, and start walking again.

I keep asking him questions about his new town, his new life, even though every answer cuts right through me. But I want to know what he's been up to, what he left me for, and I kind of despise the fact that it might've been worth it. He might love his new life more than he ever loved me.

I lead us back to the hotel the executives are staying at and his face twists in confusion when I start to say goodbye. "You're going to walk the rest of the way by yourself?"

He must be remembering our place on the east end of town— that would be a long, concerning walk to take right now by myself. But I don't live there anymore, I haven't for years. "I'm in Solana now, just down the street."

His eyes widen with surprise at the name; it's a building we always used to love. It's the place where we wanted to live, together. "How fancy."

I smile but it's half-hearted. "Well, goodnight," I say, giving a half wave and starting to turn away because I'm not sure how to act with him. In some ways, it's the same, but in others, so horribly different.

He laughs, a big, real laugh and my eyes close at the sound. "Can we not be friends?"

"Friends?" I turn to look at him and his eyes are deep pools sucking me down into the depths of his panic and desperation.

"You do know what the word means, right?" he teases, and I shoot him a glare. "We were always friends, weren't we?"

"We were never just friends, Warren." I shake my head, hating that I'm saying this, but there's a difference between being friends and what we were before we dated. "I knew I was going to love you from the first moment we met, and I'm pretty sure you've said the same thing before. We've never been *just* friends. I don't think I know how to just be your friend."

His face falls so fast it feels like a weight dropping on me, crushing me. His voice is so small when he speaks, it's practically nothing. "Can we try?"

My eyes close, my breathing gets hard. I've wanted so many times to hear him say those words, to try to make things work, but to hear them now, knowing he wants to try, but as only friends, isn't what I want at all. But we have to work together for the next two weeks—there's no avoiding it—so I sigh, and even though each word feels like acid in my throat, I say, "Yes, we can try."

His blinding smile has a tear forming in my eye and before I know what's happening his arms are around me and I'm pulled into his chest. I don't know if he realized what he was doing until it happened because we both freeze. But then his arms are tightening around me and it's like every single pore on his body is reaching out to me, pulling me in, trying to absorb me so I'll never leave again. Or maybe it's my body doing that to him.

I suck in a breath when his hand moves into my hair and holds me against him, but then I breathe in his scent and I'm unravelling in his arms. He smells the same, bright and warm and comforting, like the perfect summer day. I can't handle it. I push away from him and stumble back a few steps. There are tears in my eyes and there's pain in his—both of us breathe heavy. I can see the rise and fall of his chest through his perfectly tailored suit and I have to force my eyes away from how well he's filled out over the years.

"Goodnight, Warren," I say.

He dips his head towards me. "Goodnight, Analise."

A shiver runs through me because he still says my name like it's something to be worshipped. I can see the moment he realizes he must've done it again because his whole face shifts into sadness. "See you tomorrow?"

I only nod, then turn and walk away. I stop when I get around the corner to catch my breath.

What is he doing to me?

When I get home, I flop down on my bed and groan. I pick up my phone to text Ali, but there's already one waiting for me.

ALI

So, was Mitch cute? I want to hear everything.

I laugh, forgetting that she has no idea who Mitch really is—that there is no Mitch.

ME

Kallia tomorrow, early. I have A LOT to tell you.

ALI

I'll be there!

$$\mathcal{S}ix$$

My eyes flash to Warren's desk for the hundredth time in the past hour, lips turning down into an even deeper frown.

He was out all last week for a cousin's wedding in Maryland, but he's supposed to be back today. I even triple checked his Outlook calendar to make sure it hadn't changed to *Out of Office* today too. But it's already lunch time and there hasn't been any sign of him yet. I sigh and lock my computer before heading over to meet Ali, Trent, and Sterling. After that first day I joined them for lunch, it was like I'd been here all along. I was added to their group chat, joined them for lunch daily, and spent many evenings with them.

Ali is the leader of the group, making the decisions and rallying everyone together. Sterling is the life of the group—every day is a party with him around. He's everyone's biggest cheerleader and I've never seen him without a smile on his face. On the other hand, Trent is the quiet, reserved one. He watches over everyone like a mother hen and does his best to keep Ali and Sterling out of trouble. They've told me I'm the opinionated one, the one who always speaks her mind and will fight to the death with words for the people I care about.

Ali and Sterling are usually the ones getting us into interesting, and sometimes heated, situations, and Trent hates any confrontation, so I'm the one who gets us out of them. Our differences balance the group dynamic. I've never left one of our outings without having a new story to tell and laughing more than I ever did before I met them.

Lunch today was no different, although today, all attention turned to me when I finally admitted what had me distracted after Ali badgered me most of the hour. That spiraled into Ali and Sterling going back and forth with "I knew it," and "I told you," and "Should we invite him out with us?"

For once, I'm just as quiet as Trent is. Even as we head out, Ali and Sterling continue to brainstorm ways to find out if he likes me too or set us up.

"Isn't the quarterly department meeting today?" Trent asks on the walk back to the office and Ali and Sterling stop walking.

"I totally forgot about that," Ali says, wide-eyed.

Sterling checks his phone. "It'll be close, but we should have enough time."

They nod and take off in the opposite direction of the office.

"What's going on?" I look to Trent for answers and find his eyes on Ali's retreating form. I glance away before he snaps out of it. He doesn't know, but I often catch his eyes clinging to Ali when he thinks none of us are watching.

He keeps his head down as he starts to follow them, and I follow his lead down a road I've never walked before. We pass a building with a red door that, at first glance, appears to be a house, but then I catch sight of a logo—an acorn with what looks like wind swirling around it. It looks like there's a bar inside, so I make a mental note of the name—The Dizzy Acorn—to tell the others about later. We'll have to check it out sometime.

"It's their tradition to get coffee from Stella Lei before the quarterly meetings. They dragged me along last quarter when I was new, and now, you're part of the tradition too." Trent smiles. He might not be as high energy as Ali and Sterling, but you can see how much he likes being a part of the adventures they create.

We reach Stella Lei and my jaw drops. It's a high-end jewelry shop showcasing diamonds of every size and shape, but off to the right there's a small coffee counter with a gigantic diamond chandelier overhead where Ali and Sterling are grabbing the four coffees the barista just finished making. Even the coffee cups are extravagant here—white with black polka dots, and the sleeves are blush pink with the Stella Lei logo in a beautiful teal that matches the lid.

I don't have time to take it all in before Ali shoves a latte into my hands and herds us all out the door.

"We need to go," she says. And when she uses that serious voice, we all listen.

While we're waiting for a traffic light to change, I take my first sip of the coffee, and my eyes fly open.

"It's good, right?" Sterling raises his cup in camaraderie.

"Why don't we go here more often?" I quickly take another sip before the light changes and we're off again.

"The prices are exorbitant, but the coffee's so good, so we settled on once a quarter before this meeting."

"Well, I already can't wait for the next one."

The three of them share a look as we hop on the elevator and Trent hits the number twelve. "I doubt you'll be saying that in two hours."

My smile falters. "They're that bad?"

"You'll see." Ali smiles at me as the elevator doors slide open. "Meet back here in two minutes."

"Sounds good," I say.

I start walking toward my desk to drop my purse off, but I freeze when I see the one person I've been dying to see all day storming towards me.

But he doesn't look happy to see me at all.

"No, that doesn't sound good." Warren stops in front of me. "You're late."

"The meeting doesn't start for five minutes."

"I know," he says. "That's the point."

I glance around, but there's no one to explain. "I don't understand."

"Come on." He gently grabs my arm and starts leading me away. "We need to go."

I look back at Ali and shrug at the question in her eyes, ignoring the insinuation that's there too. I have no idea what's happening either. "I'll see you guys in there."

"I like what you did with your place, by the way," Warren says. "I think the average house price of our neighborhood has skyrocketed with all that landscaping."

He's referencing the plethora of plants that found a home in my cubicle while he was gone.

"I'd invite you in for a house tour, but it seems I instead need to report a case of breaking and entering."

"The door was open?" He's pulling me along at a brisk pace to the only meeting room that can hold our entire department but looks over with that amused smile he always seems to wear around me. I laugh and he finally slows down as we near the meeting room.

"Oh, thank god," he breathes as we enter the room, and he leads me toward the front corner of the room. "There's still two seats available."

I glance around the room and get even more confused. The seats around the large conference table are almost full but there are rows of seats still empty in the back. "There's still plenty of seats available."

"Look at the ground," he whispers once we've taken our seats.

With so many people in here, I didn't immediately notice, but when I look closely, I see that the back third of the room, where the majority of the seats are—and the only other remaining seats —is completely made of glass. I gulp wondering what would have happened if I had to sit on a pane of glass, twelve-stories up for two hours. My hands shake just thinking about it and I set my coffee on the table in front of me so it doesn't spill.

He saved me from that. He *knew* and he made sure I wouldn't be put in a position that terrified me. He remembered the one joking comment I made about heights in our first conversation and saw through to the truth beneath.

"I see your feelings on heights haven't changed," he says, and I smile as I shake my head. "What about the people?"

"They're still pretty great." I look up at him and smile at the brightness I feel being around him again. Forgetting all about my fear when his face squishes together as he smiles. "Thank you."

His eyes shift down to the coffee and his brows raise. "Stella Lei, how fancy."

"It's tradition," I say and raise my cup at Ali, Trent, and Sterling who just arrived and head to the seats on the glass.

Ali narrows her eyes in, what I'm assuming is, a question as to why I'm sitting over here, and I nod down at the glass floor. She of all people should understand. Her eyes widen in understanding, and she whispers to Trent and Sterling who nod to me in a sort of apology.

Ali was right. I'm not looking forward to another one of those meetings. It was all numbers and updates that have nothing to do with what my team works on, except for ten minutes that focused on projects I'm involved in.

But there was one intriguing piece of news from the meeting.

"Congrats on the promotion," I say once Warren and I are back in our corner. "Why didn't you say anything?"

"I had to make sure you wanted to be my friend for me, not

just my soon-to-be superior title. You know how it can be." He shrugs and I fight back a laugh. "And since you're talking to me more now than you did before, I think it's fair to say my intuition was correct."

My mouth drops open, incredulous. "Are you talking about last week? When you were gone all week and I *couldn't* talk to you?"

"You could've texted."

"I don't have your number."

"So, you would've texted?" He raises his eyebrows.

"You obviously wanted me to," I tease, and he picks up one of the foam basketballs on his desk and lightly throws it at me. I laugh and a smile pulls on the corner of his lips.

"How about I drop the breaking and entering charges and we call it even?" I say.

He laughs. "Deal."

Warren heads off for a meeting at the end of the day, but something stops me before I leave the office. I *want* Warren's number. My eyes land on the foam basketball and I have an idea.

I smile as I finally get on the elevator and soar closer to being on solid ground by the second, hoping that Warren sees the foam basketball I put on his keyboard and it makes him look at his plastic hoop where I left a sticky note with my number and the message: *Ball's in your court now.*

I'm not even home when my phone dings with a new message.

WARREN

Breaking and entering much?

ME

Where do you think I learned it from?

WARREN

I'll meet you tomorrow. 8 a.m. at Kalla Coffee?

ME

My usual spot at my usual time . . .

Now we're creeping into stalker territory.

Should I be worried?

WARREN

I'll take that as a yes.

ME

I'll blow a kiss to the tree outside my window for you tonight.

WARREN

How'd you know that's my favorite perch?

ME

One of the birdies told me.

WARREN

Damn it.

I should've known they couldn't keep their mouths shut.

All they do is chirp.

ME

Pretty sure that's called a bird song.

WARREN

Pft, if that's singing then I'm better than I thought.

ME

I'd pay to see that.

WARREN

Then you can buy the drinks to get me drunk enough to actually do it.

ME

You've got yourself a deal.

The last time I smiled like this because of text messages was in middle school. He makes me giddy, my chest flutters, heart races, and a smile that lives up to my last name is permanently etched onto my face. We don't stop texting all evening, and even then, we only stop because I drifted off to sleep sometime after 2 a.m.

Seven

When I get to Kallia, Ali is already waiting for her order, practically bouncing in anticipation. I get in line, but she grabs my arm. "I already ordered yours, now out with it; tell me everything about Mitch."

"You're not ready for what I'm about to tell you," I say, pausing for effect and her eyes scream at me to continue. "Mitch . . . is actually—"

"Warren?" she says just before I can.

My face twists in confusion. "Wait, how did you know that?"

She shakes her head and I realize her eyes are locked on something—or someone—behind me. "No, Warren is *here*."

I turn around and I see the Warren from eight years ago, the one who showed up to Kallia after our text exchange with the brightest smile on his face. Looking back, it hurts to know that he was already falling in love with me then, because when I blink, the older Warren is standing there, with the same two blue tulips he started bringing me not long after those texts, but with the hesitant smile of someone who's uncomfortable, unsure.

"Wait, *what*?" Ali grabs my arm so I look back to her and I can tell she just absorbed my words. "You knew he was here?"

"Clara messed up," I explain quickly because Warren is headed in our direction. "Mitch is actually Warren Mitchell. *He's* the CFO of the company acquiring mine."

"No. Fucking. Way." Her eyes widen.

I nod as Warren approaches and gives Ali an awkward wave. I never really asked if anyone kept in touch with him after he left, and no one ever brought it up. I assumed Ali didn't speak directly to him but kept tabs on him. He and Trent were the closest; I wonder if they ever talked.

"Hi, Ali." His voice is small, like he's prepared for a verbal assault from her, which is a fair assumption knowing Ali . . . and what he did to me. "It's been a while."

"And who's fault is that?" she asks with a perfect smile on her face. Warren shifts on his feet and I look down as a small smile blooms on my face.

"I know, it's on me," he says, and both Ali and I are taken aback. It's not that Warren didn't take accountability back then, but he deflected most things with humor. She was expecting a joking response—I was too. "I'm sorry. I really have missed everyone."

I have never seen Ali speechless, but right now she's staring at Warren like she's seen a ghost. His smile falters a little and he excuses himself to go order.

"What happened there?" I snort once he's out of earshot.

She shakes her head, turning away from the spot he was standing to look at me. "In so many ways, he's the same, but he also seems so different. More mature and steady."

"Somehow more attractive too," I say with a sigh, then snap my lips together when Ali glares at me. I look around as if searching for whoever said that, and my gaze lands on him.

The feel of his body under my arms as he hugged me last night flashes through my mind and my gaze moves up his body taking in all of the changes in daylight. He's put on some weight, but it appears to be all muscle mass. His tailored pants hint at the curve of muscles on his thighs, and his chest and arms fill out his dress shirt and suit jacket far better than they ever did back then. When I get to his face, he's watching me with a smile. His face is shaved, his honey hair has grown a little bit, and the last lingering bits of baby face he had have faded into a strong jawline that is highlighted by the smile he's wearing.

"Be careful, Ana," Ali says, and I almost jump. She looks at Warren, gaze drifting down to the flowers in his hand. The familiarity of it all weighs on us like a dusty blanket of memories. One that lies forgotten, in a dark corner of the attic for years, but is bringing everything back now that it's found the light of day. "I know you still care for him, but you've been a mess since he left. And he's only back for a short time. I don't want you to get hurt again."

"I know." I use all my will force to take my eyes off him. He's the same man I loved, but he's grown up—and he grew up well. "I'm doing my best . . ."

"But . . ." she adds, when I trail off.

I sigh. "But, it's *him*, Ali. Do you know how often I've dreamed of him coming back here, of him finally explaining what happened back then, of us getting to live the life we always dreamed of together? We were so good, until things ended. And there was no closure, no explanation. He's my one that got away. What if I can get him back?"

"He could be seeing someone else," she says, lips pressed together tightly. She was our biggest cheerleader back when we were together, but after what he did, she's not his biggest fan—understandably. Even I wasn't able to recognize myself after he left. I pulled myself together, but I know she's worried about what it'll do to me if things end badly again.

Hell, I'm scared of what will happen to me too.

"He's not," I say, too fast, and her eyebrows raise in question. "We went to Il Piacere last night—"

"Analise—"

"Before you say anything, it was all eight of us from work, and it got booked before I knew he was here." Her face says: *that doesn't make it any better.* "After, I decided to walk home, and he walked with me—"

"Are you kidding me?" She cuts me off again, louder this time. I shush her and grab her arm to pull her further away from Warren who's moving to wait for his coffee. "Did he explain why he left? Did you talk about anything?"

I drop my gaze. "I stopped him before we could get that far. I was too scared to hear what he might say so I just said we'll be professional while he's here."

She's shaking her head, exasperated. "I can tell you right now, that's not going to happen."

"What do you mean?" I say, hurt by her casual dismissal of my plan.

"What I mean is, you might say it's only professional, but he showed up here this morning with blue tulips like he always used to, and you still look at him like he's your sun. That's not keeping it professional."

My face falls because she's right. I don't know if we'll be able to pull off professional.

"You have bigger things to worry about today, though," she says, and I nod. My gaze drops; I can't look at him. He doesn't know what today is because he wasn't here for it. That reminder keeps my thoughts in check. "Call me if you need me. If not, I'll see you tomorrow after work?"

"Yeah, I'll be there." I reach out and squeeze her hand as an answer to the other comment. Ali has been my rock though the past five years. She held my hand through the funeral, held me as I cried when I realized I'd lost two parents even though only one of them died, and has dropped everything to show up for me when I needed it.

"What's happening tomorrow?" Warren rejoins the group with a smile, and Ali and I look at each other wide-eyed, silently trying to figure out how to get out of this.

His smile turns to a smirk, and I know then he knows exactly what's happening tomorrow—we've been going to the same bar for eight years, we're predictable—but he wants us to invite him.

When we don't say anything, he adds, "You know I've been thinking about checking out The Dizzy Acorn while I'm in town, maybe tomorrow would be a good day for it."

I groan and roll my eyes. "You're impossible. Yes, we're going to The Dizzy Acorn tomorrow." I glance back at Ali and she's frowning. But hanging out with the group is better than being alone with him again . . . right? I shrug at her, and she sighs as if in acceptance that this is going to happen one way or another. "You're welcome to come, although I can't promise people will be happy to see you."

Ali tries to cover her laugh with a cough but Warren has the good sense to look hesitant about accepting, although he still does.

"I have an early meeting," Ali says, "but it was nice to see you, Warren."

"You too." He smiles. "I'm looking forward to Wednesday."

Ali just looks at me one last time before heading out the door and leaving me with the one person I want to be with, and the one person I shouldn't be around.

"Oh, these are for you." He hands me the flowers on the walk to the office. I take them reluctantly, acting as if I'm doing him a favor by taking them off his hands but I get butterflies when his fingers barely graze against mine. "I survived a warzone trying to get these."

I laugh despite myself. "I take it Lola remembered you and wasn't happy?"

"That's an understatement." He shivers and I laugh again. "You might not think of flowers as dangerous, but she sure knows how to weaponize them. I had thorny stems thrown at me, and she yelled something about how she hopes one of them poisons me, so there's that. I almost had a heart attack when she grabbed the shears."

The first time I went into Lola's to get the flowers on my own, Lola asked what happened and has held a grudge against Warren for it. She's the kind of little, old lady who doesn't forget anything either.

"Are you smirking at my pain?" He nudges me with his elbow.

"I can't deny that injuring you is a thought that's crossed my mind many times." I smile at his gaping expression. "It'd be nice if someone else did it for me."

"Okay, I probably deserve it from you." We stop at an intersection, waiting for a walk signal. "I'll give you one hit. I won't even try to block it." He pats his bicep and my eyes strain to see every detail his suit jacket is trying to cover. "Come on, I can take it."

"I'm not going to hit you," I whisper, looking around at all the people watching us. The signal changes and I push his arm to get him to keep walking. His arms feel bigger, stronger than the last time I held them. My hand clenches by my side so I don't reach out to touch him again.

"At least, not when you're expecting it," I add, just loud enough for him to hear. I laugh when he glances over, trying to figure out if I'm joking or serious.

I don't know what the answer is either though.

When we get to the office, Peter, Mac, and Jason are in the lobby waiting for the elevator. Jason greets me with a tight smile but only greets Warren with a frown. Peter and Mac are looking at each other with small smiles, almost as if they're silently communicating.

"I hope it wasn't too hard to find your way here," I say, since Jason isn't being a good host.

"Yes, Clara showed us around before dropping us off last night." Peter smiles. "It's a beautiful town."

"I'm glad you like it. I've always loved the charm of the downtown area."

Peter's smile is so genuine and kind, he's not what I expected from the CEO of a health-tech startup. His eyes flash to the flowers in my hand and I see intrigue cloud his features, but he doesn't ask anything as we all board the elevator.

Warren and I are in the back while Peter, Mac, and Jason stand in front of us. Jason keeps glaring over his shoulder at Warren, eyeing our coffees from the same shop, the flowers in my hand, and surely considering how we were laughing as we walked into the lobby earlier. His anger is so obvious and he's acting the exact opposite of how we're supposed to be acting towards the people who are buying our company that I can barely contain my laughter. I cover it up with a cough, but everyone glances my way.

Thankfully, it's only a short ride to floor three—both for my fear of heights and the strangeness of this silence.

"Let's meet in the conference room before the meeting," Peter says to Warren when he starts following me in the opposite direction, to my office.

He nods then leans into whisper, "See you soon," before walking off with Peter. My chest constricts as he walks out of sight. I'm already much too comfortable having him around and it's barely been a full day. *Fuck.* It's going to hurt when he leaves again. It's going to hurt so bad.

"I don't like that guy." I jump when Jason speaks, not realizing he's still standing right behind me.

I turn on him. "You don't need to like him, but you do need to be respectful and professional."

"I'm sure I don't know what you mean." He looks angry that I'm not siding with him.

"What you did today, can't happen again." I emphasize each word. "These people are here because they bought our company. We are supposed to be welcoming."

"You're not my boss, you know."

My lips press into a hard line. And he wonders why I've never wanted to go out with him. "Want me to bring this up to Clara? Because I sure as hell can bet you she'd be on my side for this one."

He scowls, and I fake a smile before walking away, saying a silent prayer that he doesn't follow me.

As I replace the wilted flowers in my office with the new ones Warren got for me, I can't help but think: *Jason may not like him, but I sure as hell do.*

Eight

AUGUST CURRENT DAY (TUESDAY)

The eight of us are packed in the main conference room while Peter stands at the front of the room, talking through slides of the company vision and mission. It's basically what I expected. They want to create an insurance company that only has value-based care contracts with providers. Most established health plans are slowly shifting their current fee-for-service contracts over to value-based care ones anyway. So, in some ways, it's nice to start solely with that intention, but there are still plenty of providers that are hesitant to switch over.

The current fee-for-service payments are simple—one payment for one service, and the more services performed, the more payments they receive. Value-based care is trying to flip payment focus from quantity to quality based. These contracts can get extremely complicated and there are many different components to them, but essentially, they all, in some way, have a variable payment that's tied to patient outcomes. For a primary care provider, that could mean managing chronic conditions so there are fewer ER visits. For a surgeon, that could mean fewer post-op complications.

It can require more management from providers, and since the payment is variable, if they don't manage their patients well, they could end up earning less.

When I'm looking at developing our strategy for these programs, these are all pieces I have to take into consideration. And our programs get deployed by all health plans in our system; we don't work exclusively with anyone—which is my main concern after reviewing the materials they sent ahead of time.

It's why I start getting giddy when the financial slides pop up in Peter's presentation. I have *a lot* of questions, and I don't think they have the answers to them.

"Moving on to the financial projections," Peter says, standing in front of the screen. He glances at Warren to make sure he's prepared. "Are there any questions regarding the calculations sent over?"

"Yes, I have a few," I chime in, and Warren looks up, weariness in his expression. This is his area, and as much as I don't want to admit it, he knows how I am. I only smile though, because he *should* be weary. "I noticed that the only place you're accounting for the impact we'll have on the company is in the cost of healthcare savings. Are you planning on changing our company's strategy away from consulting? Because I can't help but notice that the savings projections are only a fraction of the revenue we currently generate."

Warren clears his throat and sits up straight. "Yes, looking into the matter we found that it's a conflict of interest for an in-house team to also consult out to other insurers."

"Is there no way to keep it out-of-house then? So that you can still get the savings, but we can also keep our current business?" I push because this is important to me. I started working here because I truly cared and believed in what we were doing, and this feels like a fundamental shift in our core practice. "It seems like such a waste of all the expertise and the reputation we've built here over the years. Besides, if we do things the way you've modeled here, your savings projections are way too high."

"What do you mean?" Peter asks, intently focused on every word I'm saying.

"I'm assuming you used the ten percent savings from our experience files?" I direct the question at Warren, and he nods. "Right, well we're only able to achieve that level of savings because we have multi-payer alignment. With these programs, we've found that the providers are more engaged and attentive when, say, seventy percent of their members are part of a value-based care program, as opposed to if five percent are. And if they have five different sets of metrics to track from five different programs, they'll end up only focusing on the one they believe will make them the most in return. As a result, they put more work into achieving the guidelines and striving to improve when they don't have to change their practice for a few members. If you take away the consulting side of this business, you take away the buy-in of the physicians and the savings will not be what you're expecting."

Peter turns to look at Warren who's shuffling through his papers. A smile pulls at my lips as he fidgets, searching for an answer—this part of the job never gets old for me.

"I haven't been able to find a legal way for us to do that," Warren says.

"Well, let's keep looking," Peter says to Warren, then looks at me. "Work with Miss Summers on this to make sure we're capturing all of the nuances of the business."

Warren nods and looks at me out of the corner of his eye. There's not a single drop of frustration or resentment in that look, but there is something I know all too well—heat.

"Okay, moving—" Peter starts.

"Actually, I have one more question," I cut in with a sweet smile that the men I've worked with in the past have learned to fear. "Assuming we're able to find a way to make this work, that should generate enough additional revenue to keep our staff on.

So the layoffs you have planned won't be necessary, is that correct?"

Everyone in the room goes still. The people on my side look at Peter with confused and angry expressions. The people on their side look surprised and hesitant.

"Sorry if that wasn't common knowledge," I add, unfazed by the dead silence surrounding me. "But there's no way that the expenses you projected here accounted for everyone we currently have on staff. Which is understandable considering the revenue projections that are here, but in the case that we keep the consulting side alive, we can't make what we do work with only half our staff."

"Yes"—Peter clears his throat—"that can be reevaluated after we hear your proposal." He pulls off a good faux calmness, but I catch a slight shake in his voice that gives him away.

Clara, Serge, and Jason start grumbling amongst themselves —I'm sure they had no clue this was coming until I mentioned it. Warren is jotting down notes and Mac is looking through her materials in preparation for her part of the presentation that's coming up. No one else sees it, but as I continue to sit tall, Peter watches me with interest, and I swear I see the corners of his mouth slowly turn up into a smile. I nod my head at him and his eyes light up as he returns the gesture.

I can tell just from the short time we've been in this meeting that Peter is a good boss. He listens to his employees and trusts them. He even trusted *me* with no reason to. I can see why Warren went to work for him; he's everything our old bosses at Triniti weren't.

"Damn, woman, are you gunning for my job or something?" Warren walks into my office towards the end of the day with a smile on his face. "That was brutal."

"Did you expect me to hold back because I knew you?" He

might've only worked with me for a little while, but even then I wasn't afraid to be the one person with a differing opinion, or push back on what I thought was a stupid decision.

"No, I always knew that you'd grow to be a great leader, but that was something else entirely," he says, with awe in his eyes. "You were clear and concise. You fought for your people, but you did it using logic, and you somehow tore down every counter argument we could've made before we could even say it. It was incredible . . . *you're* incredible."

"You're only just realizing this?" I tease to cover the butterflies blooming in my stomach.

"Maybe I'm just now remembering what I've always known." His voice is softer, more intimate, and my lungs forget how to breathe as my eyes stay locked on him. Time compresses, the size of the world shrinks, until there's just us two and every moment we've shared together—real and imaginary, past, present, and future.

Someone coughs outside my office and I'm jolted back into reality. We both look around and catch Jason glaring at Warren through the open door as he passes by.

"He really doesn't like me, does he?" Warren chuckles.

"He despises you." I laugh and add, "He probably blames you for not being able to get a date with me, even though I've been turning him down since I started working here."

I keep laughing but slowly realize Warren is silent. His jaw is tight, his lips pressed together, and his hands are gripping the seat so firmly I'm worried the armrests might snap right off.

"You okay?" I ask slowly.

He takes a few deep breaths before answering. "That hurt a lot more than I expected."

My breathing stutters on the way in. I try to lighten the mood, but my voice comes out as a whisper. "That some douchebag guy is interested in me?"

"That you might've said yes," he says, looking up at me. "If not to him, then to someone else. That you could've been moving on and I would've deserved every ounce of pain that brought me."

I'm shaking my head before he's even done. Tears well up but I try to keep them from spilling over because anyone could walk by at any time. "What are you trying to do to me?"

His eyebrows pull together. "I'm not trying to do anything."

"But you *are*." I barely let him finish his sentence before I start again. "*You* left, Warren. You left and then you broke up with me. So you don't get to sit here and say things that I wanted to hear six fucking years ago."

"I know, but—"

"No buts," I say, trying to keep my voice at a whisper when I really want to scream at him. "I just want to know one thing. If I didn't happen to be working here, would you have even told me you were going to be in town? Would you have tried to reach out? Because I don't think you would've."

"I—"

"Oh, there you are, Warren." Peter appears in the doorway of my office, and I place a smile on my face. He glances between us. "Could you stop by the conference room when you're done here?"

"We just finished up," I say before Warren can speak. "I need to get going anyway. I'll see you guys tomorrow."

Peter smiles. "Have a good night, Analise."

I just nod as my smile waivers, because with where I'm going tonight, it's bound to be anything but a good night. "You too."

Warren glances back before he leaves and I'm not sure if the look in his eyes is because of how our conversation went or because he could read the hesitation on my face about my night. It shouldn't matter to me, but it's all I can think about on the drive to the suburbs where I grew up.

I take a deep breath after I park in front of the familiar tan house before I work up the nerve to get out of the car. Even though I only come back once a year now, it doesn't get any easier.

"Hello?" I call as I unlock the door with my spare key. I don't even try to knock, it'd be useless.

The lights are off, but I hear noises coming from the kitchen, so I head in that direction. I flick on the lights as I move through the house until I reach the kitchen and there he is, digging through the liquor cabinet.

At least he's off the couch. That's a good sign, right?

"Did you bring bourbon?" he grumbles out in a slur of words.

Maybe not.

"Hi, Dad," I sigh. "Nice to see you too."

"Whatever, do you have bourbon or not?"

"No."

"Useless fucking bitch," he grumbles loud enough for me to hear, and I flinch, even after all this time. I still hope that one of these times I'll walk through that door and find my old dad—the kind, sweet man who showed up to every volleyball game I played in growing up. Instead, he grabs a bottle of whisky and drinks it straight from the bottle. "Just like your mother."

My teeth grind together in frustration. "You didn't start drinking bourbon until after she died."

"No one asked you." His voice raises.

Why do I still come here? Why do I put myself through this each year?

My eyes shift to their wedding picture still hanging on the wall. *She's* why.

"Could you not drink for one night?" I plead. "If not for me, then to honor her memory?"

It's the five year anniversary of her passing, and I don't think I've seen him sober once in that time. He stares me in the eyes as he lifts the bottle he just found to his lips and takes a long swig.

"She'd be so disappointed in who you've become." I try a different route, anything that will make him put down the drink even for a minute.

His eyes flare with anger, and before I can register what's

happening, the glass cup on the counter is flying at my head. I manage to move out of its direct path, but it shatters on the wall behind me and I'm close enough that shards of glass fly toward my face. As the sound of glass stills, I press two fingers to my stinging cheek, pulling them away to find a line of blood.

"How dare you tell me what she'd feel," he spits at me. "She fucking left us; she doesn't get a say anymore. Fuck her and fuck you. Get out of my house."

"Dad—"

"Get the fuck out," he screams as he reaches for another glass.

I turn and walk out before the contents of my stomach end up on his kitchen floor, and heave in a breath when I step onto the front porch. My eyes widen when the handle on the door turns, and I run down the driveway to my car. He must be really drunk if he's following me out here. He usually forgets about me once I'm out of sight.

I stop to catch my breath in the car, but he starts stomping down the driveway, so I put the car in drive and go. I call Ali over Bluetooth on the way home with a tight voice and one hand pressing a napkin to my cheek and ask if she can meet me at my place.

She must've heard the distress in my voice because she shows up with an overnight bag and immediately comes over to comfort me where I've been since I got home: curled up in a fetal position, sobbing, on my couch.

"What did he do to you?" she whispers as she strokes my hair. She takes the damp towel from my hand to wipe the skin around the cut and I wince.

"Threw a glass at me," I choke out between sobs.

"Analise," she says, voice cracking, "I don't think it's safe for you to go there anymore."

"She wouldn't want him to live like this."

"But she wouldn't expect you to fix it." Ali met my mom a lot before she passed. My mom loved to meet us for lunch in the city and dotted over Ali like a second daughter. "She would tell you that you can't help him unless he wants to help himself."

My eyes close—she's not the first person to tell me that. But what if he never wants to help himself? Am I supposed to just stand back and let him keep hurting himself?

Ali puts on a rom-com, and once my tears ease up, she helps me take care of the cut on my cheek then grabs us the emergency ice cream we have on hand for occasions like this.

"He blames her for leaving, and he can't get over it," I say once my tears have stopped and I've had some time to think. "He pushes everyone away because of it. Did . . ." I bite my lip, considering my words before I finish the sentence. "Did I do the same thing with Warren?"

She looks taken aback by the direction of the conversation. "You have more right to be angry than he does. Warren chose to leave, your mom didn't have a choice."

"But I just keep holding onto this anger," I say. "I won't let him explain, even though he's tried to multiple times now. And no matter what I still feel for him, I won't let him get close to me."

"You have to decide if there's any explanation he could give that would make you forgive him," she says. "But if there's no chance of you forgiving him, then you need to acknowledge that for yourself, and you need to tell him. Because from what I saw, he's looking for your forgiveness."

Could I forgive him? For leaving, for not giving any explanation, for not reaching out for six years. Is it possible to forgive that?

I already know the answer.

But the real reason I won't hear him out is because I'm scared of how easily I'll forgive him. How quickly I've already handed my heart back over to him, even if he doesn't know it.

I'm scared of how easy it is to love him, and how much I still do.

Nine

SEPTEMBER 8 YEARS AGO

I rush down the sidewalk, pushing people out of the way as gently as possible despite the glares being thrown in my direction anyway. My mood immediately brightens when I spot Warren through the window of Kallia, sitting at our table in the corner with two cups of coffee in front of him.

"Sorry I'm late," I huff, out of breath from half-running the whole way here, and dropping into the seat across from him. He slides my iced mocha over to me and I finally start to relax after I take the first sip of the perfectly balanced sweet and bitter drink. As I set down the cup, I realize he's staring at me with quirked eyebrows and the corner of his mouth curls up into an amused smile. "What?"

And then I realize what he's wearing—a light gray T-shirt, black chino shorts, and black boat shoes. My head tilts in confusion, but after a moment my lips press together.

"It's Labor Day, isn't it?" I say, looking down at my black knee-length dress, beige blazer, and nude heels. He laughs and my cheeks heat. "Why didn't you remind me?"

"I figured when you said *see you tomorrow* last night that you forgot we didn't have work today. I thought it'd be more fun to just show up here at our usual time and see what happened."

I try to glare, but I can't stay mad at him when he flashes that face-squishing grin.

"Now, come on, finish up your coffee. We have plans today." He smirks at my shocked expression.

"We do?"

"Of course, we do. You think I came all the way over here just for coffee?" He raises an eyebrow at me, and my smile grows. "It's a beautiful sunny day, and I'm with Miss Summers after all, so we're going to enjoy this weather."

I blush again and take a sip of my drink before he can see the color on my cheeks. We text practically 24/7, and he's now a normal addition to lunches and evenings out with Ali, Trent, and Sterling. But he hasn't asked me out yet and I'm starting to question if he feels that way at all or if it's just me trying to wish it into existence. But then he goes and does something like this and that warm, hopeful feeling comes flooding back.

"Where are we going?"

"First, to your apartment," he says, eyeing my outfit. "I'm thinking you'll want to change."

After I throw on shorts and a cute top, we walk around the city, going in and out of any stores we find but barely looking at the merchandise. We're shooting questions back and forth about silly things like favorite colors and movies, until he asks, "Why'd you want to become an actuary?"

"It's not that great of a story." I shrug but he still looks like he's hanging on my every word. "I was always good at math growing up, and when it was time to start thinking about colleges, I figured majoring in math would be best. But I had no idea what I could do with a math degree. As I started touring different schools, I met with the math departments. Applied

Math and Pure Math didn't pique my interest—they were too heavily focused on proofs and theory. But then, I met with the head of an Actuarial Science program. I was immediately drawn to it because I could see the real-life impact of it from the beginning, and it was more than just math. It combined statistics, math, finance, a bit of economics, and business. I knew then I was going to major in it and haven't looked back since."

"And how do you like it so far?"

"The exam process is annoying," I say, and he laughs. There are two levels of certification for actuaries that are achieved through a series of exams. The first level requires seven exams and some online courses and is generally required as you move up in a company. The second level is an additional three exams and three courses and is generally optional. "But it's been good so far—about what I expected. It just feels like a job right now though. I hope that one day I can find something I'm super passionate about to focus on. What about you?"

"My story is less interesting than yours." He smiles at me as he holds open the door to the next boutique store we find. "I was a finance major because my dad always wanted me to follow in his footsteps and I always looked up to him. But when my parents got divorced my freshman year, I realized he wasn't the hero I'd made him out to be in my head. I still got the finance degree but learned about actuarial science from a friend and started studying for the exams. My dad wasn't happy when I turned down an internship at his company for an actuarial internship, but I think it was meant to be."

My heart drops into my stomach. "I'm so sorry. Is he happy for you now?"

Warren takes a deep, shaking breath, and I get the feeling he doesn't often talk about this. He glances over at me with sad eyes but turns away again to continue. "I don't think he ever really got over it. We talk here and there but I don't see him often —he still lives in New York. My mom moved back to Boston, where I grew up, and I go visit her as often as I can. She's amazing, you'd love her."

I look down, color flooding my cheeks at the off-handed comment. Has he been thinking about me meeting his mom? But I frown as I consider the rest of his story. I can't imagine what it would feel like to have a parent who isn't supportive. I've been blessed with parents who are there for me no matter what I choose to do.

Before I can say anything, he clears his throat and turns to look at me with a smile. "Hungry?"

I can see in his eyes that he doesn't want to talk more about this, so I smile back and nod, hoping I'm adequately conveying how grateful I am that he shared that piece of his life with me.

After stopping for a quick lunch at a cute, little bistro downtown, we end up at a place called Buena Park. I grew up near here, yet I've never been here before. As we walk the winding paths through green grass with red maple trees spread across the park, I can only imagine how beautiful it must be in autumn, the green leaves replaced with bright oranges and reds as far as the eye can see. When I look closely, I think I see lights in the trees—they must be beautiful at night too.

Families flock around the man-made lake at the bottom of the hill—feeding ducks, having picnics, and strolling around as we are. But as we steadily climb in elevation, there's less and less people. It turns into more of a hike than a stroll and I'm glad I opted for shorts and a tank-top instead of the sundress I almost put on.

"This is one of my favorite places in town," he says as we reach the top of a hill with a viewpoint through the trees that overlooks the city.

From afar, the Triniti building—with its reverse tiering that my fear of heights hates—stands out with its unique design. I can appreciate it here on solid ground.

My fear of heights isn't triggered when I'm standing on earth. It's the manmade objects I don't trust—like buildings, bridges, and airplanes. I shiver at the thought of them, even though my hair is sticking to my neck because of the sweltering heat.

"I can see why," I say, trying to hide how winded I am from that hill.

When I look over, he's looking at me with a huge smile. "It's even more beautiful at night, with all of the lights. It's like a sea of stars."

"I'll have to come back and check it out sometime." I already wanted to come back before we got up here, but now it's a must.

"How about Friday at eight?"

"What?" I breathe, my body going still. The hot air suddenly feels cold compared to the bright, warm feeling spreading through me.

Color floods his cheeks as he locks his hands behind his back and glances to the left. "There's an incredible Italian restaurant just down this path, on top of the hill. I'd like to take you out on an official date." He swallows and looks back to me. The mix of hope and fear in his eyes is so charming my chest constricts. "Don't worry, there's a parking lot over there so we won't have to do this hike again," he adds, and I smile. I'd do this hike anytime if there was a date with him at the end of it. "So . . . what do you think?"

"I think . . ." My smile grows. "That it's about damn time." I throw my arms around his neck. After a moment, he wraps his arms around my waist like it's the most normal thing in the world and lifts me off the ground. "I'd love to go on a date with you, in case you didn't catch that," I whisper into his neck.

He chuckles and spins me around. I can feel his joy, and his relief, in that move. "Thanks for the clarification."

After he puts me down, I ask, "So, if our first date is on Friday, then what does that make today?"

"Well, tonight is the completion of a deal we made months ago . . ." He looks at me, curious if I'll know what he's talking about.

My eyes widen. "I'm getting you drunk and you're singing for me?"

He laughs as he nods. "Ali, Trent, and Sterling are meeting us for dinner and then we're all going to karaoke, yes."

"And until then?"

He shrugs. "That's whatever we want it to be."

I reach out and grab his hand, his fingers immediately lacing with mine. "Like this?"

He squeezes my hand, and a sweet smile is on his face. "This is perfect."

"Am I seeing things or did you and Warren walk in here hand in hand?" Ali has me cornered in the girl's bathroom at the burger place we decided on for dinner. We haven't even gotten our food yet, but I didn't fight when she made some excuse to drag me off here. I saw it in her eyes the moment we walked in—if we didn't talk about this now, she'd have brought it up at the table in front of everyone and made it ten times more embarrassing. "Spill."

"We're going on a date on Friday," I say, and she squeals. I'm trying to play it cool, but I'm practically bouncing with excitement.

"Finally!" she screams. A woman walks into the bathroom and shoots us a funny look having heard Ali's yelling. We fight laughter as she walks into a stall, and Ali leans closer to me. "You better tell me everything."

"I will." I blush and try to calm her down before we walk back out to the table.

She isn't subtle as she smirks at us from across the table, especially when she notices Warren's hand reach for mine under the table after we're done eating. I kick her under the table, but Sterling and Trent keep smiling at me like they know exactly what's going on without needing any of her hints. *I wonder if Warren has ever talked with them about me.* They could have known he felt this way before today—like how Ali has known I've been into him since my first few weeks here.

Now *that's* a strange thought. That the others have known more about our true feelings than we have this whole time. I tighten my hold on his hand and don't ease up until we leave to head over to The Dizzy Acorn for karaoke.

The week after the quarterly meeting we came to check it out, thinking that it wouldn't be anything special, but we've found ourselves back here multiple times a week since.

Warren and Sterling are the only ones from our group singing tonight—Warren to complete our deal, and Sterling because he's the life of every party. As they flip through the song catalogue, Ali and I grab the first round of drinks. When I make it a point of putting Warren's drink on my own tab, she gives me a suggestive look. I roll my eyes, but a smile grows on my lips.

"Did you decide yet?" I ask as we sit down and pass out the drinks.

Warrens sips his Blue Moon and winks at me over the bottle. "It's a surprise. But Sterling's ahead of me on the list."

The bar isn't as crowded as a Friday or Saturday night, but there's more people here for this than usual. Eventually, Sterling's name gets called and we all scream and cheer as he takes the stage and gets the whole crowd off their feet for a fun rendition of "Sweet Caroline" by Neil Diamond. The whole bar sings the backup vocals at the correct time, and he even gets off the small stage and weaves through the bar, putting an arm around strangers who are eagerly willing to sing a line into the mic with him. When he gets to us, we're the loudest of all. By the end of the song, he's back on stage, and he takes a bow to a roar of cheers.

Warren gulps, face pale, as his name is called. He seems nervous as he takes the stage and it's so damn charming. Our eyes meet and I wink at him. He smiles and visibly relaxes.

His song starts and my jaw drops the second I see the name —there's no way it's just coincidence that he chose *this* song. But then, he starts singing and it's not very good—like, at all—and I'm torn between laughing and crying. I feel the eyes of the rest of the table turn to me and I can't keep a grin off my face.

"Is this—" Ali starts and I just nod.

Yes, it's "Summer Love" by Justin Timberlake.

He's singing a song about Summer, about love, and he's looking right at me. I forget about the other eyes on me and I gravitate slowly towards the stage, caught in eyes that haven't left mine since he began. With the spotlight on him, he's glowing. He's the sun—the center of the universe, of *my* universe. As he sings the last words, my smile is so big it's probably taking up half my face. He steps down and walks right up to me. There's shuffling around the bar as the next person gets called on stage, but I couldn't tell you where it came from.

"So, was it worth the wait?" he breathes, eyes locked on mine. Nothing else, no one else matters to me right now.

"Well, the birds have better pitch, but they don't sing for me." A blush stains my cheeks just thinking of how sweet that was, how sweet he is. "So you definitely have them beat there."

"If it were up to me, the whole world would sing just for you." His hand lifts to gently brush across my cheek and tuck a lock of hair behind my ear. I stop breathing. Eyes wide, all I can do is stare at him in awe. "You make everything come alive. I thought I knew what blue was until I looked in your eyes. I thought I knew red until that perfect rosy color flushed your cheeks for the first time. Now, I think I was colorblind before I met you. And the warmth I feel when you smile that bright smile just for me, the flutter I get in my chest when you always have the perfect, clever comeback to my banter. Every feeling I had before I met you feels dull. You are everything, Miss Summers, and absolutely nothing else compares."

A tear drops down my cheek, which he quickly wipes away. I shakily say, "Maybe I need to get you drunk more often if you're going to start talking like this."

He chuckles and runs his hand down my arm to lace our

fingers together—goosebumps spring up across my body. "I've been a coward. I've felt this way since the first day I walked back to my desk to find you deep in concentration across the way. With the first words from your lips, I was a goner, but I'm only now telling you. And now that I've started, I don't want to stop —so drunk, sober, or anything in-between, get used to hearing it."

"I may be Miss Summers," I say, squeezing his hand, "but Summer is nothing without the sun." I can't stop the blinding grin from growing on my face as I add, "*You're* my sun, Warren."

His face breaks into one of those squinty-eyed smiles that makes my heart skip a beat, especially knowing I'm the one who put it there. "Would it be cliché to say, I can't wait to fall in love with you?"

I smile, catching the reference, but feeling the need to speak the truth instead. "Would it be cliché to say I think I already am falling?"

"Think?" A smirk pulls at his lips and the look in his eyes has me clenching every muscle below my waist. "I guess I need to up my game."

I raise an eyebrow in jest. "You're the one who *'can't wait'* to fall in love, so I think it's me who needs to step up my game."

His arms wrap around my waist and pull me closer. My heart pounds in my chest as his lips move to my ear to whisper, "I was just quoting the song, but the truth is, I'm most definitely falling," before pulling back to look at me.

Our faces are only inches away, lost deep in each other's eyes, leaning closer until I can feel the gentle brush of his lips against mine, but they're not close enough to fully touch.

"Seasons change, you know," I whisper against his lips, looking into eyes full of light.

"But my feelings never will." His words are so strong, so sure, so resolute. There's not a drop of doubt in the pool of sunshine that's occupying the space my heart is supposed to be. I believe in him. I believe in us.

His lips gently press to mine and they're as warm as the sun. Liquid gold spreads through my body, flows through my veins. The longer his lips stay pressed to mine, the brighter it gets until I'm convinced that if I open my eyes I'll be glowing.

I don't know how long it takes to melt away, but I'm about to drop into a puddle of sunshine on the floor of the bar when one of his hands moves to grip my hip, the other moving to the nape of my neck to angle my head so he can deepen the kiss. With a gasp, my arms wrap around his neck, and I pull myself closer as my mouth opens to him. I let him kiss me deeply, explorative as we learn each other's rhythm and synchronize into a beautiful harmony.

When we finally pull away, my body stays sealed to his. No more than a few inches are between us as we stare wide-eyed, and both breathe heavily.

"Now that," I whisper, "was worth the wait."

His eyebrows raise and a grin grows on his face. "Now *that's* the reaction I was looking for."

I playfully shove him and roll my eyes, but the smile on my face gives me away. "Don't let your ego get too big over there, Mitchell."

He laughs. "Do you need another drink? I'll get us another round."

"I thought I was supposed to be paying for the drinks tonight."

He shrugs. "I did get that promotion; the money's burning a hole in my pocket."

The corners of my lips tug up into a smile. "Of course. That's the only reason I'm into you anyways."

Both our smiles grow until we're laughing.

"I'll be right back," he says, before kissing my cheek and heading over to the bar.

When I get close to the table, Sterling whistles and the look on Ali's and Trent's face echo the sentiment. My cheeks heat but I haven't been able to stop smiling since that kiss. *That kiss.*

Warren just kissed me. I just kissed Warren. My mind keeps playing it on repeat; I don't want to ever forget a single detail about this night.

"I thought we were just here for karaoke, not to watch the two of you suck each other's faces off for ten minutes," Sterling teases.

"It was not ten minutes," I counter, only getting more red. *Was it?*

He only raises his eyebrows and presses his lips into a thin line. I press my hands to my cheeks in an attempt to cool the heat pooling there.

"What Sterling is trying to say," Ali cuts him off with a pointed look, "is we're happy for you guys."

"Yeah, it's about time," Trent adds with a smile. "I was getting sick of hearing how much he liked you. Now he can tell *you* and spare me."

So, he *did* talk to them about me. I want to ask what Warren told him, but after glancing back at Warren and finding him already smiling at me, I realize I'd rather wait to hear it all from Warren himself.

Warren kisses me goodnight on the skinny sidewalk outside of the brick-front of the bar. It's not even past midnight, but it's late enough that there's not a car in sight and it gives us the illusion of being the last humans alive in the city. Maybe it's that feeling, or the alcohol in our veins that keeps us sealed together long after we know we should pull apart—especially since Ali, Trent, and Sterling have made their presence increasingly obvious.

"All right, we get it," Trent groans eventually, and it's what finally breaks our spell. We both look over at him as he continues, "You're both adults and can make decisions for yourselves, *but* the three of us have collectively decided that everyone will be heading back to their own apartments tonight."

He looks at us with a glare that says *just try to argue with me and see what happens*. I almost laugh at how serious he is, as if he's expecting us to argue. But Warren and I already made that same decision earlier in the night. We knew how tempting it'd be to explore this feeling. How easy it'd be to skip steps and end up in bed together at the end of tonight, especially with all the drinks. But we want to do this right—there's no need to rush things.

A shiver runs down my spine as I recall his last words on the topic, *"Besides, I want to be completely sober our first time, so I won't forget a single glorious moment."* When I asked how he knew it'd be glorious, he said, *"Because it'll be with you."*

With his arms still around me, he can feel the shiver, and from the smile growing on his face, he knows what I'm remembering. It makes it harder to walk away.

"See you tomorrow." Warren looks at Ali and Sterling before turning back to me. His hand runs across my cheek once more and his lips press to mine one last time. "Goodnight, Analise."

"Goodnight, Warren." I turn my gaze to Trent as Warren moves to stand with him. "And goodnight to you, mother hen."

The corner of his mouth quirks up even though he still acts like he hates the nickname. Trent is always the one making sure we're on time, following the rules, and generally not getting too rowdy—which is a big ask with this group. With a wave, our groups split, Warren and Trent heading northwest to their buildings, and Ali, Sterling, and I heading east.

The next morning, as I enter Kallia out of breath for the second day in a row, he's already there with our coffees in hand and two blue tulips.

Ten

AUGUST CURRENT DAY (WEDNESDAY)

I'm exhausted.

I barely slept last night—Ali stayed up as late as she could manage watching movies with me, but even long after she was asleep, I stared at the TV. I wasn't even watching the movies, just hoping it'd eventually hypnotize me or lull me to sleep so I could stop thinking so damn much.

About my dad.

About how to explain the cut on my cheek if I can't cover it with makeup.

About the company.

About how to save the jobs of these people that I had a hand in hiring.

About Warren—mostly about Warren.

About if I should let him explain what happened six years ago.

I want to know—I want to know so badly, which is the exact reason I won't let him tell me. He's been back for two days, and I already feel the pull between us growing just as it did back then. If nothing changes, then eventually, it'll get too strong, and everything will come out in a rush just like it did at karaoke that night eight years ago. But this time everything that comes out might not be good.

Warren was at Kallia again this morning, waiting with two coffees in hand, but as we walked to the office, I didn't hear a word he said.

"Analise?" he asks, concerned, and it's that tone that snaps me out of it.

"Huh?" I look up, trying to figure out what street corner we're at. I'm not sure how long I zoned out for.

"Are you okay?" He's regarding me with the intensity of a current lover—not a past one. "You've barely said a word all morning."

"I'm sorry." I sigh, looking at my reflection in the building behind him to make sure the layers of concealer Ali helped me put on this morning to cover the cut and redness are still doing their job. It's sore as hell and has me worrying others will be able to notice, but it's not swollen, and the makeup covered it better than I expected. His eyes pass over my cheek without stopping. "I didn't have the best night."

"Do you want to talk about it?" he asks, hopeful, but I shake my head, thinking of what happened and all that he wasn't here for that led up to that point.

"Not particularly."

"Oh, okay." His face falls but I just turn to keep walking. I still feel so empty right now. Trying to conceal an entire part of my life is draining. *Dealing* with that part of my life is draining. I'm just trying to make it through the day at this point, going through the motions.

He follows, but looks distressed.

A block later he stops and turns to me. "Does this have anything to do with the texts I sent you last night?"

Now, it's my turn to be confused. "What texts?"

"You didn't get my texts? Your number's still the same, isn't it?"

"Yeah," I say, then trail off. After I called Ali, I didn't look at my phone for the rest of the night and I never checked it this morning either—now that I think of it, it's probably dead. I don't remember charging it at all, and it was already in my bag this morning. "Oh, I haven't checked my phone since yesterday afternoon."

"Analise, are you sure you're okay?" He puts his hands on my shoulders and examines my face in excruciating detail—but still, thankfully, misses any signs of my injury. My heart flutters at the care and worry in his eyes, and I know I probably shouldn't, but the feeling of needing to be held by him is so strong that I just throw my arms around him and bury my face in his chest. He freezes. "Okay, you're really starting to worry me now."

I laugh for the first time this morning and his body relaxes around me as his arms slide over my shoulders and around my back.

"I'm sorry I didn't see your messages," I murmur into his chest.

"I feel stupid for bringing it up," he says. "I was just worried you were mad at me."

I smile. "No, I'm not mad at you . . . this time."

His body shakes around me as he chuckles and I melt a little bit further into him.

"You know, I think I might prefer it if you were." He squeezes tighter. "Because at least then I would know what was bothering you instead of being completely in the dark and having no clue what to do to help."

"For now, you just being here is enough," I whisper. And it is —I feel better just being around him. He's the one I've wanted to turn to every time something bad—or good—happened the past six years.

But he wasn't there.

And I want to make sure I'm not falling back into him just

because he's here and it's easy. We need to talk before I can let myself want this again.

I squeeze him one last time before pulling away, my smile not as bright as it was a moment ago. "Now, come on, we have a meeting in a few minutes."

The day is busy for both of us and, other than the meetings we're in together, reviewing our business model, or going through what he's researched already to see if we can keep the companies separate, I don't see him much. But the first chance I get, I read his messages, and they make my whole day.

WARREN

I have no excuse for not reaching out over the past six years. All I can say is that there wasn't a single day that passed that I didn't think about reaching out, that I didn't almost reach out. I made a huge mistake back then and I never knew how to explain why I did it. Most days I couldn't even justify to myself why I did it. I know I hurt you and I will never blame you for not trusting me or not wanting to be around me, but I just wanted to say I'm glad the universe brought us back together—if only to give me the chance to apologize.

A few hours after, late into the night, he sent a second message.

WARREN

Come to think of it, I probably should've made sure this is still your number . . . if it's not, I apologize to you, stranger, for the heartfelt message.

That one made me laugh.

At the end of the day, I go to find him and stop outside one of the conference rooms with a smile on my face. He's deep in concentration and the way one of his eyes narrows as his mouth twists to the side makes me feel like we're back at Triniti. I could never resist staring at his cute, concentrated face even then.

He looks up and does a double take when he notices me watching, a sly smile growing across his face. He motions with his head for me to enter.

"You almost ready to go?" I ask, now glad that he'd been invited to this outing earlier in the week. It saves me the trouble of finding an excuse to invite him myself.

"This feels a lot like déjà vu." He smiles. "Catching you watching me while I work and heading out together after."

Even I can't stop the smile from blooming on my face. "Don't get ahead of yourself."

"I wouldn't dream of it." His smile turns wicked and his voice lowers. "You know I like to take it slow until you're begging for more."

My heart starts racing and I try to subtly press my thighs together, aching for the friction the memories tease. His eyes slowly drift down my body and his smile grows more devilish.

I scowl at him. "All right, if you're not ready to go in five, you're walking alone."

"Oh, I'll be ready," he drawls, and I turn to leave before I get myself into trouble—or more trouble than I'm already in, because who am I kidding, I'm in *trouble*. But when he adds, "Analise," in that slow, sexy voice, I have to grab the doorframe to stabilize myself because my legs have gone weak. He chuckles as I walk away, and I spend the next minutes trying to compose myself before he's ready to go.

"Wow, this place hasn't changed at all," Warren says when we step into The Dizzy Acorn. He stops and takes a look around until his eyes stop on the chalkboard next to the bar—the trivia leaderboard. A slow smile grows on his lips. "No one's beat our score yet?"

"Are you kidding?" I grin. "No one can beat *The Summers*."

The bar is more crowded than usual for a Wednesday night, and as we're weaving our way through the crowd, a man stumbles back into the woman in front of me and it causes her to splash her drink onto my face and all over my blazer. I gasp as a sticky, brown liquor drips down my sleeve.

I'm so distracted by the drink all over me that I get bounced around the crowd, unable to find my footing to keep pushing through, until a warm, sturdy hand links with mine and light pressure on my lower back guides me to the table where our friends are waiting with questioning glances at the dark stains on my tan blazer, as well as the reality of Warren being here, and Warren's hand in mine.

I pull my hand away, even though the warmth is comforting, and smile at the group. "So, in case anyone doesn't know yet, Warren is in town."

He waves but his attention is solely on me. "Sorry, guys, can you give us one minute?" He grabs my hand again and pulls us off to the side of the bar that's not as crowded and flags a bartender down. "A glass of water and two Blue Moons."

I look over at him, eyebrows raised, and he hesitates. "That's still your favorite, right?"

"It's perfect."

"Good." His smile is blinding. "Now, take off your jacket."

I cough out a laugh. "What?"

He grabs a stack of napkins as the water and beers get set in front of us. He hands over his card, then says, "Come on, jacket off."

When I don't move fast enough, he reaches out and unbuttons the blazer, gently sliding it off my shoulders, and my traitorous heart starts racing. After dipping the napkins in the water, he starts to wipe the liquor off my arms then lightly dabs at my chin and cheeks.

Our eyes meet and he keeps slowly dabbing, but without reason now. I lift my hand to his and squeeze. "Thank you."

"And here take this." He slides his own blazer off his shoulders and holds it for me to slip into.

I hope he doesn't catch the sharp intake of breath that slips through at the sight of him in just the fitted button-up. I turn quickly so he doesn't catch the color in my cheeks and slip into the suit jacket. I take a deep breath of it, savoring the smell of him I've been missing before turning back around. His hands move to the lapels, and he pulls it snug around me.

"It smells good," I say. "It smells like you."

He smiles but then his eyes rove over my face and rage builds in them. His hands tighten on the jacket. "What is *that*?"

I tilt my head, unsure of what he's asking about until his hand reaches for my cheek and I remember the layers of makeup that covered the cut. The layers that must've gotten wiped away by the water and the napkins.

"It's nothing." I turn away and look down. "I'm going to use the restroom. I'll be back at the table in a second."

He almost doesn't let me go, but I grab my purse and walk away. Shame creeps up my face and shows itself as red on my cheeks. I'm almost certain he only let me go because we just got here and by my reaction, he could tell there's a lot to this story, and there's no way he's going to let this be for long—not with how angry he is. But what do I say? The truth requires a lot of background explanation that's heavy for day three of reconnecting.

The cut doesn't hurt so bad anymore, but it doesn't look pretty. It was deeper than I originally thought so there's a small scab that formed, and there's a bright red ring of skin surrounding it. It looks more severe than it is; it's not a big deal.

After adding new layers of makeup to cover the evidence of last night's disaster, I head back out and smile when I find Ali, Trent, Sterling, and Warren all laughing together.

"Hey, guys," I say as I approach. "Sorry about that, I guess someone didn't like the color of my jacket."

Ali looks conflicted about Warren's jacket on me, and my jacket on the back of his chair. I discreetly shake my head at her. *It's nothing.* But it's definitely not nothing—not to me. Trent and Sterling both look unsure how to act with the two of us in the same room again—Ali must not have told them what she knew —and when Warren pulls out the chair beside him for me, they look between themselves.

"In case this hasn't been covered yet," I say, breaking the silence first, "Warren is the CFO of Vitality. I didn't know he was coming. We're working together, but he goes back to D.C. in a week and a half. So, let's stop being weird about it now."

Sterling laughs, his body relaxing, and guilt rolls through me realizing he's probably relieved I'm not going to break down and cry even though I'm nowhere near drunk enough to reach that stage even on a bad day. I owe them a lot for putting up with me and taking care of me on those nights. I've been such a mess, but they loved me just the same.

"What I wouldn't give to be a fly on the wall in your meetings," Sterling adds, still chuckling. While the others are still deciding how to handle this, Sterling pulls us all easily into smiles. "When you two were on the same side it was a deadly combination, but on opposite sides? That has to be entertaining for everyone else."

The corner of my lip pulls up as Warren laughs and answers, "She ripped me to shreds in a meeting the other day."

"Yeah, because your proposal makes no sense at all," I say immediately, and catch Ali laughing under her breath.

"Maybe from your side," he adds, turning to look at me. A lighthearted smile is still present on his face. This is why things worked so well between us —we could leave work at work. If we ever disagreed about something work related, it never transferred to a personal fight. In fact, I always suspected he liked it.

The more heated things got in a meeting, the hotter the passion in the bedroom became.

"What about the side where all the work Transcend has done to further value-based care and create an environment where providers and patients can thrive will be undone by this decision?" I ask, and for the first time in this conversation, his smile falls away.

"Well, shit." He runs a hand through his hair and takes a long sip of his drink. "When you put it like that, I feel like an ass for even suggesting it."

"You should," I add, trying to act serious, but a teasing smile is creeping on my face. Ali and Sterling can't hold it back and laughs sputter out. Warren's smile is back too. "I told you I'd fight for what was best for my company, and it definitely isn't your plan."

"Don't worry," he says, softly, fondly, *sweetly*, and my eyes widen when they meet his. "You eviscerated my plan so completely that after you left yesterday Peter told me to focus on helping you find a solution while we're here."

I'm trapped in his stare and the emotions I find there—emotions I've told myself for so long that he couldn't still feel. Sterling clears his throat dramatically and I blink rapidly as I turn back to the group. I don't know what I feel right now, what I want. This whole situation is not what I expected it to be, yet our connection is still what it's always been. He's still every-thing I never stopped loving, and he's still leaving again next week.

I don't know where that leaves me.

"Enough about work." I smile, but it's not as natural as it should be.

Sterling leads us to a new topic and as conversation picks up, everyone seems like they're growing comfortable with Warren being back—everyone except Trent. He still wears a frown and looks between us with trepidation. I narrow my eyes at him in question and he looks away. I glance at Ali and she just shrugs.

Trent was closest with Warren; I expected him to be happiest that he was back.

Did something happen between them after we broke up?

Ali forces us all out onto the dance floor once the crowd thins out a bit and the playlist switches over to more upbeat music. It's not long before he grabs my hand and pulls me into him as the music slows. Slow dancing in the middle of a crowd has always been our thing and I feel trapped in this moment, in this memory, with him. When I finally get the courage to look up into his eyes, he's frowning, and his jaw is clenched tight.

Instinctually, I reach up and run my fingers down his cheek and across his jaw. His eyes widen as I ask, "What's on your mind?"

He nuzzles his cheek into my hand, his five o'clock shadow scraping against my skin, and I shiver at the feeling. He speaks into my hand when he says, "Are you going to tell me who did that to your face, or am I going to have to interrogate every person I know you were in contact with yesterday?"

I stop dancing. My arms go weak and would've dropped if he hadn't caught my wrists and pulled my hands to his chest. I whisper, ashamed of the truth. "I'm sure I have no idea what you're talking about."

"Are you going to make me wipe off the fresh layers of makeup you added earlier to prove a point?" He stares at me, and when I don't move or speak, he moves his hand to my cheek. I press my lips together in preparation, but when his thumb hits a spot that's still tender, I flinch and grab his hand to stop him. Anger flares in his eyes. "Analise, I swear if you don't tell me what happened I will turn into a fucking FBI agent and track down whoever did this."

"Right, because you're just so good at everything," I deflect, looking away.

"Analise." His grip tightens on my hands.

I hesitate. I've wished he was here to talk to so many times, but now that he is, I don't want him to know.

But if things continue down the path they are, I don't want us to fall into the same patterns we did last time—not saying how we truly felt when things weren't ideal, withholding certain important facts that had large implications on our decisions. I close my eyes and sigh. I don't have a good enough lie anyway.

"It was my dad," I mumble, so low that he can't possibly hear me over the noise in the bar.

"What was that?"

I take a deep breath then look up at him with tears in my eyes. "My dad did it."

Now it's his turn to go completely still. "Your . . . dad?" he croaks out, blinking and shaking his head. "But . . . he was . . ."

He trails off, but he doesn't have to finish.

I know.

My dad was the dad everyone loved to be around. He was the one always telling cheesy jokes that you couldn't help but laugh at. He was an amazing man and an even better dad. He and Warren were so close back then. I can see in his eyes— Warren can't connect that man with the cut on my face.

I blink and tears drop down my face. Before they hit my chin, his hand is there wiping them away. That simple gesture crumbles the last of my walls. The last of my resolve to keep him at a distance, to not let myself get too close, disappears. I don't want to keep pushing him away, not when it feels so much better to have him close.

"A year and a half after you left, my mom died."

"Your mom died?" He pulls me into his arms, but he has no clue that the worst is yet to come. "I'm so sorry, I know how close you two were."

"It happened so fast, it was probably easier that way." I shrug when he pulls back to look at me. I've had a lot of time to come to terms with all of this. I don't need him to fix me, I've already fixed myself. "It was hard for me, but I dealt with it. I got through it. My dad didn't." I look away as another tear falls. "He didn't know how to deal with it, so he turned to bourbon, and he never stopped. He's not himself anymore. I tend to avoid him as much as possible, but yesterday was the anniversary of her death and I try to at least visit him then. She'd be so sad to see what he's become, and I miss having my dad, but when I try to help him, he doesn't react well." I gesture to my cheek. "Yesterday, he threw a glass cup at my face."

The way his face darkens at the words has me quickly adding, "I moved out of the way in time, but it shattered against the wall and a shard got me."

"Are you fucking kidding me, Analise," he says so loud that everyone near us looks our way. I glance around and catch Ali's eyes, who takes one look at my tear-filled eyes and gives me a smile of encouragement knowing what I'm telling him. Noticing where Ali's gaze has gone, Trent looks over and frowns. "I don't care if he is your dad. I want to fucking kill him for hurting you." His hold on me is tightening and his breathing picks-up. "What if you hadn't moved out of the way? What if that shard flew into your eye? You could've been seriously injured."

"But I wasn't," I say softly, trying to calm him. My hand moves to lay against his chest. His heartbeat is wild and fast. I don't think I've ever seen him this angry before and it brings more tears to my eyes. This anger is for me, because someone hurt *me*.

Because he still cares for me.

His eyes widen. "That's why you reacted the way you did when I brought up your dad the other night." I nod as he whispers, "I'm so sorry. I didn't know."

"I know," I say, matter-of-factly, and the unsaid words are clear: *Because you weren't here.*

His face crumples in pain, and I don't try to comfort him. No matter how much I'm enjoying having him back, he's acting like he's looking for something more than friendship between us again and I don't think I can do that unless he understands and owns up to all of the hurt he caused. I'm not the same girl I was six years ago who was willing to overlook the signs that were right in front of her because he said he loved me. If we ever try again, I need to know things will be different.

"Are you going to see *your* mom while you're in town?" I ask after a few minutes of silence. It's only about a two-hour drive from here instead of the eight-hour drive—or a flight—from where he lives now.

"I told her I'd try, but I didn't know what free time I'd have this trip." He always wears the sweetest smile when he talks about his mom. "She loves coming out to D.C., and I still call her weekly, but she'd love it if I finally made it back home."

"You haven't been home recently?" I ask, pretending I don't know this information already. Because he doesn't know that while he hasn't been back home in the six years since he left, *I've* been to his home.

"No." His voice is small and he looks down at our feet that are only shuffling side to side at this point. I want to ask about the red flush on his cheeks, but I have a sneaking suspicion it'll only bring us back to the same silence we just got out of.

I would tell him about my visits, but considering I already had plans to go to Boston this weekend long before he got here, it might be fun to make this a surprise.

At the end of the night, I walk with Warren back to his hotel and we both pause outside, not wanting to separate and risk ruining this bridge that's building between us. One storm could bring it crumbling down, but a few more connections and it'll be strong enough to bear weight. The distance between us is shrinking, but it's not gone just yet.

"Oh, don't forget this," he says, breaking the silence as he hands me my stained jacket.

"Right, thanks." I take it and look down at the jacket I'm wearing—his jacket. I suck in one last breath of his smell before starting to shrug out of it. "I guess I should give you this back."

But before it slips off my shoulders, he grabs both sides and wraps it back around me, using it to pull me closer to him. His lips brush against my neck up to my ear. "Keep it, you look sexy as hell in my clothes."

"I—" I start but don't know what I want to say. Do I ask him to tell me everything? Do I wait for him to understand that's what I need? I don't know what the right answer is, so no words come out.

"I know, me too," he says with a sad smile. It's the first sign he's given me that he understands. That maybe, just maybe, he's trying to figure out how to tell me the same way I'm trying to figure out how to ask. He said in his text that he made a mistake and didn't know how to explain it. I hope he's trying to figure it out, because when he leans in and kisses my cheek, exactly where the cut is, my stomach does somersaults. It's so tender and intimate that my lower lip trembles and I have to hold my jacket tighter in my hands to keep from reaching out to him. "Goodnight, Analise."

"Goodnight, Warren," I say. But when he starts to walk away, I reach out and grab his hand—just long enough to make him look over his shoulder. "I'm glad the universe brought us back together too."

And it's the truth. It's what needed to happen, even if we don't end up together and all I get out of this is the closure I've been searching for all these years.

His responding smile is bright enough to light the whole city.

Eleven

AUGUST CURRENT DAY (THURSDAY)

I rush to work after spending too long talking to Ali at Kallia. I didn't have to say anything, but she knew what I was waiting for. My eyes kept flashing to the door, and I'd find ways to draw out the conversation and stay just a bit longer—hoping to see him, hoping he'd show up.

But he didn't.

I know I pulled away and brought on some uncomfortable moments last night, but that connection between us has been rebuilding one string at a time, and I don't know how much longer I'll be able to resist its pull.

I almost wore his blazer today just because I knew his eyes would be on me all day if I did, but it's obviously many sizes too large on me and would likely raise questions, so it's hanging at the front of my closet and I'm in one of my typical pantsuits.

When I get to the office, I do a quick lap, looking for him everywhere, before sulking to my office to unpack when I don't find him. *Damn, why am I so worked up that he's not here?* He was gone for six years—*six*—and now he's back for three days and I'm going out of my mind that he's late for work. I need to calm down. We have a group meeting in thirty minutes; I'll see him then. I take a few deep breaths.

I can survive thirty minutes—

Just kidding.

I can't.

I try to get some work done but my gaze keeps drifting back to the clock, counting down the minutes until our meeting. And even then, I gather my stuff and head to the meeting room extremely early. I just need to see him, to make sure this hasn't all been some elaborate dream I concocted.

Finally, people start filing into the room. Clara, then Serge, Ben, then Jason, and lastly, Peter and Mac. I'm still watching the door when Peter starts the meeting and my head whips around to look at him. My eyes are wild, untamed, worried.

I take a deep breath so no panic or surprise creeps into my voice. "Will Warren be joining us?"

Others look around like they hadn't even realized he wasn't here, but to me, this room is empty without him.

The corner of Peter's lips twitch up into the beginnings of a smile that seems to know more than it should. "He's going to be late today. Some sort of personal issue he had to take care of."

I nod and smile, but my mind runs through every terrible thing that could've happened to him. Is he hurt? Did something happen to one of his parents? Is he okay?

That's all I care about. I just need him to be okay.

The meeting passes in a blur of voices that I can't clearly make out because I'm too busy worrying about Warren. I practically run out of the room when we finish and pull out my phone the second I get back to my office.

ME

A personal issue? Everything okay?

It's as casual a message as I can make it, but I know he'll see right through it. Right now, I don't even care. Every emotion that's been kept deep down in my heart, locked away, is written on my face.

WARREN

Aw, you're worried about me.

I breathe out a sigh of relief and smile. He's okay. I don't need to hear anything else to know it.

ME

Wipe that cocky grin off your face.

WARREN

I have no such grin on my face.

ME

Liar. I know you better than that.

WARREN

And I know you well enough to know you'd do dirty things for this cocky smile.

My mouth pops open. He's too cocky for his own good . . . but damn him because he's also right. I love that cocky smile, his confidence, and the way he knows me so well. I can't even lie and say I wouldn't do dirty things for that smile. I *have* done dirty things for that smile and it's all I can think about right now.

I don't bother answering the message, but he comes marching into my office later that day with a smirk on his face and I want to lock the fucking door. He doesn't stop at the door though, he walks right over to me and leans down to whisper in my ear. My eyes close when his breath skates across my skin with the words, "If you keep worrying about me like that, I'm not going to be able to stop myself from doing dirty things to you."

My breath stutters. I'm not going to be able to stop myself for much longer either.

He doesn't stick around. He turns to go, but at the door looks back and gives me one of his sunshine smiles. "I'll make sure to let you know if I'm going to be late again. Wouldn't want you to worry." Then he walks out of the office, and it takes me a long time before I start working again.

~

"I heard we have quite a few basketball fans," I say to everyone at dinner once conversation starts to die down.

Warren looks over at me with interest. Last night he told the friend group about how Peter had box seats to the Washington Wizard's and they go to games often. It gave me an idea, and after spending a few days with this group, I think they'll be up for it.

"We try to do half-day Fridays during the summer," I start, "and I thought we could play some basketball after lunch if people are interested?"

Peter's face breaks into a smile. "You had me at basketball."

"That sounds fun," Mac adds. She smiles when she sees the joy on Peter's face but quickly looks away.

Clara and Serge are quiet as expected. Neither are sports enthusiasts and I didn't count on them participating.

"Okay, so that's four," I say and start to turn toward Jason and Ben when I notice many confused looks and one sly smile. I smile sheepishly, a flush creeping onto my cheeks that I hope isn't too noticeable. I didn't even need to look at Warren to know he was in, but he didn't give an answer out loud. We definitely played down how well we knew each other the other night, so maybe they didn't expect it, or maybe it's still weird that I know him at all. "I already know Warren won't turn down a game. Jas—"

I turn to ask Jason if he wants to play but he's glaring at Warren as he cuts me off and says, "I'm in."

My lips press into a flat line as I look between them. Jason keeps glaring, but Warren acts like he doesn't notice—it only causes tension to build in Jason's face. He's getting really angry.

Yikes. Throwing them into a competitive situation will be . . . interesting to say the least.

Ben agrees and we have six. Three-on-three it is.

I'm trying to figure out what the best team split might be when Peter asks if Warren and I have made any headway on finding out how to keep the consulting side of the business intact. Clara perks up immediately and leans in to listen. She came to find me as soon as the meeting was over on Tuesday in a panic, which is why I was so worried when she told me she accepted this offer prior to my review.

I hate the disappointment on her face when we report that even though we've been searching for a solution whenever we have time, we haven't found anything yet. The hardest part is figuring out what to search for. I would bet my life on there being a solution to this, but we just don't know how to word the question to make the answer obvious.

I promised her then that I wouldn't stop until I figured out a way around this, and I assure her again now. "We *will* keep looking."

When I look over at Warren, he's watching the exchange with a small frown, but he nods in agreement with my words.

The exchange seems to sour the mood, and everyone stands to head back. The restaurant tonight was walking distance from the office and hotel, so our group splits up and heads in different directions. Clara and Serge wave and head towards the office to get their cars while Peter and Mac want to check out the town at night. They ask if anyone else wants to join but we all decline. Ben, the quietest of everyone, heads off with a short "Night," and Jason hangs by my side like a shadow, waiting for me to say what I'm doing first.

I want to walk back with Warren, but Jason won't let that happen, unless I can come up with an excuse as to why Warren and I are leaving together. I step away from Jason and say, "We're heading to a friend's place."

Perfect—a non-public place so he can't insist on joining us.

He frowns. "Together?"

Warren steps forward and joins the scene like an actor stepping into a role they were born to play. He doesn't miss a beat. "It's someone we both knew from Triniti. When they heard I was in town they invited the old group over."

Jason glares between us, not yet moving.

"Well, we're headed this way." I point in a direction that isn't towards the office or the hotel, just so I know he has no excuse to try to walk with us. To seal the deal, I let the edge of annoyance into my voice as I add, "Have a good night."

He grumbles something I can't make out—and don't care enough to ask about—and sulks away. Once he turns the corner and is out of sight, I let out a quiet laugh. Warren's smile is full of amusement.

"I didn't think he was ever going to leave," he says.

"That's Jason for you." I roll my eyes. "It was easier with you backing up my story. We make a good team."

"We always have." His smile is gone, but there's a different kind of joy present in his features.

I smile and start walking toward the hotel and he falls into step beside me. It's quiet on the walk there, but it's a calm, contemplative quiet. It's the quiet of two people who don't need words to speak—to communicate—to understand each other. It's a happy quiet.

A wave of disappointment rolls through me when we get to the hotel. I'm not ready to leave him, but I don't have a good excuse to stay. I try to hide my excitement when he solves that dilemma for me.

"Stay for a drink at the bar with me?" he offers, and the way he smiles makes it impossible for me to leave.

"Just one." I smile.

And we both know it's a lie.

Twelve

OCTOBER 8 YEARS AGO

Everyone in the bar lets out an audible, collective groan when the answer for the next question is read—everyone but me. I try to hold back my squeal of delight that we got it right and should be moving up the leaderboard. It's been one of those trivia nights where your eyebrows pull together and your eyes narrow after every question is read, and you question if anyone knows this information at all. But even though I let out a laugh of disbelief after almost every question, Warren has been wearing a sly smile most of the night.

"How are you guys so good at this?" Ali asks when we get another hard question right and move into a tie for first place.

"His brain has so many random facts in it, I don't know how it doesn't explode." I point to Warren and glance back at him with a smile. I lean over to kiss his cheek when he smiles back.

That's my brilliant, handsome man.

At the end of the three main rounds, Warren and I are tied for first place. We had to get that last question right while the other team got it wrong to push the game to a tie, and I thought we were screwed when they read out the question. I mean, who the hell knows what the name of the commission established to investigate the JFK assassination was?

But Warren's eyes lit up and he submitted our answer immediately—no hesitation—as I gawked.

"How did you know that one? You hate history," I'd asked, but he just smiled and said, "You'll see."

I didn't understand what that meant until the answer was read and it was "The Warren Commission." I just laughed and shook my head as it was announced we were the only ones to get it right.

They don't let the games end in a tie here, especially when the scores are high.

This was the first time we were involved in a tie. They didn't happen often, but we at least understood how it'd go down. It was up to fate now.

"Well, well, well!" the game host says over the mic, trying to get the crowd excited. He's a shorter man who's trying to hide the fact that he's balding by combing his hair over, but it only makes it more obvious. He looks like he tried to dress in what he thought was "hip," but it just looks haphazard. We've been here enough for trivia that he knows our group. We try to be kind to him, but it's hard not to laugh when he gets way too into this volunteer trivia hosting job. "It seems we're going to have to pull out one of the *extreme* tie-breaker questions."

He holds out the last word and wiggles his fingers at the crowd, which comes across more spooky than exciting, and everyone looks around.

He quickly stops and clears his throat. "Whoever gets it right will not only win tonight's trivia competition and get a free round of drinks, but based on the current scores, they'll also land themselves the number one spot on the leaderboard."

Now that causes some chatter, and many heads—including our own—look over at the chalkboard of leaders. The number one spot hasn't changed since we started coming here. I don't even know how long it's been there. Every time we've played in these trivia nights, we've said we're going to end up on that board, but tonight is the first time we truly have a chance. Warren and I grin at each other like little kids who were just told they're going to Disney.

"Will our top two teams please make their way down here? Give it up for *The Summers* and *The Chumpions*." The crowd claps as we walk up. Sterling and Ali cheer too loud and I turn to glare at them, but the smile won't leave my face.

We shake hands with our opponents, who are a pair of middle-aged men who look like their job could be watching the Animal Planet channel all day. They smile at us, but I see the look they give each other—they think they've got this in the bag. I press my lips together and narrow my eyes at them, hoping I'm making what Warren calls my "scary face." Their faces pale slightly when they look at me, and I smile back with a look full of venom.

Warren chuckles softly behind me and rests a hand on my lower back. I pull my eyes off the competition and fight a sigh when they land on him. I'm so in love with him, it's scary. Literally. I'm so in love with him I'm scared to tell him because the force behind the words might be too overwhelming, especially since he hasn't said them yet either.

"Are you ready for the final question?" the host asks, and I force my eyes off him. Only once we all nod does he continue. "In what scenario can it be advantageous to form a parent company under Tax Law number seven hundred and nine? A) Litigation, B) Conflict of Interest, C) Bankruptcy, or D) Acquisition."

Each team whispers amongst themselves. Warren and I immediately rule out A and C, thinking that they don't really make sense even though we can't explain why. These questions are called "extreme" for a reason—they're meant to be about extremely obscure things very few would know about. We go back and forth on the last two options, but eventually Warren gives in and agrees to go with my choice.

Both teams stand up straight and look at each other, meaning we're ready.

"All right, both teams will say their answers on the count of three," the host says, then turns to address the crowd. "If both are right, we'll keep going through questions until one team gets one wrong. But if both are wrong, we'll do a redo with the remaining answer choices." He looks between us then starts counting. "One, two, three."

"D) Acquisition," the Chumpions say, as we answer, "B) Conflict of Interest."

It goes completely silent. The crowd holds their breath, looking between us in anticipation as the announcer makes a long scene of checking his card and looking between the two teams. "It looks like we have a winner." Warren's hand moves to lace with mine and squeezes. We'll either win or lose because of the argument I made for choice B. I swallow—hopefully it was the correct argument. "The team that has won tonight's game, and will claim the top score of all time is . . . *The Summers!*"

I squeal and turn to throw my arms around Warren's neck. His arms wrap around me immediately and he lifts me off the ground.

"How do you feel?" The microphone gets shoved between us before I can kiss him, and he recovers faster than I do.

A sinful smile plays at his lips, and he winks as he answers, "Brighter than the sun."

I smile at the answer that's just for me. *My* sun.

"The sun?" the host asks. "Like your team name *The Summers?*"

Warren nods, eyes locked on me.

"Would you like to tell us why you chose that name?"

A smile pulls at my lips, and he nods towards me, letting me answer the question. "Well, my last name is Summers, and . . . well, look at him." I gesture to Warren with a grin on my face. "He's golden, and glows like the sun. I've always joked that if we got married, he'd have to take my last name. So, we're *The Summers*."

"Aww," the host starts and eggs on the crowd to join.

Warren leans down to kiss me, light and sweet and warm as a collection of *aw's* fill the room.

"So, marriage is in your future then?"

I cough out a laugh and turn beet red.

We haven't even said "I love you" yet. We're taking it slow and doing this right, even though I have to bite my tongue every time I'm around him so the words don't accidentally slip out.

"We only started dating recently," I answer first, because the look on Warren's face has me scared—but also excited—about what he was going to say. "We have a lot of time before we have to worry about that."

The microphone starts to pull back, but Warren stops it. "But living in summer for the rest of my life doesn't sound like such a bad thing."

I lightly hit him in the stomach as a blush stains my cheeks. "You getting all sappy on me now, Mitchell?"

"I guess the summer heat thawed this cold heart," he teases with a smirk, and I laugh.

"Oh, shut up." I smack his stomach again, harder this time. "You're just playing it up for the crowd now."

The host pulls back and looks between us, smiling. "I think I speak for everyone here when I say, I hope you do become *The Summers* one day."

At the end of the night, someone brings the leader board over to us and lets us write our team name in the top spot. In my best, sunny handwriting, I write the words and add a little sun next to it. I'm about to hand the chalk back over but Warren extends his hand. I raise an eyebrow at him but drop the chalk in his hand. He smiles at me, then leans over and adds a heart at the end.

My heart stutters. Does that mean he feels the same way I do? Does that mean he loves me too?

I look up at him and get lost in those beautiful eyes.

I love you. I love you. I love you.

Before I even realize that we're both leaning closer, his lips gently press against mine, and I swear it's love I feel threaded in the tenderness there.

I love you. I lo—

"All finished?" the bartender who brought over the board asks, not-so-patiently waiting for us to give it back.

Warren hands it back without saying a word. I think I hear Sterling apologize on our behalf, but all I can hear ringing through my head are the words:

I love you. I love you. I love you.

Thirteen

The bar is a small room off the back of the lobby with just enough space for a few high-top tables in front of the bar top, where most of the seating is. There are two open seats close to the middle and I lead us over. Before I can pull out the black leather seat, it's being pulled out for me. I give him a closed-lip, nervous smile and sit down.

We haven't said a word since we entered the hotel. The weight of the what-if's, what-could-have-been's, and where-is-this-night-going hang over us, threatening to drop at any moment and break this fragile foundation we've been rebuilding. This night—this location—feels different. At The Dizzy Acorn, at work, or even when we're walking around, I have some level of comfort knowing nothing will happen. Or at least, if it did, we're weren't in a location that would be conducive to letting it go too far. But here, we're sitting in a building that he has a room in. It'd be much too easy to let it go too far.

I wring my hands in my lap and watch the way the blue light lining the arch behind the bar plays off the mirror behind it as the bartenders grab different bottles on display. It's mesmerizing, but it's not enough to distract me from the man sitting beside me, watching me with a serene but contemplative expression. He doesn't say a word but when the bartender comes by, he orders for both of us.

"It's been so weird being back here this week," he says, finally taking his eyes off me to look around when our beers get set in front of us. "It feels like I've gone back in time."

"Have you really not been back since you left?" I press my hands flat against my legs, trying to still their shaking before I reach for my drink.

He shakes his head and glances over at me. "I could never work up the courage to face what I left behind."

I close my eyes and take a long sip of my drink. I'm confident he's talking about me—us—but struggling to believe him, to trust *this*. If he still feels this way, then why did he end things in the first place? Why have I not heard from him until now?

He sighs and I look over at him, getting trapped in his molten eyes. "It's crazy how it feels like nothing has changed."

I want to smile and play along, to flirt and laugh, but I can't, because if I do, it'll be the first domino to fall down the line that leads us to his room at the end of the night without having the conversations we need to have.

I've put it off long enough. I need answers and I need them now, because I only have so much willpower left before I let my lingering feelings for him take over and ignore the logical part of my brain.

"But everything *has* changed," I say, looking away to steel my nerves for the gut-wrenching truth of the words I'm about to speak. "If you had asked me seven years ago, I would've said, without a doubt that you were the person I was going to marry." I look back at him and his face falls. "I was *sure* I was going to spend the rest of my life with you, but now . . ." I shake my head. "I don't know anything."

"Analise," he rasps, reaching out to grab my hand.

My chest tightens, suddenly scared of what he's going to say again. Maybe I don't want to know why. Maybe I should've taken the easy and fun way. My head shakes faster now. "I'm sorry, I shouldn't have—"

"I *was* going to propose," he says, so softly and it feels like I just took five punches to the chest. All my breath is gone and I'm struggling for air. I'm surprised I'm still in the chair and didn't fall out of it—I'm surprised my body is still functioning.

"What?" I squeak.

"I had a ring, I had a plan, well, I still have the ring, actually." My head won't stop shaking as he so casually says words that shake the foundation of what I thought I knew. "I was going to do it that night, on top of the hill after Il Piacere. The day I got the call, I was going to propose."

"You . . . that night . . ." I can't form words. I can't finish sentences. My entire world has just been flipped on its head. How am I supposed to act like nothing has changed?

He was going to fucking propose and instead he just left. I can't think, I can't breathe. I rummage through my purse and let out a breath of relief when I find enough cash to pay for my drink so I don't have to stay here any longer. I think Warren says my name but there's only a ringing in my ears. I don't wait, I just stumble out of the bar and into the lobby, trying to reach the fresh air, trying to breathe.

Halfway through the lobby, my legs give out and I sink to my knees. Tears build behind my eyes as my head keeps shaking. I'm trying to get air into my lungs, but it won't go. I can't see anything but that night on repeat in my head—that night when I thought he was going to propose . . . because he *was* going to. I see that perfect moment when his mouth opened, and I smiled. But the words that came out were not what I expected.

At what point that day did he decide that moving meant we could no longer be in each other's lives? That he no longer wanted to marry me?

"Analise," a gentle voice goads me out of my thoughts. He's squatting next to me with troubled eyes.

He reaches towards me, and I scramble away, feeling a little guilty for the pain that flashes across his face, but I need a second to breathe, to think. I try to stand but my knees buckle. Instead of falling, strong arms catch me. I savor the feeling for one second before pushing away.

"Don't touch me," I say through tears, a little too forcefully, and a little too loud. I don't mean ever, I just mean until I can sort through these feelings and process this revelation. He takes a small step towards me, and I take a step away. His face falls into something beyond devastation. I open my mouth to clarify, but one of the hotel receptionists walks up to us.

"Excuse me, ma'am," he says, only looking at me, and deliberately placing himself between us. "Is everything okay here?"

It takes me a moment to realize what he's implying. *Oh, god.* I can only imagine what they think after the small bit of what they've seen: a woman in tears, leaving the bar, trying to get away from a man who won't leave her alone.

"Everything's fine," I say with so much anger in my voice that it doesn't sound true.

"Are you sure?" His eyes widen and the words are slower, like he wants me to know I'm safe here.

I take a deep breath and try to put on a calm face. "He's a good friend of mine." I gesture to Warren to clarify. "I apologize for the disturbance, but I promise *I'm* safe."

I don't add that he probably should be making sure Warren is safe in this scenario too because I want to beat the shit out of him right now. I just give him a polite smile then grab Warren's arm and drag him out the front doors.

"Analise," he says first when I let go and turn to face him.

"What the fuck, Warren?" I'm almost yelling again. "You were going to propose but instead you told me you were leaving? At what point that day did you decide I wasn't enough anymore?"

He flinches. "It wasn't like that."

"Then please tell me what it *was* like?" I *am* screaming now. "Because you still left."

"You said you were happy for me," he counters, and I let out a cruel laugh.

"I was, I *am!*" I yell, then pause to take a deep breath when a look of confusion runs across his features. "You still don't get it do you? I *was* proud of you. I would've told you to take that job any day. I'm not mad that you left, I'm mad that you didn't ask me to come with you." My voice gets smaller and smaller, now only barely audible. Tears flow steadily as I squeak out, "Why didn't you ask me to come with you?"

He's quiet and when I look up at him, his face is full of pure shock. He blinks quickly, processing and I can almost see him playing back those final weeks, trying to reconcile what happened with this revelation.

"It was easier when I thought you didn't want me, because at least I could understand why you did it," I say. Nothing makes sense anymore. "But you were going to propose . . . you wanted me."

"Of course I wanted you, Analise." I can hear the pain in his voice and my heart wants to reach out to him. "You're all I've ever wanted."

I close my eyes, frustrated at how different his words are now from his actions back then. "Then how could you just walk away?"

"I didn't want to be like my dad," he blurts out and my mouth drops open. I didn't expect this to come up so fast, for him to so easily tell me the information he kept secret for so long. He takes a deep breath. "When he got his job in New York, he just told my mom she was going—didn't give her a choice. Her job, her friends, her *life* was in Boston, and he forced her to leave all of it. When they divorced, it seemed so sudden to me, but I found out later that they stopped loving each other long before that. That he thought his career was more important than hers and it pushed them apart. I was so scared that you would end up hating me if you had to move. I wouldn't have been able to stand it if things ended up that way, so I thought breaking up with you and being forced to live without you was the better choice. But I've been miserable without you."

"You do realize that you basically did the same thing, just in reverse, right?" I close my eyes. I know he was trying to be better than the example set for him, but he handled it so wrong. How could he have thought he was doing the right thing here? "You could have just asked me, given me a choice. Instead, you took the choice away from me completely. I *wanted* you to ask me to come. I would've come with you in a heartbeat."

"I was twenty-six! I didn't know what to do, and all I knew was what my dad had done to my mom and I couldn't bear the thought of doing that to you—to us. You never said anything so I thought I was doing the right thing." He looks like he's in shock, like he's just now realizing we lost out on six years of life together because we fucked this up. "Why didn't you say anything?"

"It wasn't my place to," I say. "You were the one leaving. I wasn't going to force myself into your life if you didn't want me there. I didn't want to be the girl that followed you to a new state when you didn't even ask me to come. All I needed was one sign that you wanted me there, but you never gave me it."

"I wanted you there, Analise." He takes a tiny, hesitant step towards me. "I wanted you to come with me. But your job—"

"I could've found another job," I cut him off, voice raised and teary-eyed. "There are hundreds, *thousands* of jobs out there, but there's only one you. I would've gone anywhere, done anything if it meant getting to be with you. I was so completely, life-consumingly in love with you, Warren, and you took my choice away from me."

"I thought I was doing the right thing, but the second I stepped onto that plane, alone, nothing felt right. Nothing *feels* right." I take a step back to rest against the brick wall behind me as he takes a step closer. "I told you once that I was color-blind before I met you, but life has been colorless without you. Like someone turned down the saturation on my life because you weren't there with me."

He takes another step closer and there's only a few feet between us.

I whisper, "Then why did you tell me not to get on the plane? Why did you break up with me?"

"Because I knew if I held you in my arms again, I'd never be strong enough to let you go."

I want to believe it. I want to trust it. But . . . "You weren't there when I needed you most." The words are soft, but they stop him in his tracks. Tears spring to my eyes thinking of all the pain I went through alone. "My mom died and then my dad became a drunk, and you were nowhere to be found."

"You didn't call me," he chokes out. "You didn't text me. No one told me. I didn't know any of this happened until yesterday. If I knew—" His eyes are wild, and he runs his hands through his hair. "If I *knew* I would've been on the first flight back. I would've been here, and I would've made sure you didn't feel alone for a single second."

"I don't understand." I can't breathe. "Why did you stay away if you felt that way?"

"After the day we broke up I never heard from you," he says, his voice squeaking. "Not that it was your job to reach out, but I thought you would've heard from someone that there was a ring, that I still felt that way about you. I thought you knew all of that and hated me enough that you didn't want to hear from me, so I forced myself to stay away. I never reached out because the only words I wanted to say to you were the four words I didn't ask that day that I've regretted ever since. I never visited my mom because two hours wasn't enough distance to keep me from driving to your door, dropping to my knees, and begging you to forgive me. Earlier in the week you asked me if I would've reached out if you didn't work here, and I probably wouldn't have because I thought that was what you wanted. But I also wouldn't have been able to stop myself from going to Kallia in the mornings, or The Dizzy Acorn in the evenings, hoping to catch even a glimpse of you. And once I saw you, I wouldn't have been able to stop myself from walking right up to you. From trying to figure out if there was any possibility of squeezing back into your life in any capacity. From trying to win you back and show you that I'm not the same person who left you all those years ago."

"I didn't know." I can't stop shaking my head. All of the words he's just spoken rattle around and I keep waiting for them to form into sentences that make more sense, sentences that don't make the past six years feel like a waste. "I didn't know any of it. I always thought you didn't reach out because you'd changed your mind. I thought you didn't want me. I didn't want to beg you to love me if you wanted to leave, and I didn't want you to come back just because you felt sorry for me, so I didn't reach out, even though you were the one person I wanted to talk to every day."

He lets out a soft, sad laugh and looks up at the night sky. "I really fucked this up, didn't I?"

"Yeah." The word just slips out, a whisper of a breath that brings so much pain to his face you'd think he'd just been shot. "You broke up with me by way of a thirty second phone call while I was at the airport waiting to board a flight to see you. I was heartbroken. I was humiliated. I was so confused how you could tell me you'd never leave me if you knew you had no intention of making things work."

"It wasn't like that," he says forcefully and steps closer, taking my hand in his. The part of me that has been angry all these years screams at me to pull away, but it's only a faint echo now, fading more and more with every word from his mouth. "God, no wonder you hated me if that's what you thought. When I first decided to take the job, I didn't know what to do. I was so in love with you, but I knew this was an opportunity I couldn't turn down. I wanted to ask you to come with me so badly, but I psyched myself out with thoughts of my parents. So, then I thought, it's okay, we love each other so much we'll be able to make long-distance work until we figure something out. I needed to talk to you about it but all I ever wanted to say to you was that I wanted you to come with me, and I convinced myself I couldn't ask you that or you'd end up hating me, so I just didn't say anything. I wanted to make sure you knew that I still loved you in those months, but looking back it's easy to see how it could be misinterpreted as using our attraction as a tactic to avoid talking about anything real."

Silent tears drop down my cheeks. Back then I didn't know what to think, because I *did* feel loved by him, but I couldn't understand why he didn't just talk to me or ask me to go with him. And I think a part of me was afraid that I wouldn't like the answer, so I didn't bring up my worries. In the end, we both stopped communicating in an effort to keep the relationship alive, but it's what ended up ruining us instead.

"When I got to D.C," he continues, and nothing could take my focus away from the words coming out of his mouth, "I missed you so much more than I ever could've imagined. The texting and phone calls weren't enough, I wanted you in my arms. I knew that if you came to visit, I would beg you to stay. I went back and forth that whole day, and I called you so late because I couldn't bring myself to do it before that. I forced the words out of my mouth, and I hung up right away because if I stayed on the line even a second longer, I would've taken it all back. I told myself I was doing the right thing, but every word felt so wrong. The last thing I ever wanted was to break up with you."

"I wish you had just talked to me." I close my eyes, so I don't get distracted by the way the moonlight is adding the perfect sparkle to his glassy eyes. "I wish you had told me about the reason your parents divorced sooner. I wish you told me about the ring and your fears and your feelings. I wish . . . so many things."

"Is it too late then?" His voice is small but full of emotions. "To have a second chance. To show you that I can do things right this time. To communicate. To be together."

My eyes open and lock on his lips, then slowly drift up his face until I'm looking him dead in the eyes. I can feel the weight of my next words—they'll be the tipping of the scales one way or the other. But I already know my answer, so I take a deep breath and say, "No, it's not too late."

That's all it takes. With those words, all my anger is gone and all his restraint breaks. With two steps, the distance between us is gone and he's crashing into me.

Or I'm crashing into him.

We're colliding, lips desperately finding each other after years of being lost from each other. I'm too desperate to be anything but wild, my hands clawing at his chest, arms, then back—anything that will pull him closer to me. I want to melt into him. I want to become the liquid sunshine that he's made of. I never want to be anywhere but in his arms again.

His hand slides into my hair as a buffer as he pushes me against the wall, hips pinning me in place as his tongue begins a long, slow exploration of my mouth while his other hand runs up my sides, around my waist, anywhere it can reach as he retraces the path they used to make on my body—remembering every inch he used to love so much.

My hands slowly find their way between his dress shirt and jacket, savoring the feel of his muscles with only the thin layer between skin. One of my hands wraps around to his back and when he kisses me particularly deeply, my nails gently run down his back causing him to groan into my mouth and kiss me deeper. My other hand doesn't care that we're on a public street and anyone could be watching as it starts to untuck his dress shirt from his pants and then slides up his bare chest. His hand tightens on my waist, and he must be remembering where we are too, because if we were anywhere else that hand would already be somewhere else—where I want it to be.

It's enough for him to pull his lips from mine, but he rests his forehead against me as we both fight to suck in our next breath.

"Are you trying to ruin me?" he breathes.

I smile and run my hand down his chest. "Is it working?"

"You tell me," he whispers as he rolls his hips against me and I can feel just how much he wants me, wants *this*.

"Mmm," I purr. My eyes close and my body trembles with remembrance of everything good that comes after this. "That doesn't feel like ruin."

His voice is shaky when he asks, "Then what does it feel like?"

I kiss up his cheek until my lips are at his ear and whisper, "It feels like pleasure," as I tug him even closer by the waistband of his pants.

He lets out a groan that shakes me down to my core and curses, "Fuck."

Then his lips are back on mine, but his hands aren't quite so restrained. One of his hands drifts between my legs and applies pressure over my pants exactly where I'm craving it. I moan and hold on tighter to him, so I don't slip away.

"Are you just going to tease me with that beautiful mouth, or are you going to let me take you up to my room and give you all the pleasure you can take?" he asks against my lips.

"From what I remember, you didn't need a bed to do your best work." I smile when his eyes light up.

"I never said anything about a bed," he says, leaning in to whisper in my ear. "And I know you well enough to know you're stalling."

He's right. If I was going to go up to his room tonight, we'd be in the building by now, probably making out in the elevator. And I do want that, I want to go so bad, but it feels like I just survived a war and have come back to a life that no longer feels familiar.

He drops a kiss on my cheek, and the pit in my stomach eases. Because as much as I'm feeling like I'm ready to lean into whatever this might be, so much has been dumped on me tonight and I'd like time to process this before we take it further. Before this becomes real again.

"I really want to . . ." I start, my voice trailing off as I try to find the right words.

"But it's a lot to process," he finishes for me, and I nod, letting out a breath of relief. "I know, it's okay. I'm sorry I brought it up so casually like that at the bar, I thought you knew about that part already."

"How would I have known any of that?" I pull back and scrutinize his face.

"Because Trent knew," he says, and I stop breathing. "I just assumed he would've told you."

My teeth clink together and I'm seeing red.

Trent knew. Trent fucking knew and he never said a word. All those times I cried over Warren and thought he left because he didn't want to be with me, and Trent knew he did. Trent *knew* he wanted to marry me.

"I know that face." Warren's voice pulls me back. "That's your scary face."

"Sorry, this is a lot of information." I try to smile but it's hard. It feels like my life, for the past six years, has been a lie. I don't know what to think, who to be most angry at.

"Don't worry about it, go get some sleep. I'll see you tomorrow." He lifts his hand to my cheek, and I lean into the touch.

Before he can expect it, I lean forward to kiss him and mumble against his lips, "Just make sure to think of me when you're taking care of this." I run my hand down the front of his pants, and he jolts.

"What do you think I've been doing the past six years," he says before kissing me.

"You're lying," I mumble between kisses.

"Analise." He pulls away to look me in the eye. "You're *all* I've thought about for the past six years."

"Oh, come on," I say, eyes narrowing. "You must've been with someone else at some point."

He shakes his head. "Not once. All I've wanted—want—is you."

"Really?"

He nods and a fluttering feeling cascades through me.

"Is it bad that I'm happy about that?" I smile as his arms wrap around my waist and pull me into him.

"It'd be bad if you weren't," he says, laughing into my neck before planting kisses, but he stops after a few. "Have you?"

"Hm?" I sigh, feeling drunk on his kisses.

"Have you been with anyone?" The anxiousness is evident in his voice, but he quickly adds, "It's obviously okay if you have, but I might need names." It only sounds like he's half joking.

I look him in the eyes. "I told you the first night, I never got over you. I couldn't even think of anyone else that way."

I tried dating. I tried putting myself out there again, but I never made it to a second date with anyone. No one compared to him, and he was all I wanted. One of the dates kissed me goodnight once and I went back to my place and scrubbed my lips with soap and water in tears, because I couldn't remember what Warren tasted like and some random guy's lips were the last ones to touch mine. It felt like I was losing him all over again.

"Good," he says with a sly smile on his face. "Because the thought of anyone else's hands on you drives me fucking crazy."

"It's sexy as hell when you get jealous." I lean to kiss him again, wondering how I'm going to make myself walk away.

"Sexy enough to make you stay?" he teases with a kiss, and I laugh.

"Just like our first time, it'll be worth the wait," I tease back.

"You'll always be worth the wait." He kisses me, sweetly, deeply. "Now you should probably go because if you stay another second, I'm not going to be able to let go."

"I'll see you tomorrow." I kiss him one last, lingering time. "I hope you're ready to get your ass whooped at basketball."

"Oh, Analise," he calls as I start to walk away, "you can whoop my ass anytime."

"I'll hold you to that!" I call over my shoulder with a huge grin. I've missed him. I've missed this.

"I hope you do." His smile is bright even though it's the middle of the night. "Sweet dreams, Analise."

Fourteen

AUGUST CURRENT DAY (FRIDAY)

"Teams are Warren, Mac, and Jason versus Peter, Ben, and me." I relay the split and internally laugh at the frustration on Jason's face that comes from being assigned to the same team as Warren. But when Jason's gaze lands back on me I shift out of his sightline. The way he's been looking at me since I walked up in these leggings still sends a shiver through me—in a bad, uncomfortable way. I know he mostly agreed to play to go head-to-head with him, but this was the fairest way to split the teams.

I spent hours this morning looking for a solution for our company, but the only outcome of that was a never-ending stream of groans. There *has* to be a solution. Warren stopped by to help when he could, but Peter kept him in meetings all morning, and apparently they didn't finish what they needed, so he'll have to meet up with him again this afternoon.

Both of us were more than ready to blow off some steam with this basketball game.

"All right, team strategy," I say after shooting Warren a menacing smile. I'm glad we're on different teams—I really want to win just to throw it in his face. Mostly because the way he kisses when he's worked up is on a whole other level, and with the way his eyes are trying to burn my leggings off me, I know that's what's waiting for me on the other side of this game. I may have needed time to think last night, but after I did some baking —in preparation for this weekend—and now that I've processed all the new information, I'm ready to cross that invisible line I'd drawn.

When we huddle up, I'm surprised when Ben, the quietest of the bunch, speaks up first. "I should probably take Jason, since we're the tallest."

"Agreed," I say, relieved I won't be paired up with him. And though I really want to be paired with Warren, it makes more sense to put me against Mac since we're the only females here. But before I can voice my opinion, Peter jumps in.

"I'll take Mac." I try to hide my surprise and excitement when he looks over at me. "Can we trust you to deal with Warren?"

I can't hold back my grin. "Consider it done."

From observing this group over the past week, and especially with Peter's request, I've started to wonder if there's something between Peter and Mac. They're often around each other and seem to speak a language that only the two of them understand.

When we break, and see the other team has chosen the same match-ups as us—to the obvious dismay of a grumpy Jason—I wonder again if they planned this ahead of time, especially when Peter and Mac keep smiling smugly, glancing over at Warren and me.

"You game, Summers?" Warren's face is competitive and devious as he approaches me and all I want to do is throw my arms around his neck and kiss that stupid, handsome look off his face. His eyes darken and I know he's catching every little tell on my face, in my eyes, in the way I'm positioning myself around him to give *him* the best view of my ass in these leggings.

I take a deep breath to steady my thoughts, then narrow my eyes at him. I grin back as I say, "Oh, it's on, Mitchell."

As the game starts, the teams look evenly matched. Ben and Jason both get extremely into it and start getting overly competitive almost immediately. No matter how much the rest of us are laughing and keeping it light, the two of them are acting like it's the NBA Finals, Game 7. They're so evenly matched they've essentially blocked each other out of the game since neither can get free from the other. It seems like it's going to come down to me and Mac.

Whichever one of us can shut down our man more effectively is going to win this for their team.

Warren gets the ball from Jason and pulls some fancy footwork to roll around me and make a basket. He struts over to me like he's walking a red carpet, and I scowl at him as my cheeks heat. He has always played into that air of confidence, and I see in his eyes he's doing it for me.

"You've got to up your game if you want to beat me, Summers." While he's always been turned on by me going off on someone—or him—at work, I've always been turned on by his perfect amount of cockiness. I have to link my hands together behind my back so I don't reach out to him.

"Watch yourself, Mitchell," I say loud enough for the others to hear since they've been watching his celebration with varying levels of amusement and anger. But I lower my voice to add the last bit. "Or I might have to start playing dirty."

His eyes light up, two beautiful suns burning me to the ground. "Don't threaten me with a good time."

Despite myself, my forced scowl twitches up into a smile.

I take that as a challenge and start sneaking little touches across his body when no one's looking to get his blood flowing and pull his focus from the game. From the way his eyes get darker and his breathing gets heavier, it's working—but it's affecting both of us. We've both done very little to contribute to this game score-wise, but it stays competitive mostly because of Jason and Ben.

The score works its way up to a tie game—next basket wins. Peter has the ball for my team, and even though he could find a way around Mac to score, he passes it over to me. I swear there's a smirk on his face, but I immediately shift into serious competitor mode. I'm going to beat Warren.

I fake right, then roll around him to the left, but knowing he'll have read my movement, I'm particular about my foot placement—landing right between his legs as he's trying to twist around to stop me. It causes him to trip and fall and gives me the opening I need to make the winning shot.

The ball rolls around the rim and everyone goes silent.

When it finally drops in the net my team starts cheering as Warren sits on the ground calling for a foul. After I've let him complain long enough, I walk his way. "Aw, is someone being a sore loser?"

He scowls at me for real this time. "Don't play coy, you know you did that on purpose."

"Oh, come on," I tease, getting closer. "I can't control if you trip. Or can you just not handle losing to me?"

Someone snickers behind me, and my bet is it's either Jason or Peter.

"You know *exactly* what you're doing right now," he says, just for us, when I'm standing over him and enjoying the way his eyes travel up my body. I fight a smile, but it gives me away—*yes, I do know exactly what I'm doing, and it's working perfectly.* "You're lucky this is a work event, or else things would get really dirty, really fast."

I smile and hold out my hand. "Don't threaten me with a good time," I say, repeating his words from earlier.

"Oh, Analise." He says my name like it's a prayer as he gets up off his knees, and I almost drop down to mine. I suck in a breath when he brushes his fingers up my arm and whispers, "It's not a threat, it's a promise."

He walks over to congratulate Peter and Ben and talk to his team as I take too many seconds to compose myself from those few words. All I can think about is how to get him back to my apartment without it looking suspicious.

And I get so lucky.

Jason drove here, and Ben accepts his offer for a ride back. It seems they bonded over their shared competitiveness. Peter and Mac say they're going to stay at the park for a while, but they glance between us and smile as they walk away. In seconds, it's just Warren and me. And as soon as we're out of sight of the others, I lead him away from the hotel and towards my building.

We walk in silence through the streets of this town where we first fell in love. There's a nervous, excited energy between us, just as there used to be back then. But before we even make it to my place, he grabs my arm and pulls me down an empty side street.

"Where—" I start to ask but he stops us, pushing me up against the wall and kissing me like it's his job and he's looking for a promotion.

He groans against my lips. "I've been waiting to do that since you walked up in those leggings. And then you started talking dirty and touching me during the game—I was about to lose my damn mind."

"You're easy to rile up," I mumble as his lips make their way to my jawline. "I love that burning look in your eyes when I get under your skin."

"God, I fucking love that about you." He looks me in the eyes and my heart goes into overdrive at the word *love*. "I love that you're the only person that can get under my skin. I love your wit and our playful banter. I love that you're not afraid to call me out and tease me in front of anyone. And most of all, I love the way I can see every muscle in your body tighten when I run my eyes over you because I know every memory that's making you react that way. I love that I'm the only person who knows how to make you squirm, who can make you weak with one look, who knows exactly what you like."

I stare at him, awe-struck because it sounds a lot like he still loves *me*.

His hands run up my back, beneath my shirt and I suck in a breath. "I don't exactly remember where Solana is, please tell me we're almost there."

I nod, smile, and grab his hand, pulling him along after me.

The building is a well-kept brick building. It looks quaint from the outside but the second you step into the lobby you realize how much work went into renovating the inside. The lobby floor is a white and gray marble with a few black couches and seats. There's even a small chandelier that always perfectly refracts the lights in the room.

Warren looks around in awe. We only saw it through the windows back when it had been our dream to live here. We said we'd only step foot inside once we had a place there. I kind of kept that promise—I just replaced the *we's* with *me's*. When we step into the elevator, I press the button for the second floor. He stays quiet, but pulls me back against his chest, wrapping his arms around me and dropping a kiss on the top of my head.

Many business professionals live in the skyscrapers in the city-center—tall, modern buildings completely made of glass. But here, it's quieter. I'm practically on the ground floor, and there's so much more charm than those other buildings. This place has been even better than I dreamed it would be, and now, with Warren here with me, it finally feels complete.

I lead him down the hall, my hands fumbling more than usual when I reach for my key. When I open the door to my apartment, I expect his lips to come crashing into mine again, but instead he slowly enters, his head on a swivel, taking every-thing in. I decorated the main rooms in neutral earth and clay tones. I wanted it to be cozy and warm, and feel lived in, so all the shelves are packed with decorations and personal mementos. I try to see it as he is, with fresh eyes.

It's weird to be with him in a living space that he hasn't been to, but I like having him here. He's been a ghost in this place for so long, I'm glad he finally gets to see it. If he hadn't moved, this would've been our place, our life.

A smile grows on his face. "This is exactly how I imagined your place would look," he says, and I follow him as he walks towards the shelves against the back wall and starts examining their contents. There's not much I kept from our old place, so he has a lot of new items to take in, but there is one thing I couldn't get rid of.

He sucks in an audible breath, and I know his eyes have landed on it without having to look. He reaches out and picks up the small frame.

"You still have this?" His voice is small, and when he looks at me, his eyes are glassy.

That perfect polaroid—mostly a white blur with his hand hovering above us, holding a snowball and our lips locked.

Of course, I still have it.

"It's not something I ever wanted to forget." I shrug.

His hands are shaking as he sets it down and turns towards me. Something in me shifts then. This was supposed to be fun and light, the conclusion to the flirtatious challenge during the game. But I'm suffocating in the dense reality of it—it's heavy and real. I know us, I know *me*, and I can't do casual—*we* can't do casual. This is either going to be all-encompassing or nothing at all, and I need to know which it'll be now, before I let it become everything to me.

"You're leaving again in a week," I whisper as he takes small steps closer to me. "What are we doing?"

"What feels right," he answers immediately, his hand reaching for mine and lacing our fingers together.

"Warren."

"Tell me I'm wrong and I'll walk out that door right now," he says, pleading, tears still pooling in his golden eyes. "Tell me that something has felt more right than being together and I won't say another word. Tell me that you don't still love me like I love you and I'll find some excuse to get on the next plane out of here. Tell me you don't want me anymore and I'm gone."

A tear drops down my cheek and he lifts his hand to gently wipe it away. I close my eyes and lean into his touch. After a deep breath I look right at him. "You know I can't tell you that. You know I still love you."

"That's all I need," he says on his way to kiss me. And when our lips meet, that's it. No more second guessing, no more questions, no more holding back. I give in to this feeling and to him. I give into this pull that's always been between us. This pull that will *always* stay between us.

I kiss him, hungrily, desperately, not wanting to wait another second to be with him. My hand runs up his chest, pulling his shirt over his head and he laughs. "Someone's antsy."

I seal my lips back to his and mumble against him, "You might love it when I get under your skin, but there are other parts of you I'd love to be under right now."

"Your wish is my command," he says and picks me up, not breaking the kiss.

"Bedroom is at the end of the hallway." I guide him when he starts heading toward the second bedroom that's set up as an office space.

"I thought you said I do my best work without a bed," he teases.

I laugh. "Just shut up and get me out of my clothes already."

He lays me back on the bed and slides down my body. My heart is a drum, beating along to the perfect harmony of this moment, the long-awaited serendipity of this reunion I'd prayed would happen for years.

"I've missed you, Analise," he whispers against my stomach as he pulls my shirt off. "And how bossy you are in bed."

My eyes that had just fluttered closed fly open. I sit up and gape at him. "I am *not* bossy in bed."

He raises an eyebrow at me and starts taking my leggings off slowly, *so fucking slowly*. I try to stay still but I can't take it. This is torture. I start wiggling around trying to get him to move faster.

"Warren," I complain, and he just laughs.

He only gets them to my knees before I take charge, sitting up and pulling them off before grabbing the waistband of his athletic shorts and pulling him to me while slipping them off him at the same time. He chuckles as he lands on the bed beside me, and I immediately climb on top of him.

That perfect sunshine smile is looking back at me. "Bossy," he says. And before I can respond he pulls me down and kisses me. "And I fucking love it." He cups my face and holds us nose to nose. "I love you. Always have, always will."

"I started falling in love with you when I saw you leaning against your cubicle that first day," I say, tears in my eyes. He loves me. He *still* loves me. "And I never stopped. I love you, Warren. Always have, always will."

We both have glassy eyes as we make love to each other for the first time in over six years—and it's just that. This is not just sex. This is not fucking. This is pure love flowing between two people who have been apart for too long. This is destiny taking over and righting something that has been wrong since the moment he walked away.

This is *everything*.

Even after we're done, we lie there, holding each other, staring into each other's eyes, unwilling to break this precious moment. A tear drops down my cheek and his hand lifts to wipe it away.

"I've missed you so much," I whisper, lips quivering. I still can't quite convince myself this isn't a dream. "I thought about you every day, no matter how hard I tried not to."

I close my eyes as the featherlight pressure of his lips touches mine and his thumb continues to wipe my tears.

"I hate that you're crying because of me," he says against my lips.

"These are happy tears." I pull back and smile at him. "I

hoped you would come back every day and we could get a second chance, because you're all I've ever wanted. This moment is almost too good to be true."

"It's real, it's true." He presses his forehead against mine and takes a deep breath. "*We're* real."

I kiss him one more time before rolling out of bed to get cleaned up. In the bathroom, I stare at my reflection and grin at my messy hair and glassy eyes. I look happy—I'm glowing. I've been missing my sun for so long I almost forgot what this feels like: being Miss Summers and living up to the name. It feels good.

I splash water on my face and check the cut on my cheek and am pleased to find it's receded and is only a small pink line that'll be completely gone in another day or two.

I stay in the bathroom longer than I should because part of me is scared he won't be there when I walk out. That it *was* just an elaborate dream my mind concocted to heal my broken heart. I never wanted to believe that Warren could still want me because it only made the hole in my heart larger, but he's there, waiting for me at the door when I leave the bathroom, and he kisses me again—long and slow—before heading in himself.

My heart settles in my chest and I breathe easier. Not a dream.

This is real. *We're real.*

I walk over to my drawers and open the middle one on the right-hand side, this time smiling instead of crying when I see what's inside. I grab one of the old shirts and slip it on.

When he comes out of the bathroom, I'm sitting on the bed in an oversized T-shirt and his eyes widen when he sees it, recognizing it immediately.

"I wondered where that shirt went," he says, a grin growing on his face. "You've had it this whole time?"

I bite my lip and my face scrunches up as I nod. "After you told me you took the job in D.C., I started stealing your T-shirts so that I had a stockpile in case you didn't ask me to come with you and we had to do long-distance."

His mouth drops open. "How many do you have?"

I point to the drawer, and he opens it. He pauses before he slowly starts pulling them out, one by one. His voice is quiet when he finally says, "Why did you keep them?"

There has to be at least fifteen of his shirts in there. It's kind of embarrassing, but I knew I was going to miss him like crazy and wanted to prepare. "I still wear them to bed."

"Really?" He turns to look at me and there's a rawness in his eyes that I've never seen before.

"At first, it was because I couldn't sleep well without you beside me, and they all smelled like you, so it helped." I smile nervously but his eyes are endless pools of love. "And then after we broke up, I realized it was one of the only things I had of yours and I was never ready to let go of you, of us."

"That's why you kept the picture too?"

I nod and can't stop my smile at the memory. "That was one of the best days of my life, even if it was a chaotic mess of a moment." We both laugh. "I could never get rid of it."

"Remember that first night, when I was telling you all about D.C.?" He sits on the bed behind me and pulls me into him so my back is against his chest and his arms are wrapped around me. I feel safe here—happy, in his arms. "All those things I love are things I know you'd love too. I see you all over D.C. I find myself picturing what your reaction would be to everything. Everything I do, I wish I was doing it with you."

"You couldn't let go of me either?" I whisper, the vulnerability of the question coming forward in a way that I don't usually show.

"I know from your side it felt like I did let go, but I swear I never did." He kisses my temple. "I was a stupid kid back then who was scared of a good thing. Scared that it was too good to last, so I broke it before it could break me. But I ended up breaking my own heart in the process. I don't know how to begin to ask for your forgiveness, how to begin to make up for it."

My heart tightens for that boy—the one that existed before he met me. The one who lost trust in love because of his parents' divorce. The one I didn't know about until after he was gone. The one I still hope he'll tell me more about one day, so I can tell him I love that part of him too. For now, I just keep it light and revel in the happiness of being in his arms again.

"Just never leave me again." I rotate in his arms and kiss him.

His hand comes to rest on my cheek, and he sighs. "Deal."

He leaves soon after that to meet up with Peter before joining me and the old Triniti group at The Dizzy Acorn again tonight, so I begrudgingly kiss him goodbye. Only after he's gone do I question the deal he just made me.

He's only here for another week. Am I setting myself up for another heartbreak? Because I might love him more now than I did back then, and I don't think I'll survive him leaving me again.

What's the probability it'll work this time? The probability that we'll be an *us* again?

I'm so used to having all the answers. I'm used to being sure and confident. I'm used to knowing. But I don't know the answer to this question—maybe the most important question I've ever had—and it scares the shit out of me.

Fifteen

"Remember that presentation you gave weeks ago?" Warren asks, suddenly at my cube. He must've just gotten out of his meeting, but he doesn't look happy.

"I've given a few presentations in the past couple of weeks." I laugh a little bit. "You're going to have to be more specific than that."

He leans against the wall of my cube, and I can't help but run my eyes down his body. He looks so good in dress pants and long-sleeved button-up shirts; I'll have to send a thank you card to whoever decided the dress code because they've allowed me this view every day. When I look back up at him, his eyes are dark with desire, but there's still a frown on his face. I tilt my head in question.

"The one where you presented a few options that might help stabilize our cost trends, but Rob said they decided to take the project in a different direction?"

My lips press together and I nod. I was so frustrated after that meeting because I put a lot of time and effort into developing those solutions and it felt like they didn't even pay attention to the presentation at all.

"Well, we just had a project update meeting with Ethan," he says, and my eyebrows pull together in confusion. I'm on that project; I'm supposed to be in those project meetings.

Wait, why were they presenting to the higher-ups? I thought we didn't have our next steps yet.

"Exactly," he adds, reading my confusion and its meaning. "When I asked why you weren't there, Rob looked at me like he wanted to burn me alive, and said you'd been removed from the project. But then guess what his presentation was about . . ."

My eyes widen and a pit forms in my stomach. The words are barely more than a breath when I say, "My ideas?"

He nods, solemnly. "That son of a bitch thought he could steal your ideas and get away with it. Well, I made sure everyone in that room knew who really came up with them."

My heart swells with love for him. It's been almost two weeks since we won that trivia night, but he still hasn't said he loves me yet. I've been fighting the urge to say it, and it almost slips out right now.

"Warren." I reach out for his hand, and he gives it with a smile. "You don't have to do that. If you speak out too much you might start getting left out of meetings too. It's not worth it. I just need to stop giving my opinions."

He shakes his head before I even finish and moves to squat in front of my chair. "*You* are worth it, Analise. Don't you ever let those pieces of shit hold you back. They're intimidated by your voice, by your mind, by your *power*. You are brilliant, absolutely brilliant, and they're terrified that if you're in the room it'll show how incompetent they are. Ethan thought your ideas were creative and smart, and he wants to start testing them. He also wants to meet the person who *actually* came up with them. Rob and the others want you to stop, but don't let them win. Never stop using your voice. Never lose that power. Never stop being you."

I can't form words to reply to that. I can't speak at all. I can only look at him and let all of the love I'm feeling flow into my expression. I absorb his words and weave them into an invisible armor that I will wear from this day forward. If he wants me to keep using my voice, then I will, even if it's only to see him smile like this, to feel the warmth I feel right now.

He kisses me, just once, but it's long and gentle and has me checking the time when he pulls away to see how long I have to wait for more.

The flash of a camera stuns me out of my deep concentration. I look up and Sterling laughs as his Polaroid spits out a print that I'm sure showcases one of the ugly faces I make while I work.

Warren was right, Ethan did want to meet with me, and it was refreshing to feel like someone was listening to me. He wants me to contribute to these projects at a higher level than my current role would typically allow, but said nothing of a possible promotion. He also didn't say anything about what Rob did, or if there's going to be any repercussions—although I doubt it.

It was a mix of good and bad, and I left the meeting unsure how to feel about the whole situation, but excited to hopefully prove myself with this responsibility. I've been working on the opportunity analysis for the options ever since.

"This one's definitely making the wall," Sterling says with a sly grin. His cubicle is full of candid polaroids of people in the office, and my horrible working scowls are on that wall too many times already. "Now, come on, it's time to go, and there's finally enough snow on the ground."

I save my work, grab my bag that's been packed up for hours, and smile when Warren grabs my jacket and holds it up to help me put it on. But when the five of us get on the elevator, the mood changes. All friendship and relationships are temporarily banished as we tense, planning our strategy.

The second the elevator dings on the ground floor it's every man for themselves. Trent manages to push us aside and get off first, but Warren's long legs allow him to overtake the lead and reach the front doors first. Warren stops to ball up some snow and it gives Trent enough time to get out of range as Ali, Sterling, and I exit tentatively. The snowball goes flying at Ali, but she manages to dodge it just in time and it nails Sterling in the ribs—the first victim.

Ali takes off after Trent and I bolt just in time to get out of the way of Warren's second attack. Sterling runs around, taking candid polaroids of us in the midst of the first ever Triniti Five Snowball Fight. We've been planning this since the first snowfall last week, just had to wait for enough to stick.

I drop behind a trash can just in time for it to act as a shield from another one of Warren's throws and grab some snow of my own. Out of my peripheral vision I see Warren creeping around the right side, so I jut out to the left just in time to catch Ali celebrating taking Trent down, and I beam her with a snowball.

In only minutes, it's down to me and Warren.

But when I look around, I know I've lost. He purposefully pushed me out this way, backing me into a corner between the office building and a wall too tall to scale, where not enough snow has gathered so I can't even fight back. He slowly stalks closer to me, snowball in hand, like a predator who knows his prey has given up but still enjoys the game.

"Please don't dump me for this." He winks then rushes toward me.

I try to run but there's nowhere to go and I squeal as his free hand wraps around my waist and the other lifts above my head. I brace for the hit of the snow, but he just stands there, staring in my eyes like he forgot all about the competition. And when he speaks, I forget about it too.

"I love you, Analise," he says, and my mouth drops open. My heart races and I no longer feel any cold from the ice water dripping on my head from his floating hand.

"I love you, Warren." Those words have been trying to claw their way out of my throat for weeks, so now they flow freely and happily. His face squishes up in a smile I see only for a moment before his lips crash into mine.

I hear the gentle click of the polaroid the moment before a snowball explodes against both our faces. I shriek when the hit causes Warren to drop his snowball onto my head and it falls in a slosh down the back of my jacket. It moves slowly down my back, melting and dripping.

I jerk around trying to get it out, until Warren reaches beneath my jacket to untuck the back of my shirt and let the remaining chunk of congealed snow fall out.

"Better?" He looks like he's holding back a laugh.

I glare and say, "Thanks for that. I got wet."

His eyes light up and he leans closer. "Save the dirty talk for the bedroom. It's cruel for you to say something like that in public when I can't do anything about it."

My mouth pops open and I pull away. "Get your mind out of the gutter, Mitchell."

"The words came from your beautiful mouth." He grins at me and his face squishes together. It's so damn adorable I trace the wrinkles it causes around his eyes.

"That's not what I meant, you perv."

He laughs and it sends a chill through me. "How does it feel to be loved by a pervert?"

I fight my smile as long as I can but in seconds it's fully formed. "You love me."

"And you love me." His smile might be brighter than mine is.

"I do," I whisper.

He leans in closer, and I close my eyes, ready to feel the familiar pressure of his lips against mine. But I never do.

Instead, he says, "How does it feel to be *in love* with a pervert?"

My eyes fly open, and he laughs again. I move to hit him, but he grabs my hand and pulls me closer, finally pressing his lips to mine and all else is forgotten.

"Would you . . ." he mumbles against my lips but pauses and takes a deep breath, pulling back enough to look me in the eyes. "Would you like to come with me to Boston to meet my mom over the holidays?"

My heart screams *yes*, but because of the wording I ask, "Do you want me to?"

His grin is so big it steals the air from my lungs. "More than anything."

I can feel my face lighting up at the words. "Then I wouldn't miss it. I know you briefly met my mom when she came to take me and Ali out for lunch, but I'd love for you to officially meet my parents too."

"I'd love that." He leans in and places a gentle kiss on my cheek, then nose. Before his lips press to mine again, he says, "And I love you."

"All right, lovebirds!" Ali yells. "Save it for the bedroom."

Warren and I look at each other and nod, then we rush to the snow, pelting Ali, and the war begins all over again.

At the end of the fight, Sterling gives me one of the polaroids and I laugh but fight back tears of joy. In it, Warren and I are kissing, but a white blur that is the snowball about to hit us blocks our eyes from view. You just see lips locked, a white stripe and then his arm floating above my head with a snowball in hand. It's a photo of the first time he told me he loved me and it's perfect in its frozen chaos.

I'll never get rid of this picture, ever.

Sixteen

AUGUST CURRENT DAY (FRIDAY)

I walk to The Dizzy Acorn alone. Warren just texted that his meeting with Peter ended, and he'll be heading over soon, but I have a few things I'd like to say before he arrives. It took everything in me to not text Trent last night or today and ask what has been eating away at me.

When I get inside, Trent, Ali, and Sterling are all already there —Will's parents got into town today so he's spending the evening with them prior to the engagement party on Sunday—and I don't reply when they say hi. I stomp right up to the table, look Trent directly in the eyes, and ask, "How long have you known?"

He looks up, face twisted in confusion at first until he sees the restrained anger in my shaking body and flushed cheeks, then some of the color drains from his face. His eyes widen and I know I'm not going to be happy with the answer.

"Known what?" Ali asks Sterling and he shrugs as they both look between us.

"How. Long," I grit out, hands starting to shake so violently I ball them into fists and press them onto the table.

He sighs, looking like he already regrets the words he's about to say. "I was with him when he bought it."

My legs almost give out on me as I process the words. All my weight is resting on my fists and the table shakes like it might tip.

The ring. He was with Warren when he bought the engagement ring he never gave me. I wasn't even asking about that part, but it still feels like a punch in the gut. He knew the *whole* time Warren wanted to marry me.

I close my eyes and take a deep breath, trying to keep my voice calm but the words come out through gritted teeth. "And the reason he broke up with me?"

I open my eyes to catch his flinch, and it makes it hurt more. He hoped I'd never find out about this because he knew I'd be mad—he knew he was wrong. "I called him the day after you called Ali crying about it."

"The whole time," I breathe the words, blinking back tears. "You knew the *whole fucking time*?"

He nods slowly and my vision goes blurry. I don't know if it's because of the tears that burn behind my eyes or the hurt that rages within me because he kept this from me.

"I don't understand." My voice is so small. I'm so hurt—I'm not sure if I'm even looking at him anymore. "You watched me cry over him for over six years. You listened to me speculate about every horrible reason he could've done what he did. I was miserable, and the whole time you knew. You knew that every theory I came up with was wrong. You knew that he was miserable without me too."

"He hurt you so bad," he counters. "I thought I was protecting you from more hurt."

"Don't you understand that you did the same thing he did?" I keep talking before he cuts in. "You both had some fucked-up notion that you knew what was best for me, and by withholding information you took away my choice. You didn't care what I wanted. If you did, you would've told me the truth, because what I wanted was Warren."

"He was already gone. Would it have made a difference?"

"Of course it would have." My voice raises and people at nearby tables glance over our way. "If I knew he still loved me, that he still wanted to be with me—if I knew that somewhere in his apartment in D.C. was a ring that was meant for my finger—I wouldn't have cared that he told me not to get on that plane. I would've kicked down every fucking door in the whole fucking city until I found him."

"Wait, *what?*" Sterling says.

"Did you say *ring?*" Ali's eyes are wide as she looks between me and Trent. Then her face drops, and she focuses on Trent. "You knew?"

He hesitates before he slowly nods, and she looks back at me, conflicted.

"He's going to be here soon," I say. "I'm going to get some air." I start to walk away but pause, remembering something else. "Oh, Sterling, is it okay if I bring Warren as my plus one to the party Sunday?"

"We'll make room." He smiles at me and reaches for my hand.

I grab it and squeeze. "Thank you."

"Come on," Ali says, linking her arm through mine. "Some fresh air sounds nice."

She's silent as we walk out of the door and turn left toward a non-crowded area of the brick wall. Nor does she say anything as I lean against the wall and suck in deep breaths, trying to calm down. Once my emotions are under control and my breathing settles, she finally speaks.

"I'm so sorry," Ali says. "I didn't know."

"I know." I give her a small smile. Even if she hated Warren with her whole heart—which she did after he hurt me like that— she would've told me if she knew. She would've given me the choice.

"He had a ring?" she asks, hesitantly.

"Still has, apparently." I close my eyes and start breathing deep again. If I think about it too much, it's overwhelming. The life I wanted was within my grasp, and it hurts too much to think about how much I lost. How much time we lost.

"He just told you all of this out of the blue?" she questions, and I understand her tone even though I don't like it.

She wants to make sure he didn't tell me this in an attempt to manipulate or sway my feelings. But I don't think there's a manipulative bone in his body. He told me because he wanted me to know the truth, because he thought *I knew* the truth, and when I said I wanted to go home, he let me leave. If I said I didn't want to be together after that, he would've walked away no matter how much it would've hurt him.

"He thought I already knew—that Trent would have told me." I sigh, and the concern fades from her expression. "Ali, I'm scared of how much I love him, of how quickly he's become everything to me again."

"Well, it sounds like you guys finally talked about what happened before, right?" she says, and I nod. The scary part is we haven't talked about what happens now. We're still in a very similar situation to the last time with a countdown till he leaves again. "Analise, the two of you had something so real, something that felt untouchable to everyone else. It only took a few seconds for anyone to realize that you guys were made for each other. I only hated him for hurting you. If he's what you want, then go for it. Last time they took your choice away, but this time it's completely up to you. You get to choose what's best for you, you get to choose what you want."

Always on my side, even when her boyfriend is the one my anger is directed at. I lucked out eight years ago when she was assigned to show me around.

"I love you, Ali." I pull her into a hug.

Over her shoulder, I see Warren walking up the street and a smile immediately pops onto my face. I don't need time to think about it—I know exactly what I want. I know exactly what I choose.

I choose him.

I just don't know what that means yet.

His eyes pull together with concern when he gets close enough. "What's wrong?" His hand reaches up to my cheek and his thumb brushes over my puffy eyes. When I don't answer he turns to Ali.

"She got into it with Trent," she answers, and his eyes widen in understanding, his mouth forming a little *O*.

I squeeze his arm. "We'll be back in a minute.They're at the usual table."

He nods. "I'll grab us some drinks."

"That'd be great," I say.

He leans in to kiss me so casually in front of Ali, my heart skips a beat.

"Thank you," I whisper as he pulls away.

"For the kiss or the drink or for . . . *earlier*?" His eyes are bright with mischief and desire.

A smile pulls at my lips. "Definitely the drink," I tease. "I was only ever with you for the promotion money anyways."

He laughs and kisses me again before heading in.

"Excuse me," Ali says, gaping at me. "What the hell was that? And what happened *earlier*?"

"Last night after we talked about everything, we kissed." I sound like a schoolgirl talking about a crush who kissed her on the playground. "And after lunch today we played a three-on-three basketball game with people from both companies, and he came over after."

"Oh my god," she exclaims. "He hasn't even been back a week and you're already sleeping with him again."

"That's not the point," I say as my cheeks turn red. She gives me a look that says *that's very much the point,* but I ignore it. "He told me he still loves me, that he never stopped loving me."

"Well, of course, he does," she says and laughs when my

eyebrows pull together in confusion. "He'd be an idiot not to, but good for him for finally stepping up."

I sputter out a laugh. "Ali."

"What?" She shrugs but her shoulders shake as she does. "He should've said something years ago."

"You know what's crazy," I say, leaning back against the wall and looking up at the sky that's still showing the last colors of the sunset before dusk hits. "If he had just asked me if I wanted to go to D.C. back then, or Trent told me how he felt, we could've had six years of living the life we dreamed of. We'd be married and probably have a couple of kids. We'd be doing everything we wanted to do, right now."

She lets out a long breath. "True, but life would be so different if you did. You wouldn't be living here right now. We wouldn't be as close to each other, and we wouldn't have nights like these."

"I know." I frown. I hadn't thought much about how me leaving would've affected these friendships, but we've grown so much closer in the years since he left. I wouldn't let us lose touch ever. "That part would suck, but we'd visit each other all the time. It's not that far."

"You really love him," she says softly, and I nod, a light flush staining my cheeks.

"I really do."

"I'm happy for you." She smiles, reaching out to squeeze my hand. "And Trent will be hearing more from me tonight on this."

"Don't go too hard on him, the past can't be changed now." I sigh. I just needed to get my anger out, he doesn't need to be punished further for it. "Besides I've forgiven Warren so I kind of have to forgive Trent—although, after I yelled at Warren he pinned me against a wall and kissed me until I couldn't stand, so that helped with the forgiveness thing."

"You two are worse than teenagers." She shakes her head, but we both laugh.

I loop my arm through hers to head back inside.

There doesn't appear to be any remaining tension when we get back to the table, but Trent looks like he's avoiding my gaze. I try to let it go as I drop into the seat between Warren and Sterling and take a sip of the Blue Moon waiting for me.

"How is it being back after all this time?" Sterling asks Warren.

"I've missed this," he replies, looking around at each of them. "It's impossible to find friends better than you guys. It's been a while since I've laughed this much."

I don't think I'm the only one that notices he doesn't mention the town itself. He really does love Washington D.C.—that much is obvious.

"Did he tell you he got his ass kicked in basketball today?" I chime in and laugh when his eyes narrow at me.

"That was a foul and you know it."

I shrug. "The refs didn't call it."

"We didn't have any refs." He crosses his arms, turning towards me.

"Peter didn't call it a foul."

"Peter was on your team. Of course he took the side that made him win." He's trying so hard, but the corners of his mouth are tugging up into a smile. "Jason would've been on my side."

I bark out a laugh at that. "No one gives a shit what Jason says, and I'm pretty sure he wanted to see you lose more than he wanted to win so I doubt that too."

His lips press together, and I turn back to the group with a smile. "Long story short, he lost."

"Brave of you to try to fight her on this," Sterling says with a laugh. "Have you forgotten that she could convince an innocent man he was guilty?"

That phrase got coined at Triniti when I started speaking up in meetings. People would always look over at me at the end of a presentation—if I was invited to it in the first place—because if I saw holes in an argument, I was going to bring them up.

"Have you forgotten that I'm a masochist?" Warren teases as he reaches over under the table and laces his fingers through mine. "You know I can't resist a losing fight if it's against her."

I blush and lean into him, bumping my shoulder into his chest. He kisses my temple and squeezes my hand. There's a collective groan from the rest of the table, but they all look happy for us too.

The newest wannabe DJ starts his set, and Ali stands when she realizes it's worlds better than last week's set. "Come on, we're dancing tonight."

Reluctantly, we all follow. Trent doesn't have a choice but to dance with his girl—he'll act like he doesn't like it, but a smile never leaves his face, and his eyes never leave her. Sterling is missing his dance partner but has never had a problem taking on the dance floor alone. And Warren doesn't let go of my hand, always up for an opportunity to hold me close.

As we're dancing, my eyes keep drifting to the trivia rankings—to the sign with our team name on it. Something about it is pulling at my brain, something about it feels important. I think through the day, when we tied all through the preliminary round and then on the big final question, we got it right and won it a—

Oh. My. God.

The final question. I stop dancing and just stare, hoping it'll help me remember. I remember that it was about tax codes and conflict of interest, and parent companies. *Fuck*, what was the code number.

"Are you okay?" Warren asks, looking amused and I'm sure my face has twisted into one of my entertaining, concentration faces but I don't care.

"I think I have an idea of how to keep both companies fully operational, legally," I say.

He stops moving too. "Seriously? We've been looking all week and haven't found anything."

"I know," I add. "I think we've been looking in the wrong

places for the work around. How long did Peter give us to find something?"

"We'd have to present by Tuesday if you wanted to delay the layoffs," he says.

Shit, that's so little time to research, model, and pull together a presentation. And with being gone tomorrow, and the party Sunday . . .

"This is going to be tight," I say.

"Let me know if there's anything you need from me."

"I'm starting to think you have a fetish for bossy women," I tease.

"If I have a fetish for anything, it's for you," he mumbles against my lips before kissing me. "You have no idea how fucking sexy you are when you're being a strong, powerful boss at work. It brings me to my knees every time—seeing your mind work as you shut down every counter proposal, the way the people around you look up to you like you're a goddess. I don't know how you haven't taken over the world yet."

I laugh. "Quit playing around."

"I'm not," he says, and he sounds serious. "Just take me as an example. You use that mind of yours to outwit me in most conversations, and I get turned on by your teasing comments. You boss me around and I can't get enough of it, I live to hear those beautiful lips tell me what to do. I would kneel before you daily and worship you like the goddess you are. You've taken over my world."

I bury my face in his chest to hide the dark red spreading across my face, but I hold him closer to me than he was before, and I hold him like that until it's time to go.

"So, what's the gang up to tomorrow?" Warren asks before we all part.

"We'll be helping Sterling and Will finish setting up for the party on Sunday," Ali says about her and Trent.

"Party?" He looks intrigued.

"Their engagement party is on Sunday," I say, turning

towards him. "I guess now's as good a time as any to ask if you'd like to be my plus one."

He smiles. "Of course! I can't wait to meet Will." But then he realizes something. "Are you not helping them set up tomorrow?" he asks me.

"No." I shake my head. "Sterling and Will were kind enough to plan their party on Sunday because I have an errand to run tomorrow that will take all day."

His face falls in disappointment and I can hear Ali's repressed laughter as I add, "You're more than welcome to come with me if you don't have anywhere else you have to be."

I wasn't sure how to get him to come with me for this, but I've been looking for a way since we talked on Wednesday about how he hasn't been to visit his mom in a while.

"There's nowhere else I'd want to be." He smiles, but he has no idea what he just got himself into.

Seventeen

"Where are we going so early?" Warren yawns as we get into my car.

After we left the bar last night, we stopped at the hotel to grab some of his stuff and then he spent the night at my place. We got very little sleep, but with how far we have to drive today, it has to be an early start.

"And when did you have time to make those?" He gestures to the strawberry yogurt muffins I packed safely into the back seat. When I pulled them out of the fridge he tried to grab one and I swatted his hand away, enjoying the tired, pouty face he made. He keeps eyeing them, but I made them specifically for the person we're going to see. He'll have to wait too.

I laugh. "You know I bake when I have a lot on my mind, and Thursday night I had *a lot* to think about."

"Well, if what happened yesterday is the result of your thinking, maybe you should do it more often." He reaches over to grab my chin and turns my face to look at him before I can put the car in gear. My eyes meet his just before he kisses me.

When he pulls away, I pull him back for another. "One for the road," I whisper, and he laughs.

"Are you going to tell me where we're going now?" he asks as I pull out of the parking garage below my building. I don't use my car often since I can walk to work, but it's convenient to have on days like this.

"Nope."

When I stop the car in front of Lola's a few minutes later, his confusion only rises.

"Just wait here." I smile as I leave the car running to pop inside.

It's earlier than Lola's is usually open, but today she's up waiting for me.

"Oh, Analise." Lola walks out from the back with a beautiful bouquet of pink tulips tied together with a white ribbon. "How are you doing?"

"I'm doing well, Lola," I say, taking the flowers. I wonder if he'll figure it out just from these. He might, but I don't think he'll ever expect that it's the truth . . . at least, until we get to Boston. "It's been easier this year."

She looks out the window and smiles at the car. "Because Warren's back?"

"I heard you gave him quite the welcome home party." I laugh when her smile grows. "Thanks for that by the way. It made my day when I heard."

Her raspy laugh fills the space and she pats my arm. "He deserved something thrown at him, and I knew you weren't going to do it."

"If words count, I've thrown a lot of those at him."

"Your body counts too." She looks at me with raised brows and I look away as my cheeks heat. "I always knew you two would end up together."

"We're no—" The look she gives me stops the words in my throat, because I know they're lies as much as she does. "I've always hoped we would too."

"If there ever were two people meant to be," she says, more serious than she's ever been, "it's you two. Take it from an old woman like me who's seen a lot. What you two have is special."

"You know, you're not the first person to tell me that this week." Does that make it true? "I'll see you later, Lola. Thank you again."

"Does he know?" she asks, hesitantly, when I'm almost out of the door. "Who you're going to see and why? That you see her every year?" I shake my head, and she nods solemnly. "Good luck."

I can see his brain working as I walk out with the bouquet of tulips, his face twisted in concentration. I take my time securing them into the backseat so they won't get damaged on the drive. He doesn't speak until I'm turning onto I-84 E.

"Muffins, tulips, and . . ." He looks around. "How long is the drive?"

"You'll see," I say, smiling. I think, in the back of his mind, he knows, but he doesn't believe it's actually what we're doing.

I want to distract him from asking more questions, and I want to know more about what's been going on in his life, so I ask the first thing that comes to mind. "Do you hear from your dad much?"

A smile stays on his face, despite the touchy subject, as he says, "No, not really. Mostly just around birthdays and holidays. He got remarried recently, and I think she's been encouraging him to reach out more because he asked about coming to visit."

He's so calm, so much steadier in his emotions than I remember. I'm happy to see he's not angry still, he always carried that with him even if he didn't want to talk about it.

"What did you say to that?" I glance over quickly and catch him shrug.

"I think I'm going to take them up on it. It's already progress that he offered to come to me instead of saying work was too busy and if I wanted to see him I'd have to go out to New York. I did that once and ended up exploring the city alone. If he's wanting a better relationship, I'm open to it."

"Wow," I say before I can stop it from slipping out.

He laughs. "What?"

"That's so different from how this conversation would've gone six years ago."

I catch his smirk out of the corner of my eye as he says, "Please enlighten me on how it would've gone back then."

"Well." I laugh, nervously. "If your dad had reached out back then you probably would've masked your anger with some comment about how you survived without him so why would you need him now. You only ever told me the bare minimum about that whole situation, but I always knew there was more to it than you let on."

"I told you more than just the bare minimum," he says, but I hear the question in the words as he tries to remember how those conversations went.

"No." I shake my head. "All you ever told me was that they got divorced. The first time you told me anything about why or how it affected you was yesterday, and even then, I don't think you've told me everything about the situation."

"Hm, I guess you're rig—" He pauses. "Wait, but you weren't surprised to hear the reason. You knew?"

I nod and try to fight my grin. "Someone told me about it a few years ago."

"Who?"

"You'll see." My grin comes shining through and I laugh when he narrows his eyes at me.

"Fine," he grumbles as he reaches over and laces our hands together on the center console. His voice is softer when he asks, "What about *your* mom and dad? Will you tell me more about what happened?"

I take a deep breath. "It was a heart attack. There were no warning signs, no issues with her health, we were just a family at lunch, laughing one second and the next she'd fallen out of her chair and wasn't responsive. By the time she got to the hospital, it was too late to do anything. She was being kept alive by machines and my dad had to make the decision to unplug her . . . or not."

He squeezes my hand, and I shoot him a grateful smile. It's been long enough that it's easy to talk about this part, even though I still miss her. What's hard to talk about is the ongoing pain, the ongoing impact of what it turned my dad into.

"I've always wondered if having to make that decision made it worse for my dad, if he felt partially responsible for being the one to decide to let her go." As far as I'm aware he didn't start drinking until after that. "It was the right decision. We had the funeral a few days later and I didn't think much of it when I picked him up and he was drunk—he'd just lost his wife. But as the days kept passing, he kept drinking. He wasn't eating much, wasn't moving. He was like a zombie—there but not really alive. Then his personality started changing and no matter what I did, nothing helped. Nothing made him stop. I've never felt so useless in my life. I tried everything I could think of, but he only grew more aggressive. So I started going less and less. I really only see him once a year now when I show up on the anniversary of her passing to check on him. I keep hoping, one of these times, he'll be back to normal, that he'll realize the harm he's done and apologize. But it hasn't happened yet."

"I'm so sorry," he whispers, and I think I catch the glimmer of a tear dropping down his cheek. "I know how much you looked up to both your parents, and to lose them both in such a short time . . . I can't even imagine how hard that was. I wish I had been there for you."

I wished that for a long time too. He was who I wanted to talk to for so long, but he wasn't there, and I still survived. I still made it through. "As much as I hated it, I think I needed to go through it alone. You were always the one telling me how strong I was, and I believed it because it was *you* saying it. I had to prove to myself that I was that strong. I needed to believe it for myself."

"You *are* so strong, Analise." His voice is firm but warm, and his thumb brushes across the back of my hand sending flutters through my stomach. "You always have been."

"I know," I tease, squeezing his hand and laughing when he sticks his tongue out at me like a little kid.

We continue talking the rest of the ride there, catching each other up on everything in our lives that happened over the past years.

But when I take the exit for Boston and toward his childhood neighborhood, he turns to stare at me. "What is going on?"

I don't answer; I park the car in front of the brick house he grew up in and start grabbing the items from the back seat. Warren appears and takes the muffins out of my hands, following behind me as we walk up to the door.

I knock and a moment later a tall, thin woman who looks way younger than her age, answers the door.

"Analise." She smiles and hugs me.

"I swear you look younger every time I see you, Cindy," I say.

"I knew there was a reason I liked you so much." She winks at me before addressing Warren who's just been standing there, watching us with a confused expression. "And you got my son to come home, that's a miracle."

"Hi, Mom," he says, still obviously confused as he turns toward me. "What's going on?"

I smile and put my hand on his arm. "I'll give you two a few minutes to catch up." I take the muffins from him and start to head inside.

"I already got the vase out," Cindy says, and I smile as I walk in the house and toward the kitchen.

Ever since I learned Warren hasn't come to Boston in a while, and then learned it was because of the proximity to me, I've been planning a way to get him out here. That was my motive for inviting him to come today, but I would've been here even if he wasn't. I've been coming to see Cindy yearly on the Saturday closest to the anniversary of the death of my mom since weekends are easier to make this trip. When my dad started drinking and I needed someone to talk to, she was the closest thing to the person I wanted to talk to, and she welcomed me with open arms when I showed up on her doorstep. That first time was out of desperation, but I kept coming back because it was nice to have someone older and wiser to talk to about life's problems.

We've discussed everything over the years—everything except what happened between Warren and me. I wasn't sure if she ever told him about my mom, or these visits, but by his reaction at The Dizzy Acorn when I told him she died, and now, it's obvious she never did.

I'm setting out cups of coffee and plates of muffins on the coffee table when they head in, all smiles on their matching, sunny faces.

"I'll just grab some milk and sugar," I say, and Cindy stops me.

"I'll grab it, dear."

I sit down next to Warren on the couch, and he leans into me with a smile. "*This* was the errand you had to run today?"

"I've been coming here every year since the weekend after my mom died. She helped me so much right after her death, so it kind of just became a tradition." I shrug.

His eyes soften and he kisses my cheek. "I guess I know who told you about the reason for the divorce . . . and whose side she took in the breakup."

"Well, if you bothered to visit," Cindy says as she walks in, not bothering to hide that she was eavesdropping, "I might've taken your side." She looks at me and smiles. "But probably not."

"It was too tempting to come back—to be this close," he says, looking over at me. His fingers reach out across the couch and gently pull my hand towards his. I lace our fingers together and squeeze.

Cindy eyes the movement and purses her lips. "How long did you make him grovel until you took him back?"

"Mom!" Warren exclaims, and I laugh.

"She's like a daughter to me," she says. "And I don't care if you're my son or not, I need to make sure you're deserving of her. She's been hurt too many times already. You know how mom's like to say, *I brought you into this world, and I can take you out?* Hurt her again and you'll find out just how accurate that statement can be."

"Oh, I have no intention of hurting her again, and I have never been deserving of her," he says.

"Stop." I squeeze his hand and move our joined hands to hit him softly on the leg. "If we ignore the past, like, six and a half years, you've always been deserving. But when we factor those years in . . ." I grimace jokingly and tilt my head back and forth. "It could go either way."

"All right." He wraps his arms around me and pulls me down on his lap, his hands tickling me as I squeal. "You guys are so funny. I know I was the biggest idiot for letting you go, am I going to have to hear about it the rest of my life?"

"If you plan on keeping me around that long," I tease, hoping he does, "then, yes."

"Hm," he murmurs, leaning down to kiss me. "I guess I could live with that."

When we sit back up, Cindy is sipping her coffee and watching us with a smile.

Eighteen

Warren trudges back to his desk and I can practically see the steam blowing out of his ears. He drops his stuff on his desk with a loud crash and I hear his deep breaths from my cube. He's pissed, and knowing where he just came from, that scares me.

"How was your performance review?" I ask, hesitantly.

He starts packing his things even though we usually don't leave for another thirty minutes. "You ready to go home?" He avoids my question.

I quickly save all of my files and shut down my computer. Most of my stuff is packed already but I throw the last of my items in and grab my bag. "Yeah, let's go."

I keep quiet as we get into the elevator, unsure what's wrong and desperately trying to figure out how I can make his day better. When the elevator starts moving, he reaches over, lacing our hands together, and some of the tension in my body dissipates. At least now I know for sure his mood isn't about me. I squeeze his hand and smile. His face softens as he leans down to kiss my forehead.

The walk back to our apartment isn't too long, but it feels like forever. We don't talk and I can tell he needs the silence right now. He needs to know I'm here for him, but he wants to calm down before he talks about it. I don't think I've ever seen him this angry before, though.

The second we get through the door his lips are on mine. They're desperate, willing to take anything I'm willing to give, and for him, I'll give everything—always. Our bags are dropped by the door, and we step out of our shoes as we move through the living room to the bedroom.

He pins me against the wall with his hips, his arms on either side of me, caging me in. His lips move down my neck as he whispers, "I love you, Analise. I love you so fucking much."

We never make it to the bed. We claw and rip until every last bit of clothing is gone. He doesn't waste a second before lifting me up and pressing my back against the wall. He kisses me relentlessly, until I'm gasping for breath, and he doesn't stop until I'm crying out his name and his hands under my thighs are the only thing keeping me from collapsing to the ground.

When he sets me back down, most of the tension has left his body and his face is softer, happier than it was before. We've had some good sex since our first time—which was just as glorious as he promised it'd be—but that was by far the most passionate sex we've ever had. And that's saying something because this man is all passion. It was wild and claiming like he had something to prove. Like he needed me to know he loved me. Like he needed to remind me I was his—or remind himself.

What the hell happened in that meeting?

My worries only grow as he takes a shower and I get cleaned up. I throw on one of his T-shirts that I love to sleep in, but it isn't enough to calm me. I can't sit still, so I clean up the clothes we left all over the apartment and grab two beers from the fridge. He's just walking out of the bathroom, running a towel over his wet hair, when I enter the room with the beers. I freeze and almost drop them, my eyes trailing down his body that's almost completely bare other than his boxers. I still don't understand how someone this incredible wants to be with me.

We sit in bed, drinking our Blue Moon's and put a show on the smaller TV in the bedroom. It's silent for a while, but he doesn't seem to be paying attention to the show at all. His mind isn't here, so I reach over and grab his bottle and place both of them on the nightstand. He's deep in concentration, face tight, but the movement shocks him out of his thoughts.

"Are you going to tell me what happened today?" I ask, reaching out to smooth the worry lines on the bridge of his nose.

He sighs and runs a hand through my hair but doesn't look at me. "They said I've been doing great work, and they want to consider me for a promotion soon."

"That's incredible, Warren," I say, confused why he was so upset when this is good news. "You definitely deserve it."

There's a sadness in his eyes when he finally looks over at me. "They said they *want* to, but that they can't."

"What? Why?"

"Because the promotion would have me overseeing multiple teams." He pauses, and I still don't get what the issue is here. "Including yours."

My stomach flips and I feel nauseous. Oh.

Oh.

"It's against company policy for a manager to be involved with a subordinate, and since our relationship is known, I can't get promoted as long as I'm with you." His voice grows smaller the longer he talks.

My head is shaking, my eyes wide. I was wrong earlier. It *is* about me.

"There's no position that won't put you in charge of my team?"

He shakes his head. "Trust me, I asked."

"I'm so sorry." My voice is full of heartbreak and guilt. My lower lip shakes and my eyes burn. This is because of me. I'm holding him back. He's four years older than me, he's always been in a higher position than me, but he's never been in charge of me. Everyone at Triniti knows we're together, and it never seemed like it was a problem . . . until now.

"Hey," he says, sternly, forcing my eyes back up to his. "This is not your fault."

"But it is," I squeak out.

He sits up and puts his hands on my cheeks, looking me deep in my eyes. "I'd rather have you than any promotion."

"You've been working so hard. You deserve to be recognized for it," I say, grabbing onto his arms and closing my eyes. "What can we do about this?"

"Nothing."

"Come on, there has to be something." I flop back in bed and think for a while. "I could look for another job so you can get your promotion."

"Analise."

I sit up at his tone and frown. "I'm serious. If it will help you, I'll do it."

He has to know I would do anything for him.

"Do I want to work at a place that would do something like this though?" He thinks out loud.

"Well, then you could look for another job," I chime in. "Get that promotion you deserve at a company who won't penalize you for being in love."

He laughs and my heart melts. There's the light, sunshine man I love. "You think I should?"

"It's up to you," I say, leaning forward to kiss him. "But it couldn't hurt to at least see what's out there."

Nineteen

AUGUST CURRENT DAY (SUNDAY)

For a moment, I forget the man I love is lying in my bed. But it's a beautiful reminder, rolling over to see honey-colored hair and the light scruff of a day gone without shaving. He's gorgeous with the first rays of light haloing him in a brilliant golden glow. This has to be heaven. There's no other way to explain how perfect this is, how perfect he is.

How perfect *we* are.

The way we move together and have each other memorized so completely is intoxicating. Nothing will ever compare to this feeling, this connection.

It wasn't until he was back that I realized how lonely I'd been since he left. I'd become so good at faking it, I had started to convince myself it wasn't so bad—that I could find something better, that I could live without this, that it wasn't as perfect as I remembered.

But it's better than I remembered, and not just the sex— although, that is mind-blowingly good. The way we interact, the way we're so in sync, even the way we work together is on a different level than it was before.

I think I understand what he meant when he said we felt too good to last. What we have doesn't feel like what I see other people have—Ali and Trent, Sterling and Will. They love each other, there's no doubt about it, but Warren feels like so much more than just someone I love. It feels more like our names were always meant to be spoken in the same sentence, like neither of us is supposed to exist without the other.

It's why I always thought of him as the sun to my summer. Because those two words go hand in hand, and they will for eternity. Just like I will be his for eternity, and without him, my life lacks meaning—like summer without a sun.

Tears well up in my eyes from this overwhelming feeling, this overwhelming love. He's the picture of peacefulness, and I don't want to disturb him so I quietly creep out of bed and grab the first piece of clothing I can find. After closing the bedroom door behind me, I slip on the shirt and grin when I discover it's one of his long-sleeved button-up work shirts. I roll up the sleeves, button the bottom half of the shirt that fits me closer to a dress, and start up the espresso machine.

As it brews, I pull out my work computer and start searching for that tax code I need to find, praying that it's the solution I need to make this work. It takes a few different searches, a few different wordings for the search engine to decipher what I'm trying to find, but I click on a link and gasp.

Tax Law #709. This is it.

The language of the actual law goes right over my head—it's not what I'm trained in. So I open a new tab and search for a summarized version of the law until I finally find a website that looks promising.

I skim the page looking for keywords. *In the case of an acquisition that causes a clear conflict of interest, a parent company must be established, and the entities must remain completely separate under its umbrella.*

Okay, that's good. That means we can still operate exactly as is without legal issues, they'll just have to create a parent company to manage both businesses. But wait, how is this beneficial to the company acquiring the other? It's no different than just contracting out the services since services would still have to be paid.

And why is this a Tax Law? I haven't seen anything about taxes. I reread the article, paying more attention this time.

Holy shit.

The services have to be paid but the parent company gets to write off the cost of the two companies doing business together. So, we could provide value-based care consulting services that can be written off, making the cost neutral, but still generating the savings, and still continue making revenue by consulting out to others as we have been.

This is exactly what we needed.

This is—

"What a way to wake up," Warren says, and I look over to find him leaning against the hallway entrance wearing only his boxers.

His eyes didn't get the memo that it's morning. They skipped sunrise and have gone straight for mid-day heat as they take in the scene. Me, in nothing but his work shirt, sitting at the counter engrossed in my computer as the smell of fresh espresso —that I completely forgot about—wafts around the room.

"This is going to work, Warren," I say, body humming with the feeling of accomplishment.

"Of course, it is." He smirks at me, and my body starts humming with a different feeling that only he brings out of me.

"I'm talking about work."

"So was I," he says, but that look only intensifies. "I knew it was going to work on Friday when you first told me you had an idea. You underestimate yourself, Analise. You're brilliant. In my entire professional career, I've never met someone who thinks the way you do—it's rare and beautiful."

He slowly makes his way over to me and reaches out to the buttons on the shirt, undoing the first one with slow precision. "I love your brain." He unbuttons another. "Almost as much as I love the sight of you in nothing but my work shirt."

When the last button is undone, he looks down at my bare body. His hands lift to my collarbone and slowly run down my body, gently moving the shirt out of the way so he has a clear view, but obviously not wanting me to take it completely off. His hands stop on my thighs, his thumbs rubbing intoxicating circles so close to where I want him but not moving closer just yet.

"Beautiful," he whispers and his body shudders from his ragged breathing. "So fucking beautiful."

From there, everything happens at once. The words are barely out of his mouth when his right hand moves up and dips between my legs. The groan that rips itself from my chest is swallowed up by his mouth crashing into mine. The wetness he finds there is more than he expects because he curses, "Fuck."

After that, I don't know if it's me or him who frees him from his boxers, but then his fingers slide out and he's there, pressing against me. He takes his time, slowly entering me one glorious inch at a time. My legs slowly get spread further and further until we're chest to chest and I'm shaking with need for him to move inside me.

He pulls back to look into my eyes and what I see staring back at me is a side of him I've never seen before. It's wild, but raw and vulnerable at the same time. His hands close tightly around my hips and he doesn't break eye contact as his hips roll away from me and then thrust back in.

My head drops back as I cry out in pleasure, my hands frantically reaching behind me for anything to steady myself. He keeps thrusting at a steady, relentless pace and I can barely keep my eyes open, but when I get a quick glance, I see him greedily taking in the look of my face twisted in pleasure. The look of my body in nothing but his shirt that's now hanging from my elbows, shaking from the pure ecstasy of him.

Most times we move as a unit, both chasing each other's release, but right now, this is all about me. It feels like he's trying to show me that no one will ever satisfy me the way he does, as if I didn't know that already. It feels like he's branding me with his possessive grip of my hips and his eyes scorching patterns across my body. With every thrust into me, I feel the word *mine* reverberating through me. *Mine. Mine. Mine.* I feel his claim of my body, of my pleasure, of me.

"Analise," he whispers, and I come undone.

I unravel with his name on my lips, and as I stitch myself back together, he gets woven into every thread. Any part of me that wasn't already his has been remade in his name. He is so much a part of me it hurts—and it's the most glorious, beautiful pain I've ever felt.

Tears stream down my face when I finally find my way back to the room. I am not the same as I was moments before, and I will never be the same again.

When his eyes open again, he's back to the Warren I'm used to, but I think I see a change in him too. His raw edges that he usually keeps tucked away are visible to someone who knows him better than they know themself. Those raw edges are the depths of his love, the truth of his love. That's what scared him so much before, yet here he is, laying them bare in front of me whether he intended to or not.

"What's wrong?" he whispers, reaching for my face and wiping my tears. Panic floods his eyes as he asks, "Did I hurt you?"

"No." I shake my head. "I just . . ." I take a deep breath. "I hope you know how much I love you. I hope you know I'm yours . . . completely, unequivocally. I'll only ever be yours."

Warren's lips start to tremble and a tear drops down his face, rendering me completely speechless. I can count on one hand the amount of times I've seen Warren cry, and none of them were as real as this is right now. These tears are ones that rip themselves out of you whether you're ready or not. These are tears that show you truths about yourself you're not ready to acknowledge.

"Warren," I breathe, and stand up to pull him into a hug when a heartbreaking sob leaves his lips.

His arms wrap around me, slowly at first, then sure and strong as they pull me in tighter and he buries his head into my neck. I hold on tight as his tears hit my shoulder and roll down my chest.

"I thought I'd lost you for good," he whispers between tears. "I fucked things up so completely, I was convinced you could never forgive me. I've hated myself every day for what I did to you. I don't deserve something this perfect. I don't deserve love this pure. How can I sit here and think of you as mine when you deserve more than to be sitting here in my shirt with my hands on your body? What if I fuck this up again?"

"I won't let you fuck it up again," I say, and he huffs out a laugh. I pull back to look him in the eyes and smile through my tears. "I'm serious. Do you remember why our team name was *The Summers?*"

His face twists in confusion. "Because we always joked that if we got married I'd take your last name."

I nod. "Do you remember why?"

"Because I'm golden like sunshine?"

I laugh. "Technically, yes, I did say that that night. But the night we first kissed I told you that you were my sun and—"

"And summer's nothing without her sun," he finishes for me, eyes growing wide, like he never realized what I was saying back then.

"Exactly." I place my hands on his cheeks. "You're my sun, Warren. *You.* And only you. Summer's nothing without her sun, just as I'm nothing without you. You are who completes me. You are the sunlight I want to bathe in forever. You are all I need. Yours are the only hands I want on my body, the only shirts I want to steal." That brings a genuine laugh out of him and a smile back to his face. "You are the only person I want to give my love to. So please, don't run from it this time."

"I won't run." He kisses me and our bodies sigh in unison at how right it feels.

"But if thinking of me as yours is going to result in what happened on that stool," I mumble between kisses. "Then please never stop thinking it."

He chuckles against my lips and his entire body rumbles against mine with the movement, reminding me that we're both completely naked aside from his shirt that's halfway off my body. I gasp when his hands move down to my legs and lift me up, backing us up until I'm on the stool again.

"Whatever the lady wants, she shall get."

His lips stay locked on mine this time, but it still feels just as raw as before. Like a bridge between our souls was formed and is only growing stronger the longer we stay connected in this way. This time, the words on my lips are a prayer, a wish, my deepest desire.

"I want this. I want you, forever."

I squeal when we walk into the house and run over to Sterling and Will immediately. Throwing my arms around both of them I practically sing, "How's my favorite couple on this extra special day? I can't believe we're celebrating the engagement of Mr. Raymond Sterling Holmes and Mr. William Hernandez!"

"Hey," Ali says, pretending to be offended by my comment, but we both are obsessed with Sterling and Will's relationship.

"Where's Trent?" I ask, looking around and not finding him.

Ali frowns. "He went grab us drinks as soon as you guys walked in."

I cringe. "He does know I'm not going to yell at him again, right?"

"Please don't," Sterling says just as Will says, "Please do."

We all look over at him and he shrugs. "I'm sad I missed it and no one recorded it."

I laugh and step back so Warren can be more included in the circle. He smiles at Sterling. "Congrats, man. I'm happy for you."

"Oh, you haven't met Will yet," I say. "Will, this is Warren. Warren, Will."

"It's great to finally meet you," Warren says, reaching out his hand. "I've only heard good things from this one." He nods at me, and I smile.

But Will's face is tight, his eyes are dark and angry. He turns to me. "You brought him here? After everything he did?"

The color drains from my face. *Uh, oh.* Sometimes I forget that Will wasn't around back when Warren was here. That the only things he knows about him is how much he hurt me. That he doesn't have a previous friendship and personal memories to fall back on.

Everyone is silent and tense when Trent gets back and he looks around. "What did I miss?"

Warren's face has fallen back into the vulnerable, devastated state I talked him out of earlier today and Will's constant glaring isn't helping.

"We're going to grab drinks." I grab his hand, needing to get him away from this to make sure he's okay, and pull him to the bar set-up in the backyard.

"Don't listen to him," I say, finding a quiet spot in the yard to talk. "He didn't know you before. All he had to go off of were the times I cried over you when I had too much to drink."

He looks like I just punched him in the chest but then his eyes narrow. "Wait, didn't Sterling only meet Will two years ago?"

I cringe. "This may have happened as recently as last weekend . . ."

"Analise—"

"No." I turn his face back towards me when he starts to look away. "Look at me, Warren. We talked about this already."

"I know," he says, sounding defeated. "But I keep learning more and more about just how bad I hurt you. It's killing me."

"Listen to me." I wait until his eyes shift to mine. "You can't change the past, but if you want any chance at a future, this has to stop. Yes, you hurt me, but it only hurt so bad because of how much I loved you. I could've stopped the hurt at any time if I stopped loving you, but I chose to believe in what we had. What's happening right now, us reconnecting like this, wouldn't be happening if I let go of us. I know you hate that you hurt me, I know you wish you could go back and do things differently, but let's stop letting our past mistakes hold us back from reaching our future."

Seeing this side of him is tearing me apart. I've always known how much he loved me—I've never questioned it—but we didn't have these deep, serious conversations before. We didn't share or show our emotions as unfiltered as this. The banter and joking that is the core of us has always been our way of showing how we truly feel, but this imperfection makes us feel more real now. It makes this more believable, less like a fantasy. Less like something that couldn't possibly be true. I think it makes us better.

I can see the impact my words have on him, but he's still partly lost in the past. I smile and pull on the other, teasing side of us for the rest, because both pieces together will make us whole.

"I guess I'll have to bring bossy Analise out. You love listening to her." I lower my voice into a sultry purr.

He smiles, the light coming back to his eyes as he steps closer to me. "And what does bossy Analise want?"

I smile and lean in to whisper just in case anyone else walks within earshot. "I want you to wrap your arms around me and kiss me. Kiss me until the only thing you can feel is how perfectly my body feels in your hands, how perfectly it reacts to your touch. Kiss me until the only thing you can taste is me; until all other tastes have been ruined for you because you only crave mine. Kiss me until the only thing you see is what you're going to do to me tonight when we get home, until everything before this moment fades away. Kiss me until the only thing you know is that you are mine and I am yours."

And he does. He kisses me slowly to memorize me, to claim me, to ruin me. His hands press against my back, barely moving but sending goosebumps across my body. He does exactly as I asked but he does it better than I ever could've imagined.

I don't want him to ever stop.

Someone clears their throat near us and our lips part but stay separated by only centimeters. I'm breathing heavily, body still pressed against his, trying to regain the strength in my legs that he stole from me.

"Save it for your own engagement party," Sterling says through a smile, although the intonation is anything but sunny. "Tonight is about me, thank you very much."

Warren and I laugh, finally stepping away from each other but he keeps hold of my hand.

"Sorry." Warren grins. He's anything but sorry.

Sterling shakes his head, but he can't stop his smile. "You'd think two people in and near their thirties would have learned better self-control. You two act like teenagers still."

"Worse than teenagers if you ask Ali," I deadpan, and he laughs.

"That's probably true." He pauses. "I'm sorry about Will, he shouldn't have acted that way."

"It's okay," Warren says, squeezing my hand. "It's not like I didn't deserve it."

Sterling smiles and looks between us. "I am happy to see you guys back together though." Then his face turns serious again and he adds, "Just not tonight."

Throughout the night, I catch Warren talking to each of our friends one-on-one. I'm not sure what they talk about, but he looks serious. Maybe he's apologizing for not reaching out, or just trying to catch up with each of them. But then, towards the end of the night, he approaches Will. I watch as they have an intense conversation, but at the end, Warren extends his hand and after a long moment, Will takes it.

I wonder what that's about.

"He's been going around apologizing and thanking each of us," Trent says, answering my thoughts as he sits down beside me.

My eyebrows pull together. Thanking them?

He smiles and explains, "Apologizing for not reaching out when he was gone and thanking us for being there for you all this time. He's changed in a lot of ways, but one thing that hasn't changed is how much he loves you."

"It hasn't changed for me either," I say, softly.

"I'm sorry, Analise," Trent says, and I look over at him. "I should've told you, let you make your own decision."

"I shouldn't have yelled at you like that." I sigh. "I had so much pent-up anger and yelling at Warren wasn't enough, so I took it out on you too."

He chuckles. "It's not like I didn't deserve it though."

"Oh, I never said that," I tease with a grin. "I know you were only trying to look out for me, mother hen." He laughs at the nickname. "But in the future, please don't keep things from me. I promise I'm strong enough to handle it."

He nods with a sad smile on his face. We sit in comfortable silence until everyone joins us at the table. Sterling and Will have been making the rounds with their guests and are currently at our table.

"So, Warren was telling me about this great idea you had at work that's going to save the jobs of half the company?" Trent says, and I whip around to look at Warren who's beside me.

"You don't even fully know what my idea is." I laugh. "It might not even work."

He shrugs and looks around the table. "I think anyone who

has worked with you can back me up when I say, if you have an idea, it's going to work."

Sterling, Ali, and Trent all agree and my cheeks flush.

"Do you guys want to know something even Warren doesn't know about the idea?" I direct the conversation away from me. They nod and Warren looks at me with interest. "The idea came from the final question from that trivia night when we got the top score."

"How do you even remember that question?" Trent asks.

"Wasn't it something about some law?" Sterling adds.

"Oh, yeah!" Ali exclaims. "It was some tax law, right?"

I nod and when I look over at Warren, his eyes are wide in realization. "So, that's why you first thought of the idea at The Dizzy Acorn. This whole time I was thinking my dancing was so underwhelming that you were just thinking about work the whole time."

I laugh and poke back. "Well, I did think of it while we were dancing, so you obviously weren't holding my attention *that* well."

The table laughs and this all feels so right—all of us here together joking and laughing. It always should've been like this.

"Is that a challenge?" He narrows his eyes at me.

"Feeling deficient, are we now?" I smirk and his eyes burn just for me.

"You didn't think I was deficient earlier." He doesn't bother lowering his voice when he says it, and I don't even care.

Goddamn. How much longer are we going to be here for?

"Have they always been like this?" Will asks, and Ali, Sterling, and Trent all respond in unison, "Yes."

"Like what?" I ask innocently, forcing myself to turn away from Warren, and Sterling throws an empty plastic cup at me.

When we're getting ready to head out, Will pulls me aside.

"I've never seen you that happy," he says, and I smile.

He's right, he's never seen me like this. I wasn't miserable every second of every day, but I was missing the glow I have now. He only knew me after Warren left, after my mom died, and my dad was already a drunk. I had lost so much, he really only knew a shell of who I was—of who I feel like I'm closer to now that I've had a lot of time to do some healing and Warren's back. He hasn't seen me shine so bright before.

"I haven't been this happy in a long time."

"You know, I never believed them when they told me what you and Warren were like," he says. "I always hated him solely because of how he hurt you."

"What do you mean?"

"They'd always talk about you and Warren like it was some mythic, legendary, untouchable thing, and I'd laugh because it sounded so absurd. It had to be an exaggeration, but seeing you two together today, I got it." He shakes his head like he's still grappling with this change in his opinion of Warren. "What you two have is what everyone envisions for themselves back in their fairytale age, back when we believe anything is possible and that soulmates and a one true love are what we're looking for."

"Is that not what you and Sterling have?" I ask.

"I love Sterling, and I will love him for the rest of my life, but we will never have what you guys have. That connection, that pull you have *is* the stuff of fairytales. I don't know what's going on with you two, but if he's what you want then don't let him go again."

"I don't plan to," I whisper, and hug him.

Twenty

As we walk into the office, everything is different from last week.

This time last week, I didn't know Warren was in the same town as me and now he's spending his nights in my bed. For us, this weekend changed everything, but to everyone else it was just another normal weekend.

Peter, Mac, and Clara all end up on the elevator with us, and the small talk about what everyone did this weekend makes me antsy. I can't stand straight, shifting my weight from leg to leg, until a pinky loops through mine. I glance over at him slyly and instantly feel relaxed again.

"What about you two?" Peter looks back at us.

"It was a friend of mine's engagement party," I say, squeezing Warren's pinky in mine.

He squeezes back and says, "I went to Boston to visit my mom."

When they look back to the front, we both smile at each other conspiratorially. They don't need to know that I also went to Boston and he also went to a friend's engagement party.

The elevator doors open on our floor and Peter turns to Warren. "Have some time to discuss that paperwork?"

"Of course," he answers but turns to me. "Did you need me for any of the work on the presentation?"

"There's a few numbers I need from you, but I can get most of it done without that," I say.

"I'll come find you as soon as I'm done." He smiles. He would've come to find me after even if we didn't have any work to get done, but it's a good public excuse.

In my office, as I get set up for the day, my stomach turns a little bit. It's weird, but I feel like I'm doing something wrong. I don't know if it's because of how casual and professional we have to be in front of the others, or the fact that, last time, our relationship imploded because of work, or that the start of this week means he's only in town for five more days, but *this* suddenly doesn't feel so certain, so easy, like it was this weekend.

"Knock, knock," Clara says at the door to my office. "Got a minute?"

"Yeah, come in." I gesture to the chair and we both sit.

"Have you been able to find a solution?" she asks, biting her lip and wringing her fingers. "I feel like I've failed this company. You remember when I first came to you with the idea of starting a value-based care consulting firm? You were just as excited about the idea as I was, and even though I'm the president of the company, I've always seen this as *our* company. It would not be what it is today if you hadn't been there since day one, running the strategy. But when I got the acquisition offer, I jumped the gun. I should've pulled you in sooner to make sure they'd be keeping the integrity of the company. I shouldn't have found out they were considering layoffs in a meeting, after signing the deal. Anyone that gets let go—it's on me. So please tell me you found a way to save our company, our people."

With a tear in my eye and a huge smile on my face, I say, "I think I found a way to save it."

She lets out a deep breath and just nods for a few seconds. "I'm going to hug you now," she says, a tear in her eye too. It's not until she's holding me that she whispers, "Thank you."

We've both gotten so busy that we lost some of the magic from the beginning, but right now, I feel it all again and I remember why I fought so hard for this.

And why I'll never stop fighting for it.

When she leaves, I get to work on the presentation I have to give tomorrow. I want to show the financial projections of both companies in three scenarios: without the acquisition, with the assumptions they sent over, and then my proposed way. Mostly to outline that the current proposal makes no sense because of all the lost revenue and the lowered savings impact—it would be better for them to not acquire us and just contract out our services than to go through with the changes they modeled.

It really makes me wish I was part of the earlier conversations, because Clara either did a bad job of explaining how our company generates value, or they didn't understand the business model. Even though value-based care has been around for a bit now, it's still relatively unknown to those who aren't directly involved with it, so it wouldn't be surprising if it was the latter, or even a little bit of both.

I have all the numbers I need for my side, but I need to confirm a few things with Warren in regard to Vitality's numbers. But by the time lunch rolls around, I'm happy with how far it has come and how clear of a story it tells.

"I just sent you everything you asked for."

Warren's been sitting in my office since lunch "helping" me with the presentation. He sent over the numbers I needed from him, but other than that he's just been looking at me with that enamored, love-filled look that made it hard to work even back in our Triniti days.

"Thank you for finally being useful," I tease with a smile on my face.

He smiles and his eyes spark. "If we were just in cubicles in the corner instead of an office, it'd be like nothing changed."

"It's kind of weird being back in a shared work environment and being together again." I hesitate, and maybe it's just my insecurities talking, but I don't want to just assume things again this time. If this is going to work this time, we need to talk about our feelings and concerns, not ignore them and shove them under the rug. "It's making me feel like we still have things we need to talk about."

He frowns at that, and I continue quickly.

"Last time, everyone knew we were together and at the end of the day, it hurt us," I say. "But now, no one knows, and it kind of feels like we're trying to make sure they don't find out. I don't really know how to act. It's so similar, but at the same time the complete opposite."

He's still frowning, but his eyes are soft and understanding. "Tell me what you're feeling. I don't want there to be any doubts, anything we're afraid to say."

I look down. Last time I wasn't realistic about things. I won't be so ignorant or naive this time. It'll be better for both of us if we call it as it is and have hard conversations before they blow up in our face. "You're going back to D.C. at the end of the week, Warren, and I'm staying here. We haven't really talked about what happens after this visit is over."

The hesitation and pain on his face slowly shifts into a small smile that grows on his face. It settles something in my heart, and I continue. "If we both want this, we need to figure out what it's going to look like. I know we both love our jobs, but I'm about to be thirty and you're thirty-two, starting a long-distance relationship with no end in sight isn't what I had in mind either. I like certainty; I like being in control. But right now I don't even know how to go about figuring out the probability of this working with all of these obstacles. And that scares me because last time there weren't as many variables as there are now and we didn't survive it then so what makes this time different?"

I want him. I want him in my arms each night. I want to see his sleepy smile each morning as he rolls over and kisses me. I want to have a life *together*, not together while in different cities living separate lives. We've already lost so much time, and this only prolongs the time it'll take to get where we want to be.

Jason walks by the open door and frowns. He stands there watching us for so long it halts our conversation.

"Can I help you?" I finally say to him, but he just grumbles and stalks away.

I watch until he's out of sight again before saying more, just in case. When he's gone, I open my mouth to speak again but Peter pops in. "You guys almost ready to head out for dinner?"

We both smile and nod before he walks away and we both stand and grab our things.

Before we leave, Warren turns to me. "We *will* finish this conversation. I want to figure out a way to make this work. I don't want to live without you again. Okay?"

He checks the door before reaching for my hand. I take it and he squeezes tight.

"Okay." I squeeze back.

Twenty-One

"You look beautiful." Warren smiles at me when I walk out of the bedroom dressed for date night. And while I know he means it, it doesn't reach his eyes. My stomach twists even more, making me feel worse than I already do.

The past few weeks he's been acting a little strange. I originally wrote it off as frustration and stress from interviewing. At first, he wouldn't seriously consider getting another job, but after another round of promotions where he didn't get his deserved title, he understandably got fed up. He's been actively applying and has had a good number of interviews over the past weeks.

But it's more than just that. He's been more secretive lately, cancelling our lunch plans or running out after work before coming home. At times he has even been standoffish, ignoring me in a room to whisper with Trent in the corner and changing the conversation when I get near.

If I didn't trust him so much, I might've been tempted to believe he was cheating. But aside from the fact that he's been ravenous when we get back home each night, I know that he's not the kind of man to do that. And even though I truly believe, in my heart of hearts, that he's getting ready to propose, and I've been so excited in anticipation, the change in his behavior still unsettles me.

Earlier in the week, when he told me he planned a date night for us tonight, I tried to hide a squeal. What better place to propose than on the hill outside of Il Piacere where he first asked me out and we had our first date?

He seemed excited too, and it only fueled my theories.

Until today.

Today he's been distant. The sun has set in his eyes, and his smile isn't as bright as usual. It's unnerving. Even as we walk to the restaurant hand in hand, it's in silence. I start overthinking. Is his grip on my hand lighter than usual? Is he not looking over at me because there's bad news coming tonight? Is the silence only heavy to me or does he feel it too? Is he going to break up with me here, in the same spot he asked me out, so that when he walks away he can start fresh, as if we never happened?

The negative thoughts won't stop berating me, and I try to hide the fact that it's getting hard to breathe as we're led to a table on the back patio. He pulls out my chair for me, but his smile is still dim. As he orders us lobster ravioli and a bottle of our favorite white wine—which we only order on special occasions—I'm not sure what to think. But the silence needs to end.

"How are your interviews going?" I ask. "You hear anything new?"

His face becomes more guarded. "Can we not talk about work for now?"

"Of course," I say, confused. "Did you have something in mind?"

He shrugs and the wine turns sour in my stomach. "No, I just want to enjoy a work-free evening with my girl."

Something isn't right here. I feel like I might cry or be sick—or both. This isn't my Warren staring back at me. He might as well be a stranger.

We struggle through dinner with small talk that's not even

remotely important and is so far from the witty and deep conversations we usually have. I can barely eat because the unease only builds the longer we're here.

He pays the bill, and we walk towards our bench on the top of the hill. The city below us is its usual sea of lights that's so beautiful that, for a second, I focus on the familiarity of the lights to forget the strangeness of this night.

"Analise," he says, and when I turn toward him, he looks so nervous that I let myself hope again that he's proposing. What else could explain all the strange behavior?

"Warren," I goad when he doesn't say anything else and the corners of his mouth twitch up.

There, that's a flash of my Warren. Maybe he's just so nervous it's making him act this way. He takes a deep breath, and my eyes widen in anticipation of the words: *Analise, will you marry me?*

"I got a job offer," is what he says instead, and I blink for a moment before registering the words. It's an adjustment from what I thought I was going to hear, but it's still good news.

"Oh my god," I squeal. "Warren, that's incredible."

I throw my arms around his neck and hold on tight, but he doesn't move to hug me back. My heart drops. He's been nervous, he didn't want to talk about work, and he's not hugging me back. My face drops—*no*. I never asked where the jobs he was applying for were. I knew most of them, but there were some he didn't talk about, saying it was a long shot that he'd be selected for those positions, so they weren't worth mentioning. I just assumed he was only looking in the area.

"I'm moving to Washington D.C.," he finally says. "I start in the new year."

Apparently, I assumed wrong.

"You accepted already?" I ask, pulling back. My head is spinning; what's happening here?

"The offer was too good to refuse," he says. "They called today."

"Warren." I shake my head, but a smile grows on my face. "That's amazing. I'm so proud of you."

"Really?" His hesitance is so charming, but some of that light is coming back.

This could work. I've heard Washington D.C. is beautiful, I'm sure I'll love it there too. It shouldn't be too hard to find another actuarial job there—there's a lot of good companies that operate there.

"Of course." I throw my arms back around him and this time his slowly wrap around me. "I knew it wouldn't be long until someone realized how amazing my man was and snatched him up."

"How did I get so lucky?" he mumbles before kissing my cheek. "I love you."

"And I love you." I pull back and kiss him. All of my unease disappears when he deepens the kiss.

I sigh against his lips. In a few months we might be kissing in a whole new state. I wonder what life will be like for us there.

His fingers move up to stroke my cheek and the love I see when he looks at me is overwhelming. "Don't worry, we'll make long-distance work."

Wait, what?

I stop breathing, ears ringing. Long-distance?

I stare blankly at him, not understanding at first but then I replay the conversation in my head. *"I'm moving,"* he said. Not us. Not do I want to come too. Just him.

Oh. My. God.

He's not inviting me to go with him. He's just leaving.

I've been quiet for too long—his face is starting to scrunch up with worry. I swallow to help my dry throat, but my voice is still hoarse when I answer, "Of course, we'll make it work."

He's leaving. He's leaving. He's leaving.

"I love you so much, Analise."

Then why are you leaving? Why aren't you asking me to come with you?

My voice is almost robotic when I respond, "I love you, too."
He's leaving.
Is he leaving me?

Twenty-Two

The presentation has to be perfect. There can't be a single word out of line, a single number out of order. There are peoples' jobs at stake. This is my *legacy* at stake.

"I want to take you out tonight."

I look up to find Warren smiling at me from the doorway as he watches me work. It's an expression I know well from when he used to sit next to me and catch my face twisted in all sorts of funny ways when I was deep in concentration. He called them my "unstoppable faces" because when I "focused on a problem, there was nothing I couldn't solve."

"Take me out?" I can't help the smile growing on my face. "What's the occasion?"

"We're celebrating, of course." He winks at me, and I think the hit of dopamine it gives me is visible.

"Isn't it bad luck to plan a celebration when you haven't won yet?"

He shrugs, leaning against the frame so casually and comfortably, like he's been doing it his whole life, just for me. "I'd bet on you any day, with full confidence that I'd win."

I stand up and move to make myself a coffee that just so happens to put me right next to where he's standing. As I approach, his eyes slowly travel down my body. Without my suit jacket on, I'm in just a fitted white button-up shirt and light blue tapered pants and he likes what he sees. The muscles in his jaw are tight and he takes a step into the office, reaching to close the door behind him. I raise an eyebrow at him as it clicks closed but turn to make two cups of coffee.

He steps up behind me, leaning down to press his lips to my shoulder, then up my neck. "This is what I wanted to do the moment we were alone in this room that first day," he mumbles and spins me around to face him. He captures my gasp of surprise with his lips as they crash into mine.

I'm grateful that I almost exclusively keep my office blinds closed, so it's not suspicious that we're in here together like this.

He kisses me like this is the most important thing in the world—like *I'm* the most important thing in the world. And I kiss him like this isn't my workplace, like there aren't a hundred people outside that door that could walk in and get us both in trouble. But as he picks me up and sets me on the corner of my desk, I couldn't care less. My legs wrap around him, and I pull him closer by the blue tie he wore to match my outfit.

God, Warren Mitchell is a fucking religion. No, a cult, and I drank the juice.

And I never want to go back.

Let them walk in. Let them see how perfectly his body curves around mine. Let them see how he kisses me until I can't remember anything but his name and that he belongs with me.

His hands travel from my back and thighs to the button on my pants.

"Warren," I gasp out between kisses.

"You look so good in these pantsuits," he says against my lips as the zipper goes down and his fingers flirt with the space created. "But," he adds, just as his hand finds its way down the front of my pants. I would get on my knees and beg for his fingers to never stop doing what they're doing right now. "They make it really hard to have office sex."

I don't want him to stop—I never want him to stop—but I lightly push back against his stomach and in a second, he's two steps away from me. He sucks in breath after breath just as I am, and his jaw is tense like he's forcing himself to stay right where he is even though all he wants is to bridge the distance between us again. His dark eyes are still on my unzipped pants.

He wants this as much as I do.

I take a deep breath and try to make my voice firm. "No office sex."

His eyes flash up to mine and his words are ragged. "Your body is saying otherwise."

"You could touch me in every inappropriate place on this planet and my body would react that way simply because it's your hands on me." I finally catch my breath and stand, fixing my shirt and buttoning up my pants. "Are our evenings not satisfying enough for you?"

"I have six and a half years to make up for." He steps forward and kisses me once more. "And when it comes to you, I'll never have enough."

"Well, for right now, it has to be." I kiss him again then move to open the door so he can't tempt me further. Just seeing him in his perfectly tailored suits every day is temptation enough. "We have a presentation in a few hours, and I need to make sure it's perfect."

"It'll automatically be perfect because you're giving it." He winks and I chuckle. "But do you need anything else from me?"

"I'm going to look it over a few times to make sure I'm not missing anything and then I'll come find you to do a final walk-through," I say, gently pushing him out the door. If he stays, I won't get anything done.

∿

I don't even make it thirty minutes before I'm taking all of my notes and my laptop over toward the conference rooms.

That prick has ruined my office for me.

I never had a reason to even consider office sex before, but as I sat in that room after he left, all I could think of were all the ways we could have sex in there. Couple that with the knowledge that he was only a hundred feet from the door, and I couldn't stay there any longer. I don't know if I'll ever be able to work in there effectively again—definitely not while he's here.

When I come stomping into the room he looks up and a grin grows when he sees the frustrated look on my face. "You're thinking about it."

"If I get fired, you're to blame for killing my productivity." I scowl as I drop into the seat beside him. "You have ruined my office for me."

"Oh, Analise," he purrs my name, and a chill runs down my spine. "If you believe your office is the only place I've ever imagined fucking you, you don't know me as well as I thought you did."

My heavy breaths huff out of my nose like a bull ready to charge its prey. The glass wall exposing us to the rest of the office is the only thing that stops me from climbing into his lap and letting him finish what he started in my office.

"I'd prefer to not have every place we've ever been ruined for me," I say through gritted teeth.

His face lights up the way it always has when I play along. "You do know me," he pouts.

"Well enough to know this is just as agonizing for you as it is for me." When he's so under my skin like he is right now, all I want to do is get under his. I lean in closer and lower my voice as I continue, "I know that all you can think about is your hand between my legs earlier. How my usual put-together appearance was unraveled by your touch as I sat on the corner of my desk with unbuttoned pants and my shirt untucked, and wild eyes that almost let you do every little thing you desired in that moment."

"Now that's just cruel," he murmurs, his hand moving to my leg, just above my knee, to squeeze.

"I haven't even begun yet." I smirk, and run my hand up his leg to feel him through his pants.

He hisses and grabs my wrist immediately. His breathing instantly turns ragged and his eyes dance with want. "Careful," he breathes, unable to speak louder. He's about to snap and part of me really wants to see what happens if he does.

"I know you better than anyone on this planet ever will," I say, holding eye-contact. "I know every little thing that gets under your skin, that turns you on, that makes you tick, because I'm fucking obsessed with every move you make. I have been studying you since the moment I met you—always with the goal of making you happier than you ever dreamed you could be. So every dirty, depraved fantasy that goes through that brilliant mind of yours . . . I intend to be the person to make every one of them a reality."

"Holy, fuck." His one hand grips my leg harder as the other starts shaking even as it holds mine back.

"But right now," I add, forcing myself to continue. I want to see him snap, but it can't be right now—there's too much at stake. "What may end up being the most important presentation of my career is in an hour, and I need you to use all of your focus to help me make sure this proposal is bulletproof."

He sucks in a deep breath, followed by another, and only after he's composed himself does he look at me and nod. "Whatever you need."

"Holy shit, is this for real?" he asks after I go through the presentation I've put together.

"It looks too good to be true, right?" I say. That's been my biggest worry—that it *is* too good to be true and I've misinterpreted something. "I want to walk you through all of my research to make sure you agree with my interpretation of everything. I want your complete agreement with everything in these slides, especially the financial projections. You are the CFO after all."

He grins. "Still after the title, huh?"

I laugh as I pull up the research and walk him through it.

We have some really great discussions about some of the articles and their exact interpretation and application, and at the end of it all, we're in complete agreement. My numbers, although mind-boggling, seem to be completely accurate.

"Do you want to present with me?" I ask and he shakes his head before I even finish.

"No, this was all you, Analise." The pride in his voice, in his eyes, is breathtaking. "I don't want to take credit for even a sentence of it. They should see how fucking brilliant you are."

Our eyes lock and nothing else exists to me. I smile, much too friendly for a room that has a glass wall, but I can't help it. "Looks like we'll be able to celebrate tonight after all."

"Good thing I already made the reservation."

Twenty-Three

"In conclusion," I say to a room of faces wearing varying levels of disbelief. "We can keep the consulting side of the business as is and still use it for your company at a net neutral cost because of the tax write off. It generates more revenue for the health plan side and maintains the value our company has worked hard to earn over the past years. All we have to do is set up a parent company that owns both entities and keeps them separate."

The room is completely silent.

Is that a good or bad thing?

I look over at Warren and he's sporting the largest grin I've ever seen. It makes me feel more confident.

"Any questions?" I add.

Peter stands and clears his throat. His eyes are wide as he looks at Warren. "Is this real?"

"She found the tax law and did all of the analyses." Warren makes sure that's clear up front and I wish I could kiss him right now for it. "But she walked me through every piece of research and all of the assumptions and calculations, and I stand behind every word spoken."

"Well, Miss Summers." Peter turns towards me and extends his hand. "A deal's a deal. We will keep discussing this proposal of yours, but this is great work."

"So, no layoffs?" I confirm.

"No layoffs." He laughs. "But I would love to hear how you came up with this. How did you even know about this tax law?"

My eyes flash over to Warren for just a moment, and I smile. "Now *that* is a long story that begins about eight years ago at a local bar's trivia night."

Peter stares at me and blinks rapidly. Only once he's processed what I said does he break out laughing—leaning over and using the conference table for support. "Seriously? The future of my company is based on what I assume was a drunken night out?"

"If it makes you feel better, in eight years, no one's been able to beat the score we got that night." My eyes lock with Warren's and we both join Peter in laughter when my comment makes him laugh harder.

The rest of the people slowly file out of the conference room. Jason stalks out, Serge and Ben just go on with their day, and Clara squeezes my shoulder and mouths *"Thank you."* It's just Peter, Warren, and I laughing while Mac watches us all with a smile. She seems to be wherever Peter is and my suspicions of them being together only grows.

"It probably shouldn't," Peter says, finally calming down, "but it makes me like the proposal more."

"Who says work and play can't go hand in hand?" I tease, feeling comfortable around Peter already.

"You know, Miss Summers—"

"Analise, please." I smile.

"Analise." Peter nods. "You have quite the reputation in this space; I wasn't sure what to expect when we got here. I must say, I'm pleasantly surprised."

"Reputation?" My face twists in confusion.

Warren snickers and I turn to glare at him. But when I see his face, I understand.

It was the same reputation they teased me about, that caused people to keep me off meeting invites so I wouldn't poke holes in their presentations when important people were in the room. Yes, I was good at what I did, and everyone knew it, but that was the precise reason they didn't want me around. I hadn't realized that reputation followed me from Triniti.

"Oh," I say under my breath and my face falls.

"Don't get me wrong," Peter continues, "you have a reputation for being the best, and quite frankly I think even that under-sells what you can do. But I'm starting to think the rumors that you're hard to work with come from narrow-minded men who couldn't accept the fact that a woman, let alone a subordinate, was smarter than them."

My eyes widen as I look up at him.

I never let the comments bother me. I never stopped just because people were uncomfortable, but other than with my friends, I knew it pissed people off. I'd never had someone of a higher level tell me it was welcome—no, scratch that, I'd never had a *male* colleague at a higher level welcome me speaking my mind who wasn't a friend.

"I have no tolerance for people like that at my company," he continues. "Never change, Analise."

I smile. "You know, you're not what I expected from a health tech CEO yourself."

"I'm going to take that as a compliment." He smiles back.

"It was meant as one."

My office door clicks shut just before I'm about to head home. Strong arms wrap around my waist and lips press to my shoulder then move up my neck. I sigh and lean back, resting against his chest.

"You are incredible," Warren whispers against my neck, and I shiver. "And now everyone knows it."

I turn around and place my hands on his cheeks. I just stare at him, drinking in every detail on his face until the corner of his mouth pulls up, then I kiss him, long and deep. His hands wrap around my waist and pull me closer. I keep kissing him until I have to stop, because if I kept going, I don't think I'd ever stop.

I lean my forehead against his and soak in his presence.

"What was that for?" I can hear the smile in his words.

"That." I take a deep breath. "Was because you are also incredible, and I've never thanked you."

He pulls back. "Thanked me? For what?"

"For always standing up for me, especially when I wasn't in the room. For not letting others take credit for the work I did. For not being intimidated by me, and always telling me my strength and my voice were my superpowers. For making sure I didn't let their words stop me." A tear drops down my cheek and he kisses it away. "I took for granted your unwavering support, and I don't want to do that ever again. If I'm incredible, it's because you helped make sure I was."

"Analise, you shouldn't have to thank me for doing the right thing—for treating you the way you deserve."

I kiss his nose then his lips. "You have always been one of the good guys. I have always been so grateful to have you in my life."

"I love you," he says between kisses. "I will always love you."

"Can you take me home now so we can continue this," I mumble.

Home. Home is not a place, it's a feeling. A feeling I've only ever had with him.

"I wish I could, but we have reservations tonight and I need to run by my hotel room first. I left my date night outfits there." He smirks and I laugh.

"You brought date night outfits?"

"Just in case." He shrugs and I shove him away, but he grabs my wrist and pulls me back into a deep kiss. "I'll be at your place as soon as possible."

I'm just zipping up my dress after doing my hair, makeup, and taking about ten minutes to figure out how the many straps on this dress work when there's a knock at the door. I run over and throw it open without looking before I move to the dining table to steady myself as I slip on my heels. "Hi, I'm almost ready to go."

He doesn't say anything, so I glance up before leaning down to buckle up my heels just in time to catch the door closing, a bouquet of blue tulips dropping onto the table, and Warren dropping to one knee before me.

I stop breathing. If the table hadn't stopped my fall I would've stopped standing.

He's not doing what I think he's doing, is he? Because that would be absolutely insane.

Wouldn't it?

But if it's crazy then why has my stomach morphed into butterflies made of that liquid, sunshine gold that has his name on it? Why is my heart trying to claw its way out of my chest to land in his hands where it belongs? Why is my mouth forming the word *"yes"* that's been waiting to come out since that night?

Lips press to the inside of my thigh, just above the knee, as his hands snake down to the straps on my heels. A stuttering laugh of a breath slips out as my eyes flutter closed.

"Who's being cruel now?" My voice isn't steady at all, nothing about me is steady right now. I was just preparing myself for him to propose, I must be going insane. And I really do start to lose it as his lips travel across my legs as he straps on my shoes.

"Oh, I'm sorry," he whispers against my thigh and my leg twitches. It's physically impossible for my body not to react to him. I can feel his smile grow against my skin. "Is there something else I should be doing down here?"

"I can think of a few things," I mumble, letting my head drop back until cool air replaces every place he was touching me and my head snaps back up. He's watching me with eyes that make me feel like nothing else exists in this world but me and him. Like I'd float away if it wasn't for this connection between us that never went away no matter how much distance or time separated us.

He shakes his head like he's waking up from a dream. "How is the most beautiful woman in the world somehow mine?"

"Yours?" I smile, loving the way it feels to say the words that have always been true. I have always been his . . . but he once walked away from being mine. So, I snap my legs shut in front of his face.

His eyebrows pull together at the wall blocking where he was planning to go. "Is there something wrong with that?"

"Oh, not at all." I stand and with a finger under his chin guiding him, he follows. I slowly unbutton his cream-colored short-sleeved button-up. "I have always been yours. I will *always* be yours."

I kiss him as my hands run down his bare chest and move to his belt and the button on his navy-blue chinos. He kisses me back without hesitation, pulling my dress up over my hips, but before he can go any further, I reach behind him and pull out a dining chair. He pauses and pulls back to look at me but with one light push on his chest, and with his pants and boxers around his ankles halting movement, he has nowhere to go but down onto the chair.

He watches me, eyes burning, as I place my legs on either side of the chair and slowly lower myself down. As I get close, I reach down to pull my underwear out of the way and position him in place so I can lower myself right onto him. He groans and drops his head back, closing his eyes and I fight to keep mine open, wanting to take in every second of this as he did when the roles were reversed. But *god*, he feels so fucking good.

Once I'm all the way down, I roll my hips and he curses, his hands flying to grip my hips. He tries to move but I keep him pinned down so he can't move until I let him. I lean forward and thread my hand into his hair. After pressing my lips to his neck, I move them to his ear. "I think it's you who needs the reminder that just as I will always be yours, you will always be mine."

As I speak the final words, I lift up and drop back down—over and over. I don't stop moving, not letting him make a single move or recover. I savor every little noise he makes and the way he freely gives himself to me—the way he surrenders himself to me.

I know he doesn't give it lightly. I know it's precious and delicate, and I know I will treasure it for as long as I live. His love. Him.

When he comes back to the current moment, he's still breathing heavily. His hands ended up threaded in my hair and he kissed me as he fell apart with my name on his lips. He holds me like he never wants to let me go.

"Analise Summers," he says between breaths. "There is not a single part of me that has not been yours since the moment I first laid eyes on you." He kisses me before I can speak. "And I know I've been gone the past six years—I know I'm the one who walked away—but I never stopped loving you. I've had six years to think about everything I'd do if I ever saw you again. Six years to think about everything I wanted to do with you that I never got to."

"I hope I haven't seen it all already," I tease and kiss him.

"How about we forget the reservation and I'll show you more?" His arms wrap around my back and his lips bury into my neck. "We'll be late by now anyway."

"Not if we run."

He laughs into my neck and tries to protest when I start to stand.

"How about we make the reservation, so we have the necessary energy for the rest of the night?" I smirk at him over my shoulder as I pull my dress back down after cleaning myself up, and toss him a wet washcloth to clean up with. I will never get over the way he watches me like he would be content if I was the only thing he ever saw for the rest of his life. The way he looks at me like I'm his reason for being alive.

I have to look away or we *won't* make the reservation. "Besides, I'm only in this for the money, so I'd better get a free dinner out of it."

He laughs then crosses the room and pulls me into his chest. "It *would* be a shame not to show you off to the rest of the world in this dress."

He kisses me deeply before grabbing my hand and leading us, running through the streets of Hartford. And when he orders our favorite white wine for special occasions and toasts "To the most brilliant and beautiful woman in any room," I feel cherished beyond belief.

I don't think any two people smiled and laughed more than we did that night. As we ran hand in hand through the streets of the city where we first fell in love. As we solidified that love all over again.

Twenty~Four

After lightly knocking, we slowly open the door and step into the middle of a party that has been in full force for a while now. Sterling's been talking all month about how he's going to make this the best New Year's party since Warren leaves in a few days. I've been struggling to be excited about this since it marks him leaving. I've been holding out hope—avoiding buying a plane ticket to visit him—just in case he changes his mind and asks me to go with him.

But he still hasn't, and I don't know how to enjoy this night when it feels like a celebration of the end. But damn him, because every time he smiles and talks about his new job, I'm so fucking excited for him I can't even be mad.

"It's nice of you to *finally* join us," Sterling says with a glare when we find him with Ali and Trent in the center of the room. Anyone semi-cool from work is here and there are a lot of familiar faces of some other frequent patrons of The Dizzy Acorn, but we only know them well enough to smile and wave in passing on our way to the core group.

"Sorry." I try to convey the feeling in my face even though I didn't want to show up at all. "I couldn't decide what to wear."

Which isn't technically a lie, but it's not why we were late. The issue was that with each dress I put on that was a no, Warren would take his time slowly stripping it off me and teasing me until I was at my tipping point. Then he'd pull away, smirking, and say "next" as I begged for his fingers or tongue to keep going just a little bit longer.

That happened over and over until I put on the dress I'm wearing now—a black, skin-tight tank dress with short sleeves, and an A-line mesh dress over top that, at first glance, appears black until any hint of light hits it, then it sparkles and shines. I saw it in his eyes when I walked out of the closet that this was the one. His eyes slowly moved down my body then back up and when they met mine again, they were as bright as a summer day.

He swallowed, and as if he couldn't speak, he curled his finger in a *come here* motion. He'd been sitting on the bed in nothing but his boxers like he'd been waiting for this moment all night. I slowly stalked across the room, heart racing in anticipation. I'd stopped caring what time it was long ago.

"Is this one coming off too?" I asked, and smiled when a huge, wild grin grew on his face.

He shook his head just as I got within reach. He reached out to grab me and pulled me down, flipping us over at the same time, so I laid on my back on the bed and he hovered over me. Steadying himself with one hand, the other dropped to my thigh and moved up my leg, pulling the dress up. I lifted my hips to let him pool the dress around my waist.

"I want you to keep this one on," he said and then kissed me.

My underwear had been on the ground since the second dress, but now his joined it, giving him free reign to settle between my hips and slide right into me with one slow move. I groaned in relief, ready for what I'd been begging for all night.

But when he started moving it was as slowly and lazily as the kisses he placed on my neck.

He was taking his time, like he planned to keep this up all night. And if I wasn't about to lose my damn mind because of all the buildups and letdowns, I would've let him. But as his hands traced lines up and down my body I whimpered.

"More," I gasped, barely able to think past all of the things he was doing to my body right now that were just shy of what I needed.

He hummed against my skin, pretending not to know what he was doing. I tightened my legs around his waist, trying to control the momentum but as I pulled myself flush against him, he lowered us back down to the bed, letting more of his weight push against me to keep me still.

"Warren." I was practically crying by that point, but he just kept lazily kissing me.

Before I exploded from the buildup of pleasure he wouldn't follow through on, I flipped us over and took control. I don't know if he wanted it to play out that way or if he was just too awestruck to stop me, but he watched me move on him like it was something holy.

That time, as I approached the edge, he sat up, placing one hand on my hip to help me keep my rhythm and the other into my hair to pull my lips to his. As he kissed me, both of us too far gone to be anything but sloppy, he whispered, "That's right, take what you need. Take everything. It's all only for you. You're in charge."

And I did. I took everything he gave, but I gave him everything in return so we both fell over the edge together.

Before we got off the bed to actually get ready to come here, he looked me right in my eyes and said, "I'm so fucking in love with you, Analise Summers."

"I'm so in love with you, Warren Mitchell," I'd said back. But as we chat with people at this party and everyone asks about

Warren's move, I have to excuse myself. The more I drink, the more my fears creep to the surface and my smile is slipping.

I walk into the kitchen, which is mostly clear of people, and search for a bottle of the good alcohol I know Sterling keeps hidden away and didn't put out for this party. I'm pulling it out of the back of a cabinet above the fridge when Ali walks in and laughs at finding me standing on the countertop, balancing to reach what I'm looking for.

"Want a shot?" I ask, looking over my shoulder with a cheeky grin and grabbing two of the nice glasses when she nods.

I place them on the island and fill both, then immediately pick mine up, clink it against hers and take it. The burn as it goes down my throat is a welcome distraction from the hurt I'm feeling so I fill it again and take a second shot as Ali finishes her first.

I cough as I set the glass down. "Ugh this stuff is horrible, what is it?"

"Bourbon." Her face twists like she didn't enjoy it either, but her eyes watch me carefully. "Did something happen?"

"I just needed a break from hearing him talk about how excited he is to move and start his new job." I sigh. "I *am* so excited and proud of him—he deserves this—but I just don't understand why he hasn't asked me to come with him."

"He *still* hasn't said anything about it?" Shock flashes across her face but she tries to hide it because she knows it'll hurt me, and it does.

I shake my head. "He still tells me how much he loves me, and I know it's true—I see it, I feel it. Hell, there are still times I think he's going to propose—we're there, we're both all in. I don't understand why he wouldn't at least bring it up if he felt that way. So, then I start to wonder if maybe I'm seeing us as something more than what we are. Maybe he doesn't want to be with me anymore and this is his way to let me down easy."

My lips start shaking and I regret the shots. I'm an emotional drunk and that's not how I want tonight to go. I want to have a good memory of these last days together.

"I don't think that's what it is at all," Ali says. Her eyes are sad, but I can hear that she believes the words. "You might not see it, but I promise you the way that man looks at you is evident of a man in love." Her eyes shift to something behind me, and she smiles. "See, he's looking at you that way now."

I turn around and when my eyes meet his, I lose the ability to breathe. She's right—there's nothing but love staring back at me. There's never anything but world-ending amounts of love when he looks at me, but with the extra weight of the bourbon running through my veins, I can't smile like I want to. Instead, when I blink, a tear drops down my cheek and that's all it takes for his face to twist in concern and him to part the crowd of people like the Red Sea on his way to me.

"He loves you, Ana," Ali says and squeezes my arm before heading off to where Trent is.

When Warren reaches me, he threads his hand with mine and leads us off toward the guest room in Sterling's place that's off-limits to the guests of this party. If anyone saw us sneak away, they'd probably assume we were having a quickie in here. But if it got back to Sterling, I know Ali would tell him what was up. Because Sterling is the kind of friend who would come bursting into the room if he thought we were having a quickie in there to chastise us—not that we know first-hand, we're not *that* bad, although I'm sure everyone else would roll their eyes if we said that to them because we *are* pretty bad.

And if I'm willing to admit we're pretty bad, that probably means we're really bad.

"What's wrong?" As soon as the door is shut behind us, he pulls me close but keeps far enough back to look in my eyes.

More tears fall and I curse the semi-drunk me who thought taking shots would help anything. I open my mouth and the words come tumbling out like an avalanche. "Tell me we'll be okay. Tell me we'll make the long-distance work. Tell me we'll get through this."

His eyes widen. "Analise."

I haven't brought my fears up to him because I don't want to ruin his excitement. I don't want to make him feel bad for even a second for taking this incredible opportunity. I don't want him to feel bad about leaving Hartford behind, but I don't want to get left behind either.

"I am so proud of you, Warren, and you are so deserving of this job." I place my hands on his cheeks. "I just love you in a way that has become part of who I am. There's not a single part of me that won't be ruined if we don't make it. I need you to tell me we're going to be okay because I want you *and* I need you, forever."

He kisses me, hungrily, desperately. He kisses me until we're both out of breath and standing with our foreheads pressed together, breathing the same air.

"Analise, I promise you we'll make it through this." I almost drop to my knees just from those words, but he keeps me upright and continues talking. "You are my life. Since the first moment I laid eyes on you I haven't wanted to look anywhere else. I don't want to even think about what a life without you would be like—it would be cold and colorless. It would be lacking everything good in this world. I promise you we'll be okay because I would be ruined too if we weren't."

I kiss him, overcome with happiness. He doesn't want to live without me either.

But I'm too drunk to think about how his words all lead to the conclusion that he'll ask me to come, but he still hasn't. I'm too drunk to realize that he's also had a lot to drink and might be saying more than he should. I'm too drunk to realize that I should be worried about how he's going to keep these promises instead of just being happy he said them.

"How much longer until you take me home?" I whisper

against his lips, letting myself fall into him and get lost in his touch.

"We probably should stay at least till midnight, considering it's a New Year's party." He laughs and it feels like everything is right in my world when I hear that sound. "Are you tired already?"

I stretch on my tippy toes to whisper in his ear, "Oh, I have no intention of sleeping tonight." Then I kiss his cheek and walk out of the room, only looking back once I've opened the door and finding the brightest smile shining back at me.

Twenty-Five

"Why the pantsuits?" Warren asks as his hands run up my legs and tug me closer to him.

"Warren," I caution even though my resolve on this issue is slowly slipping away.

We got into the office early today, so I didn't fight him when he closed my office door behind us, but I haven't changed my mind about office sex. But I know he knows that if he keeps going and unbuttons my pants, I'll let him. I'll let him slide them off me, lift me onto the edge of the desk, and have me right here, right now. But I've spent so long building my career, and I won't jeopardize that. And the sexiest thing a man can do is listen and respect what you say, so the fact that he doesn't push me makes me love him more.

His lips leave my neck, and he laughs, moving to take a seat across the desk from me. "I wasn't asking because of that, although I'm glad you're still thinking about it."

I narrow my eyes at him as I sit in my chair. "Then why were you asking?"

"You always loved your work dresses and skirts and how

they made people more uncomfortable when you were being all badass and shit." The grin on his face makes me laugh, but underneath there's a warmth seeping through me that he remembered that small detail about me.

"The last time I wore a dress to work was my first day working here." I know how he'll react to this story, so I brace myself as I say, "But you have to promise me you're not going to kill anybody after I tell you this."

His eyes darken and the muscles around his jaw tense. "I can't make any promises when you start a story like that."

"Of course not." I sigh. "Well, I'm sure it wouldn't surprise you to hear that Jason is known as the office creep. But on my first day, I saw it—the way his eyes were always on my legs or my body. The way he positioned himself around me. It felt like I was chosen as his next target."

Warren looks like he's about to storm out of this room and go find Jason right now. I glare at him until he settles back in the chair.

"I was at a point in my career that I didn't need to make that statement with the dresses, so for my own comfort, I switched solely to pantsuits."

"I didn't think it was possible to hate that guy more than I already did," he grits out and I laugh because the reason he hated him before was so petty, but this is a legitimate reason. "How has he not been fired?"

"He's Clara's cousin, so unless we have solid proof it's hard to approach her about it." I tried, since I was who she trusted most aside from him. But anytime I did, she'd talk to him and come back with comments like *"Oh he didn't mean it like that"* or when it was about a female on his team not getting a promotion because they wouldn't go out with him she'd say, *"That's not why, he said Matt shows a lot more promise"* even though we all know who did the work on that team. "Everything he does is just on the safe side of that immediately fireable offenses line, but it's bad enough that I've had to move all the females from his team to mine so they could get their promotions and not have to work in that environment."

Understanding washes over him and his eyes widen. "And you keep his attention on you, so he won't bother them as much. That's why he still thinks he has a chance with you."

I shrug and look away. I'm not sure I ever made the conscious decision to do it, but it took one look of discomfort from one of the younger girls on the team for me to stop openly showing my disgust for him and start directing his attention my way as much as possible. "I can handle him, and my position is high enough that he can't do anything to my career. But if one of those girls got hurt or did something they didn't want to do because they felt powerless, or like it would hurt them at work, I'd never forgive myself."

He's quiet long enough that I look up and am surprised to find awe instead of anger on his face. "I said it when I first got here and I'll say it again, I can promise you that these people look up to you like you wouldn't believe. And rightfully so because you are not only an amazing leader, but an amazing person."

Color floods my cheeks even as I shake my head. "I'm just doing the right thing."

"But so many don't."

I look back at him and we just smile at each other.

"We should probably go say our hello's before we get caught in here," I say.

I narrow my eyes in question when his smile grows. "You're thinking about it again."

As much as I fight it, my smile grows in return because I know exactly what he's referring to and he's right. We're sitting on opposite sides of the desk, if someone walked in now it'd look like we were just having a meeting. But I can't stop thinking about damn office sex, so being in here feels like we're doing something dirty.

"How did I ever get work done at Triniti?" I ask, staring at him and never wanting to look away. "Because you are such a distraction."

I stand and walk towards him as he says, "I think you mean you're just so in love with me, I'm all you can think about, and when we're in the same space I'm all you can focus on."

I can see that it was a joke in his eyes, but I lean over, kiss him, then whisper against his lips, "That's exactly what I mean."

His hand moves to the back of my neck when I start to pull away and drags me back for another kiss before I step away.

I open the door, so we actually get to work, and jump back when Peter is on the other side, arm raised like he was just about to knock.

"Good morning," I spit out, breathless.

Warren chuckles from his seat and Peter glances between us, a small smile growing on his face. "Good, you're both here. Have a minute?"

I nod and gesture for him to join us. I compose myself as I move back to my chair and Peter takes the one beside Warren.

"What can we help you with?" I ask when no one else speaks.

"Are both of you free for dinner tonight?" Peter says and I blink a few times before registering what he said.

"I am," Warren answers first, but he looks as confused as I feel.

"I'm free too," I add.

"Great." He stands and I'm thrown off again. *Is that all?* "Right after work, at the steakhouse next to the hotel?"

"Sounds good," I say as he walks out the door and leaves us looking at each other like what just happened was all a dream.

"Any idea what that's about?" I ask and he shakes his head.

"Not a clue."

~

"Ready?" Warren's head pops into the doorway of my office and the way the evening sun shines into the building and reflects through his hair makes my lungs forget how to function. He's glowing. He's golden. He's gorgeous.

And he's *mine*.

It's too much—this feeling, this love. Him being back. Him leaving again in three days. I turn thirty in a few months for fuck's sake, he's almost thirty-three, and we're about to start a long-distance relationship—again—when it didn't go so well the first time. We've got to be out of our damn minds.

But I see him standing before me now and I know I'd rather do long distance with him for the rest of my life than be with someone else. I love this man more than I love anything in this world. He is the beat of my heart, adding a beautiful melody to my life, the breath in my lungs keeping me alive, and the colors of a sunrise, shrouding my world with the promise of a new beginning.

"You need to stop looking at me like that," he says, and it sounds more like a groan. "We're about to go to dinner with my boss, who is now technically your boss too, and when you look at me like that, I lose all my sensibility. I have no control."

I smirk at him. "Is that such a bad thing?"

"God, no." The words come out as a laugh. "I love when you look at me like that. But why don't we get through this dinner first, then you can look at me like that all night."

"Fine, I can act normal around them." I grab my bag, shut off my computer, and walk towards him, leaning in when I'm beside him. "But in my head, I'm always looking at you like that, just so you know."

His eyes close and he takes a deep breath. As if on instinct, his hand drifts to my hip and squeezes. "Now you'll have me thinking about that all evening."

"You would've been thinking about it anyway." I look around to make sure no one's around before kissing him on the cheek. "Now, come on. It's time to go."

We meet up with Peter and Mac at the elevators, he hits the down button and as we step into the elevator I glance over at Warren who shrugs. He's as in the dark about this as I am.

Is it just the four of us? I had assumed this was going to be a larger group. *What the hell is this about?*

We exchange polite small talk on the walk over and until we get seated. But it's not till we get our drinks that Warren decides to broach the question looming over our heads.

"What's this about, Peter?"

I'm not sure whether to be worried because Warren, the CFO of Peter's company, doesn't know what's going on here, but Peter smiles and the sincerity of it eases my mind.

"This isn't traditionally how I'd like to do this," Peter starts, looking at me. "I haven't even had the chance to run the idea by Warren, but since you two know each other, I'm hoping this can be more of an open discussion."

"What idea?" Warren chimes in, voicing my question as well.

"Miss Summers," Peter starts, and my lips press together. He laughs. "Right, Analise. I know we've only worked together for less than two weeks, but you might just be the most impressive person I've met in my entire professional career." His smile turns sheepish as he looks over at Warren. "No offense."

Warren laughs and I can't fight a smile as he raises his hands in surrender and says, "No complaints from me. I completely agree."

I want to look at him like I was earlier—letting all that love shine through—but I know I shouldn't do that here. His eyes flash to me for just a moment, but they darken just enough in that time that I know he understands what I'm thinking.

"Good, because I would like to offer her a new position," Peter says and my jaw drops, but Warren's smile only grows with pride. "We have some work to do to establish this parent company, but I want you in charge of our strategy, and I mean all strategy—for both companies."

My mouth is open, my excitement is rising. This sounds like an incredible opportunity—too good to be true.

"We can work out the details if you're interested. This is intended as a promotion so you can expect a pay increase, and I would like you to be in D.C., with the rest of the executive team, but that wouldn't have to happen right away."

This pitch just gets better and better, a real reason to move to the same city as Warren. I can practically feel the excitement radiating off of Warren too. This is perfect. This is everything I could've asked for.

"The position would report to Warren."

I don't breathe because it would sound like I'm dying if I did. This *is* too good to be true.

This isn't going to work.

I want to cry. I want to scream. But instead, I keep a smile on my face even as the sunshine fades from my eyes in time to the sun dipping below the horizon outside.

Peter and Mac are still smiling at me, and I don't look away even though I no longer hear the words coming out of his mouth. I can feel Warren's gaze on me, the intensity of the expression. I can feel the understanding radiating off him—that I was just offered a job that would put us back in the same position as the one that caused our downfall.

Under the table the heat of a hand rests atop mine, trying to comfort me, but it sends a shock through me that threatens to let the tears spill out. I have to pull away and I hate myself for it. I can't think about this, talk about this right now.

"So, what do you think?" Peter says and I take a deep breath.

"It sounds incredible," I say, too robotic, but only Warren notices the shift. "Is it okay if I think about it?"

"Oh, of course." He laughs. "No rush."

The waiter approaches with our food and I've never been more thankful for an interruption, even though my stomach is twisted in knots, and I don't think I can eat a single bite.

I risk a glance over at Warren as we start eating and beneath his believably calm mask, I see the devastation etched across all his features. Whether it's for me, or for the situation, or both. Or because I pulled away from him. No matter what it is, it's not okay. I won't let us make the same mistakes we made before. I won't run away because it's not ideal. We planned on long-distance before this and we can still do it.

I won't lose him.

Under the table I reach over to give his knee a light squeeze and the instant relief that flows through his entire body lets me know everything will be okay. I love him and he loves me. The rest can be figured out.

Twenty-Six

The same man that's been running trivia as long as we've been coming to The Dizzy Acorn is haphazardly getting everything set up. It looks like it's his first time running this even though he should have it streamlined by now. Whatever works for him, I guess, but it's not how I work and it gives me anxiety just watching.

Thankfully, Trent gives me the perfect out when he whispers, "Now."

That's my cue.

I get out of my chair, giving Warren a kiss on the cheek as he pulls his arm off my shoulders with a knowing smile. I know we're both thinking the same thing—*it's about damn time.*

"I need to talk to you," I say, leaning down when I get to Ali's seat. I don't have to say anymore, she just stands and walks with me off to the back of the room.

The bathrooms are located down a skinny hallway on the side of the bar, far enough from the main room that the sound doesn't travel here well. This has been our spot whenever we need to talk after a long day so it's not suspicious of me to ask even though I have ulterior motives this time. I promised Trent I'd keep her out of there long enough for him to talk to the teams playing trivia tonight—most are also regulars like us so I have no doubt they'll happily agree to his request—but I actually do need to talk to her.

"Did something happen?" she asks as soon as we're inside and finish checking that we're alone.

"Peter, the CEO of Warren's company," I clarify when she looks confused at the name, "offered me a job."

Her eyes squint and her brows pull together. "Well, isn't he your boss now too?"

I laugh, I'm not explaining this well. "Right, but he offered me a promotion I guess?"

"Oh my god," she exclaims, and I jump from the volume of her words. "Analise, that's incredible."

"I'd have to move to D.C.," I add, and her excitement fades fractionally but she smiles.

"You and Warren could be together then."

My lips tremble at that, falling into a frown. "The position reports directly to the CFO."

I wait for her to realize who the CFO is because I can't bring myself to say his name in that sentence. Her face falls when she remembers.

"No," she breathes and all I can do is nod. "What did you say?"

"I said I needed to think about it, because I didn't want to say no right away." I know she doesn't need a reminder of why I'm hesitant to take this. That to me, this is setting us up for ruin again when we just mended the fractures between us.

"Did Warren say anything about it?"

I shake my head. "I haven't let him yet. They offered it to me yesterday after work and when we got home, I cried, and he just held me. I think he knew I couldn't talk about it then, but he knew what I was thinking too. I'm going to talk to him tonight, but I can't take it, right? They didn't know we were together when they offered it and telling them would only make it more complicated."

"Ana." She only uses that nickname when she wants me to listen, when I *need* to listen. "Technically, he's your boss now anyway, there's just a few people in-between. I think this is something you're going to have to face regardless of if you take the job or not."

Shit. She's right. I hadn't really thought about that since this acquisition is so new, but actuarial departments report up to the CFO.

"But if you don't take the job, are you just going to stay here while he goes back? When does the long-distance end? When do you get to be together?"

I look down and twist the sole of my sneaker into the ground, thankful to not be in heels. I wear those far too often and my feet are glad for the break tonight. "I thought we'd figure that out at some point," I mumble, knowing exactly what her response is going to be before she says it.

"You thought that last time too."

And there it is. My greatest fear. That this time will end exactly the same, that we're doomed to be an almost and not a forever. I want to do this differently, but what if it doesn't matter in the end?

I finally look up to meet her eyes and give her a small, grateful smile. "I'll talk to him. I don't want this to be the same as last time."

"Good." She reaches for my hand and squeezes. "You guys deserve a happy ending after everything you've been through."

We head back to the table, arm in arm. The trivia host looks like he's just about ready to start asking for team name submissions—perfect timing. I slyly glance at Trent and he gives me the smallest nod but it's enough. I smile as Ali takes her seat beside him.

Little does she know she's getting her happily ever after tonight.

"Do we have to go get our sheet?" Warren asks when I sit down, and I laugh.

"You know there was this magical discovery that happened in the past six years." I'm smirking as I pull out my phone and hold it up for him to see. "It's called technology, maybe you've heard of it."

Back when we won it was still a paper and pencil process, but about two years ago it switched over to a fully electronic process that's so much easier, and makes the games go by faster since there's no reading of answers or manual collection process.

The corner of his mouth quirks up even though his eyes try to glare at me. He takes my phone and looks at it with a puzzled face. "How do I use this *technology* you speak of?"

My grin grows, and I lean in to kiss him as I take my phone back. I unlock it and lean into him as I pull up the website. "What's our team name?"

He doesn't answer so I glance up at him and he's looking at me like I'm insane. "You better be joking."

I laugh as he takes the phone and enters *The Summers* and adds a sun emoji next to it, but before he can hit submit, I take it back and add a heart emoji—so it's just like the one we wrote up on that scoreboard all those years ago.

After I submit it, I look up at him and his eyes are glassy. His hand comes to rest gently on my cheek and holds me like I'm the most precious object he's ever touched. He leans in so slowly it's like time keeps pausing to let me soak in each second of him looking at me this way.

He pauses when his lips are just touching mine. "I'm still taking your last name."

"I've heard all this before," I whisper even though my heart flutters and my hands want to reach out and pull him closer.

"I won't make the same mistakes again," he says before pressing his lips to mine.

We only separate because the microphone makes a squeal that has everyone cringing.

"Is this right?" The mans voice flows through the speakers. "Do we have trivia royalty in the house with us tonight?"

The other tables start looking around confused, but our table understands. He can see the team names and just pieced together that ours is the same as the number one spot.

"Is this actually *The Summers*?" he asks.

"Yes!" Sterling shouts immediately and he and Will start pointing at us.

My cheeks flush as all eyes in the room turn to look at us. The attention suits Warren and he beams down at me.

"Come on up here." He gestures at us. I shake my head, but Warren stands and pulls me up with him. He smirks at me, and I swear he's doing this just to get me back for the technology joke. I roll my eyes and let him drag me up to the microphone.

"You guys really are the same *The Summers* who have held first place on the leaderboard for five years?" he confirms.

Warren nods, but I lean to the microphone and say, "Closer to eight years now, but yes that's us."

There are a few cheers from our friends and others who have been coming here just as long and remember us from that night. I laugh and out of my peripheral vision I think I see someone I know, but when I look over, there's no one there.

"If I remember correctly," the man continues, "you two were talking about marriage back then." I stop breathing, my head whipping over to glare at him, but he doesn't see. "Did that work out? It appears you two are still together." He gestures at my hand in Warren's.

"Well . . ." I start but Warren grabs the microphone. Smart move.

"We aren't married." The room boo's him and I glance over at him with a smug expression and mouth a "boo" too. He laughs. "I know, I know. I made some mistakes that drove us off course for a while, but with all of you as witnesses I swear I'm going to marry this girl one day."

My face gets hot, like I've spent the day in the sun, and it's probably as red as if I did too. Some people in the crowd cheer, but they're all looking at me. A nervous laugh slips out as my eyes flash to the table of our friends—all four of them are wide-eyed but Sterling has a huge grin on his face.

I take the microphone from Warren before he can say anything else. "All right, I think he's had enough to drink tonight already."

"I haven't even finished my first drink." He leans into the mic and gets a chuckle from the crowd. He's so damn charming.

"Don't we have a game of trivia to start?" I look back at the man, desperate, and he reaches for the mic.

Just before it leaves my hand, Warren leans to it and says, "I'm going to marry her."

Another laugh comes from the crowd and as soon as the mic is out of my hand, I turn around and playfully shove him. I see the glow in his eyes. He wanted to embarrass me a little bit, but every word he spoke is the truth. It's because of that knowledge that, when he wraps an arm around my waist and tugs me into him, I slide my hands up his chest and around his neck.

"So, you're going to marry me one day?" I ask, voice low even though the mics aren't near us anymore.

Before he can answer Sterling yells, "Kiss!" and it starts a chant that shakes the bar.

His arm tightens around me as his other hand comes to rest on my cheek. I let him lead the movement, hold me, and pull me closer. When his lips meet mine, I savor the gentle, sweet kiss and when his lips part, mine follow, letting him kiss me deeply. It's the kiss of two people who have spent years memorizing each other, who know that this is who they want to kiss forever.

Emotions swell in me, and I let them out as a small groan while he kisses me. The noise sends a shock wave through him, and his hand squeezes my hip like it's trying to stay put since it knows where we are. It's enough to make me pull back and smile. If we kept kissing, neither of us would be able to stop ourselves from taking it too far for our current location.

We take our seats to the low whistle of Will and the jokingly scandalized but happy faces of the others.

When trivia starts, we get more serious. Mostly because we're supposed to be rigging the game for Trent and Ali to win. Thank god we switched over to this digital version so we can see where the scores lay because everyone getting zero would be too suspicious. Now we can choose which questions to get wrong based on the current standings and make sure they're on track for the win.

With only five questions left, Trent and Ali are in second, and none of us can figure out who team JSON is who's in first. It's a pretty large margin, and considering Trent talked to everyone beforehand, it's a dick move to not help out here.

There's some confrontation on the other side of the room, and as the next five questions pass, JSON gets them all wrong, and Trent and Ali get just enough right to end up in first place.

All of us let out a sigh of relief when the results pop up.

Ali squeals, they haven't gotten first place before, and their score just squeaks them into fifth place of the overall standings, so they'll get to put their names on the board.

"Looks like we have a new winner." The man's voice rings over the speakers. "Where's team TrentAli?"

Ali waves her hand, not afraid of the attention and Trent swallows nervously. They're invited up on stage which isn't a normal thing if there's no tiebreaker, but since Warren and I got called up earlier it's not as suspicious. Maybe everything worked out perfectly after all.

After asking them their names, the man says, "There is one more question you have to answer before you can add your name to the board though."

Ali looks back confused and while she's distracted Trent pulls a box out of his pocket and gets down on one knee. When the man doesn't give her the question she looks back to Trent for help and her hands fly up to her mouth. Tears immediately cloud her eyes.

I've never heard it this quiet in here as Trent says, "Alison Jennings, will you marry me?"

I don't know if he had planned to say more or not. He's shaking and is obviously nervous from this attention, but he looks at her with nothing but love in his eyes.

She's practically bouncing as she nods her head and says, "Yes," before reaching down and pulling him up to kiss him. All of us cheer, our table loudest of all as he slips the ring on her finger.

Twenty-Seven

My knee bounces with excitement as I ride in the backseat of an Uber on the way to the airport. I'm going to Washington D.C. today. I'm going to see Warren today.

He hasn't even been gone a full month, but I'd commit crimes to see him for only seconds. He's been pretty busy settling into his apartment and job there, so even when we were able to Face-Time, he'd often end up falling asleep on the call. I didn't mind though, I'd just cuddle up in his T-shirts I've been collecting since he told me he was leaving and pretend it was his arms around me. Being able to see him sleep just as I've always been able to is a comfort I didn't know I needed.

He might be states away but he's still mine, and that's all I really need.

I booked this ticket to see him the day he left, and I've been counting down the days until it arrived. The only reason I didn't book it earlier is because I was holding out hope that he'd eventually ask me to come with him.

I close my eyes tight and try to erase that thought from my

mind. This trip is for good things only, not things I wish happened. We can still make this work, we're going to make this work.

"Which airline?" the driver asks and I open my eyes. We're pulling up to the departure's terminal.

"American," I say, and he nods.

It's only another minute before he pulls over and wishes me safe travels. I mumble a "Thanks," but all of my attention is turned to the building that will take me one step closer to seeing my man.

I just have a carry-on for the weekend trip, so I head straight to security and groan when it's a long line. I'm inpatient, anxious, excited, and I can't stand still. I'm bouncing in line, stepping side to side almost in a dance because I have so much adrenaline coursing through me. My movements draw the attention of the TSA workers, but I'm too antsy to be able to stop. Their eyes stay glued to me, probably interpreting my happiness as nervousness of being caught.

They must be so cautious of me that they bring out the dog to sniff the line. Three sets of uniformed eyes watch as I pass by the dog, it sniffs, and keeps going, but it's apparently not enough to halt their suspicions because I just happen to get pulled for a hand swab test *and* my bag gets searched. The man searching my bag asks where I'm going, and I grin.

"I'm going to see my boyfriend," I say, excitement evident in my words. I can't stop speaking, needing to tell another person about my plans. "You see, he just got a new job and moved to DC, so I haven't seen him in a month and—"

The man quickly closes my bag, fights an eye roll at the piles of lingerie he found, and grumbles, "Have a good trip."

I can't tell if he was actually done searching the bag or just wanted me to shut up. I stare at him another second before shrugging, grabbing my bag, and practically skipping towards my gate.

Once I arrive at my gate. I pull a book out of my bag. I try to read but I can't focus, so I plug in my headphones and put on a TV show I downloaded last night. But a few minutes later I couldn't tell you a single thing that happened, so I shut that off too. The only thing that holds my attention is the screen with the words Washington D.C. and boarding in fifty minutes. I watch it count down.

Forty-five minutes.

Thirty-five.

Thirty.

Hurry up.

I'm shaking so much I almost miss my phone vibrating, and I practically squeal when it's his name I see. The people sitting around me glance my way, but I'm too happy to care.

"Hi, my love," I coo into the phone. "I'm at the gate just waiting to board. It's taking forever though."

It's quiet on the other side—a chilling quiet that sends a shiver through me.

"Warren?" My voice waivers, suddenly uncertain.

"You're already at the airport," he says, his voice is cold and distant. I don't recognize it. I don't like it. "I was hoping to catch you before you got there."

"What do you mean?" I squeak, my stomach twisting. Something's wrong.

"You shouldn't come see me." His words are matter-of-fact, emotionless. They're a knife that's slicing through me. They're my greatest fears coming to life.

"Is it not a good time?" I try to be understanding, a lot is changing for him too. I could just be getting ahead of myself. "I can resched—"

"No." He cuts me off with the one word that feels like a fatal blow to my heart. "I don't mean you shouldn't come now. I mean you shouldn't come ever."

"What?" The word barely makes an audible sound. He didn't say that, did he? I heard wrong. I had to have heard him wrong.

"This isn't going to work, Analise." He continues as if he doesn't hear me. "We were kidding ourselves to think it could."

"Warren—" I start.

"Goodbye, Analise." His voice wavers for just a moment before the line goes dead.

I keep the phone to my ear, staring straight ahead. That's it? That's all he's going to say? After everything we've been through, he's not even going to give me an explanation?

All of my adrenaline turns into anger and I call him back.

"Motherfucker," I curse under my breath when it goes straight to voicemail. Did he turn his fucking phone off? Did he block my number already?

The longer I sit there, my anger slowly fades to sadness and pain. The reality of what just happened hits me like a train.

Oh. My. God.

Warren just broke up with me.

I thought I was going to spend the rest of my life with him. Fall asleep in his arms, wake up to his kisses, and grow old with his banter. Our path was set, clear skies, no turbulence—a smooth ride. But I guess we veered off course and entered the Bermuda Triangle when I wasn't paying attention, because now everything is lost, suddenly disappeared. That life, that path, no longer exists and I don't think it'll get rediscovered.

Sometimes those lost planes and ships get found years later, or in shows they just reappear, unaware that so many years have passed in the real world. But that's not realistic. Warren doesn't make impulsive decisions. If he's breaking up with me, then that means we're done for good.

What the hell happened to all of those promises he made me not even a month ago? How do you tell someone you'll love them forever, that you can't imagine your life without them, and then break up with them over the phone a few weeks later?

He told me he loved me enough that the distance wouldn't matter.

He told me we would make it work.

But it took less than a month to settle into life without me. To leave me. There wasn't even enough time to try to make this work. He just gave up on me, on us.

"Flight 5044 with service to Washington D.C. will begin boarding momentarily." The voice over the intercom is cheery and happy and I want to yell at the attendants. There's nothing to be happy about. How can they not see that the world is ending? *My* world is ending. And they're *happy.*

Five minutes until boarding.

It now counts down until my heart will shatter beyond repair.

Slowly, the people around me stand and get in line. Pre-boarding begins. Then the groups start, but I just sit and watch everyone else move on with their life as mine stays frozen. I sit and watch until the last person has gotten on the plane. Until they've called my name over the speakers. Until they've given up on me—just like he did—and finally close the doors. Until the plane leaves the gate and starts barreling towards the person I want to see more than anything in this world, without me on it. Until the tears start to flow and I grow tired of the judging stares.

I text Ali and ask her to pick me up from the airport—I don't want to be alone right now—then I slowly trudge out of the terminal, leave security, and pass baggage claim. The airport isn't far from us, so it's not long before her red car stops in front of me. I've been holding it together as well as I can but as soon as I shut the door behind me I break down.

I sob.

I wail.

I can't breathe.

I don't want to breathe.

Her hand grabs mine and it grounds me enough to grit out, "He broke up with me."

"He *what?*" she screams.

"He called and told me not to get on the plane."

I'm hyperventilating. There's too much air but it's not doing its job. I don't want it to. I need to breathe. I don't know what I want. Except him. I want him to call and say he made a mistake.

But he never does.

Twenty-Eight

AUGUST CURRENT DAY (THURSDAY)

Warren walks out of the bathroom and runs a hand through his wet hair on the way to bed. I'm already in one of his old T-shirts, curled up beneath the covers, and the sight of him shirtless sends a thrill through me. This beautiful, sunshine man loves me—*still* loves me—and I won't ever understand why. But who am I to question what's meant to be?

He crawls under the covers and when he rolls over, so we're face to face, the corner of his mouth pulls up. "What's that look for?"

I smile as his hand finds my hip beneath the covers, and my shirt, to pull me closer. "You're like a *man* man now," I say.

His eyes narrow at me like I'm crazy, but a beautiful, bright laugh comes out of his mouth. "What does that even mean?"

"Back then, we were still immature kids, even though we acted like adults. We were still on that short high that comes from finally having the freedom you craved your whole life. We thought we had everything figured out, but looking back, I knew nothing." He laughs and I reach to trace the wrinkles his scrunched-up face causes. "And don't get me wrong, you were attractive as hell back then, but now you're all filled out." I run my hand down his arm and back up his chest. His body shudders beneath the touch. "Your muscles and jawline are more defined. But more than that, there's a calmness, a sureness about you that I never felt back then. It's like something settled in you and that change helped you become the man you are today."

I expect him to kiss me, to pull me closer, but instead, he takes a deep breath and starts talking about the things we never discussed before.

"On the way to Boston, you were right that there was more about my feelings on my parents' divorce that I never talked about. I don't think I ever consciously understood those feelings until recently. But before I met you," he starts, a small smile on his face even though his eyes have dimmed like the sun on a cloudy day, "nothing about me was settled. I was a mess. I was a different man than I was starting the day I met you. It was like a piece of me had always been missing, I wasn't balanced, and then you showed up and suddenly everything made sense in my world."

I shake my head slightly, not believing that I could've changed him on day one—that he could've been different before the day he met me. He just smiles in return and some of the sun peeks out from behind the clouds. "I know you heard about what caused the divorce. That their marriage was over long before they told me, but they played the part of a loving couple in front of me until I went off to college. Then they couldn't separate fast enough. But I stopped believing in love for a little bit because of them. If the two people I thought loved each other more than anything could end so quickly, what chance was there for me?"

Even though I'd guessed how he probably felt about it all, the words still cut through me like a knife coming from his mouth.

"In college, anytime a relationship started to get semi-serious, I'd bolt. I didn't trust it so I left before I could get hurt." He won't look at me during this part, and my heart breaks for the shame he still feels. "I never wanted to tell you about it because I feared you'd look at me differently. I always used humor and banter to cover anything real and I hurt so many people, but at the time all I could think was not to let myself get hurt."

"But then I walked back to my desk that day to find your face twisted in concentration and a warmth ran through me I'd never felt before." He finally looks up and my eyes widen. In that look I start to understand why he always seems to say my name as if it was holy, or as if I was his savior, because maybe I really did save him, or a part of him at least. "So, of course, I led with humor, but then you played along and shot back with the perfect counter and it almost knocked me off my feet. We only had one conversation, but I couldn't stop thinking about you. I spent so long avoiding anything serious and then I spoke to you for a few minutes, and I wanted to get on my knees and beg for you to give me a shot, to go out with me, to never leave."

I laugh and lean in to kiss him, looping my leg with his to help me pull closer. "If it makes you feel better, I totally would've given you my number that first day. Then you wouldn't have had to berate me when you got back from your cousin's wedding a month later, and it might not have taken you two months to ask me out."

He chuckles against my lips. "I did come on a little strong after that wedding. *God* I was such a mess while I was gone. I should've been happy for them, celebrating, but I was more annoyed that I had to be away from you right as I was starting to believe you could be into me too."

"Then why not ask me out sooner?"

"I was scared you'd change your mind about me," he says so fast it's like a bullet to my chest.

"Warren," I breathe, the word barely there.

"I'd spent so much time running I was worried that, now that I'd found someone to be serious about, they'd run," he adds. "So, I waited—absolutely too long—but that day I couldn't take it any longer. I couldn't wait another day to ask you out. Then you hugged me and said yes, and when you took my hand you officially became the sun in my world. Everything I did, thought, and wanted revolved around you."

"And then you sang a song about summer love." I smile, remembering how off-key he was. But that key fit right into my heart.

"It was more about loving Miss Summers." He kisses my nose. "I know I said I was only falling for you then, but I was so fucking in love with you already."

"If I hadn't loved you before you sang for me, that would've sealed the deal." I laugh. "But I didn't want to scare you off."

He rolls over so he's hovering over me, and I let my hands roam his bare upper body. His lips move to my neck and my eyes close. My whole body hums and it feels a lot like the word *more*.

I'm just about to slip my hands under the waistband of his boxers when I turn to stone because he says, "I went to therapy in D.C."

My breathing gets deeper. He doesn't pull back to look at me, he just keeps his head buried in my neck as he talks. "Walking away from you completely ruined me. I hated myself so much for what I did I fell into a deep depression. It took some convincing, but eventually I listened to one of my friends and went to see a therapist. He helped me finally deal with all the things I never talked about—all the things I avoided and hoped would just go away but never did. Helped me realize that the way I acted in college, and running from you were because of unresolved feelings I had about my parents' divorce. That I made a mistake with how I handled leaving last time. That I didn't communicate the way I should have, and that hiding parts of myself didn't help us in the end. He helped me finally be ready for this. For us."

"Thank you for telling me this," I say, softly, running my fingers up and down his back. It's different, hearing it from him, hearing everything. My heart aches for our younger selves who both messed up, who didn't fight for the love we knew we had. Yes, he walked away, but I let him. I didn't fight for him, for us, the way I should've. I didn't communicate the way I should've either. I hid my fears and let them ruin us. He might've made the bigger mistake, but my hands aren't clean either. "I'm proud of you for getting help. For healing."

"Last time, I loved you with everything I had but I didn't give you all the parts of me," he says, finally pulling back so I can see his face. My fingers moved to smooth the pain and worry off his face. "This time, I want you to know all of me, to love all of me, because I still love you with everything that I am."

"Warren." My lips curl up into a small smile. "I have always loved every part of you, even when I didn't know them all. There was never anything you could tell me that would make me love you less."

"Really?" he asks, skeptically. A real, big grin spreads across his face and my heart kicks into overdrive. He leans down to brush his lips against mine. "What if I told you I killed someone?"

I laugh, shifting beneath him so more of our bodies press together. "The only time I've ever seen you angry was when someone hurt me. So that would have to be the reason, and how could I be that mad when you were just protecting me?"

With a smirk, he leans down to press his lips to my neck again. I lift my hips when his hand runs up my leg, lifting the shirt, then hooks into the waistband of my underwear and pulls them down to my knees. I shimmy out of them completely as he removes his own.

"I love that you know me so well," he whispers against my neck as we start moving together. Each movement is so rhythmic and in-sync, like we'd mastered a piece of complicated choreography, but in reality, we've just mastered each other. And there's nothing better than that.

"I . . . love . . . you," I gasp out before his lips crash against mine.

As the tempo picks up and our breaths get shorter and heavier, I can't help feeling that these shared breaths between us are all I need to survive.

It's not until we're cuddling and getting ready to fall asleep that I tell him I'm ready to talk about the job offer—that I finally communicate the way we needed to back then. "What happens to us if I don't take this job? How do we make this work if I'm here and you're there?"

"Analise," he says, his touch turning gentle and tender as it encourages me to turn around. His hand rests on my cheek, and it settles the loose wire hovering over the fuel in my gut—stopping me from exploding with worry. "Listen to me, I don't care where you are in the world. D.C., Hartford, hell if you had to move to Tokyo, I'd wake up in the middle of the night just to hear about your day. I lived without you once and I refuse to do that again, even if it's through texts and phone calls, I want you. In any way I can have you."

"Really?" It just slips out, but the warmth from his returning smile evaporates the rest of my doubt. He chuckles and kisses my nose, then cheek, then lips.

"I understand why you're worried about taking the offer, and I don't blame you for feeling that way," he says, but I know what he's going to say next. I know because I've thought about every angle of this, every possibility. "But Peter is not like our bosses at Triniti. It wouldn't be an issue like it was then."

But my eyes burn. How can he say that so casually after everything we went through last time?

"Even if I knew for sure that was the case." I take a deep breath and open my eyes. "I couldn't accept it without him knowing about us first. I won't leave it to chance."

He hesitates, but asks, "Do you want to tell him, or do you want to turn it down?"

"I don't know yet." I have worries both ways, but I need to decide what will be best for *me*. As much as I might want to, I can't make this decision solely for him.

Twenty-Nine

Even as a shiver runs through me and goosebumps spring up my bare legs, I can't wipe the mile-wide smile off my face. My gaze clings to the corner of my desk, and my breath quickens as I remember what occurred there this morning. I let out a deep breath as my eyes flutter closed and my hands rub my bare lower thighs.

Damn him.

Damn that beautiful, perfect man for getting me to wear a dress to work. And without even asking me to.

Ever since he brought up the idea of office sex, the work dresses that had gone long unnoticed in the back of my closet started screaming to be worn. It's crazy how something that sat like trash in the back of my closet for so long became treasure overnight because the right person was around to admire it.

But the office sex was definitely worth it.

I made up some excuse to get him here early, then locked the door behind us and sealed my lips to his.

I didn't even care about his smug tone when he whispered, "I thought you said no office sex," against my neck. Or that I responded, "Only this once," on a shaky breath that was full of longing for him to pull my dress up faster.

All I remember is how he whispered, "Bossy," before complying after I'd said, "I can think of many more productive things for your mouth to be doing than sassing me right now."

I thought if he was heading back to D.C. tomorrow I might as well have some memory to tide me over, but I don't think I'll ever work again in this office. I'll just stare at the corner of the desk where I had perfect, early morning, try-to-keep-quiet sex with my perfect man.

Is this how happy people think?

It's been a while since I thought anything was perfect, but now everything is perfect because of him. Because I'm with him. Because he's here. Life is sunny and bright. There's not a cloud in my mind's sky.

Or at least there wasn't, until Jason comes stalking into my office like he owns the damn place and suddenly there's nothing but storm clouds. He's not a person I want around on a good day, but the look on his face now terrifies me—especially since he closed the door behind himself.

"Have a nice night?" he spits. He's a coiled snake ready to strike, and I need to watch where I step.

With a cheery voice and smile I say, "I did, thank you." But the gears are turning in my head, trying to dissect his words, what they could mean, and what the hell the dark insinuation that lies just beneath the words that's turning my stomach is.

I stand up and try to subtly shake off the nerves that have been growing the longer he stands there glaring at me. Moving towards my coffee cart as an excuse, I hope to be able to get him out of the office as soon as possible. But the second I step around the table I know it's the wrong move. Greedy eyes rove over my exposed legs and the feeling I've spent years trying to forget and save others from, the feeling that made me put the dresses in the back of my closet in the first place, washes over me. I'm struggling to stay afloat in a stormy sea.

I try to walk towards the door, but he shifts into my path and it's not until I move to go around him that I realize I've played right into his hand. He corrals me away from the door, trapping me in the space between the desk and the blinds I always keep closed because I hate it when people look in the room as they walk by. It's ironic because right now I'd give anything for someone to walk by and be able to look in. To be able to help.

My eyes dart around the room searching for a way out of this. Trying to figure out a way to get past the man slowly stalking closer to me, caging me in, trapping me, like a damn circus animal.

I take a step closer to the blinds, hoping that if I can find a way to open them, someone will be able to help. He clicks his tongue at the movement and closes the distance between us before I can reach them. His body presses against mine, pushing me into the wall and making it hard to move. I'd rather sink into the wall or melt into a puddle on the floor than have him this close to me.

"Nice dress," he says, darkly.

A hand lands on my leg just below the hem and my body twists and pulls, trying to get away from him, but his size and strategic positioning keeps me from being able to stop him as his hand slowly inches higher.

"Get your hands off me," I grit out. My lips shake and tears prick at the corners of my eyes.

His smile only grows with my discomfort. "I've grown tired of this cat and mouse game we're playing. I think it's about time you pay up for all the teasing you've been doing."

"Excuse me?"

"Don't act like you don't know what you've been doing." His hand slides up just under my dress and bile rises to my throat.

"I *said*, get your hands off me," I say, louder this time. Hopefully, loud enough to be heard outside. I push off of the wall as much as I can, and his hand leaves my leg to push my shoulders back to the wall—hard. I groan as my shoulders and head hit the wall, but it makes a loud thump that shouldn't sound normal from the outside. *Please, someone hear.*

"Tell me," he says, leaning closer. I try to press my body as flat against the wall as possible, but I can't get away from him. "Would you fuck me too, if my title was CFO?"

My eyes widen and my jaw drops open. He knows. How the fuck does he know?

But then my teeth clank together. *"Have a nice night?"* he'd said when he first entered. And at The Dizzy Acorn last night the name JSON for trivia, and the moment I thought I saw a familiar face in the crowd but then they were suddenly gone.

"You were there last night," I say, not needing to phrase it as a question. I'm such an idiot for not considering that possibility from the start of this all. He could've been there any night when we were publicly dancing and kissing.

He sneers. "At least now I know why you've turned me down all these years. I wasn't high enough on the corporate ladder for you."

He moves in even closer, and I squirm, trying to find any additional distance to put between us. "It doesn't matter what your title is, I'd never fuck you. The only reason I ever pretended to be interested was to save the other girls in the office from this. If Clara wasn't your cousin you'd have been fired ages ago."

"You little fucking whore." He moves, barricading my upper body with one arm and moving the other back to my thigh, not bothering to move slowly this time.

I cry out, "Stop," and start kicking the heel of my foot against the wall, trying to make any more noise that I can. He quickly hooks his leg around mine to stop me, and I can no longer do anything to stop this other than cry and yell.

"It's a good thing Clara is my boss then," he says as his hand continues to creep up under my dress.

No, is all I can think, all I can say. My eyes close, I can't watch this happen. I want to be anywhere but here right now. I want to shrivel up and die. I want to burn alive and take him down with me.

I need help, but no one is coming. No one knows I'm in trouble.

"Actually, *I'm* your boss now," a voice says from the door and my eyes fly open.

Peter stands there, accompanied by Victoria and my tears come faster now. Tears of relief.

Jason hesitates before finally taking a step back and my limp body drops to the ground. There's pain from my knees hitting the ground hard, but pain is better than what was just happening. I'm sucking in breath after breath as if I'd just been choking and can finally breathe. Peter creates a path for Victoria to cross the room to check on me without crossing Jason and I focus on her kind smile as she crouches in front of me.

"Are you okay?" she asks.

I nod and take her hand to help me up. "How'd you know?" I whisper.

"You have always protected us from him." She squeezes my hand, and my lips start to quiver. "So, we've always made it a point to look out for you too, especially when he wanders in here."

I close my eyes and nod, a few more silent, grateful tears slip out. "Thank you."

"No," she says, and I open my eyes again. Tears fall from her eyes. "Thank *you*."

We both look over as more people show up at the door, but it's just Mac with a security guard in tow. I just watch as Peter instructs him to detain Jason and remove him from the premises.

"Your personal items will be boxed up and shipped to you," Peter says. "You will not set foot in this building again or I will have you arrested for trespassing."

Jason's mouth looks like it's moving but I don't hear anything he says as he's led out of the room and down the hall. I just shake my head in disbelief.

He's gone. For good.

I meet Peter's eyes, and he says softly, "Can we chat for a minute? If you're not comfortable being alone in here we can go somewhere else, or have someone sit in with us."

"In here is fine," I say. But then my eyes stray back to the wall I'd just been pinned against, and I shudder. "Could we keep the door open though?"

His smile is kind, understanding and he nods. "Of course."

Victoria squeezes my hand one last time before leaving and walks off with Mac. I gesture for Peter to take a seat, but as I take a step to head back behind my desk, I see him. Just out of my original sightline, Warren stands glaring at the door they took Jason out of. His fists shake at his sides and his body is rigid with anger. His eyes are trying to scorch Jason alive.

He's so mad he doesn't even notice me standing here. I glance back at Peter who stopped to look at what caught my attention too. I bite my lip, considering, but when Warren takes a step towards the exit door I don't care if it gives us away.

"Warren," I say, harshly, as a command to stop.

His head whips over to me and he freezes mid-step. I shake my head, my eyes pleading for him to not go after Jason and do something that will get *him* in trouble. His breathing deepens and his head looks between me and the door, considering.

"Please," I add, quieter and some of the tension leaves his body as he looks at me. His eyes look me over, trying to make sure I'm okay. It looks physically painful for him not to come over and make sure I'm not hurt.

I gesture with my head for him to go back to the conference rooms. Trying to convey with my eyes that I'll come find him as soon as I can. He lets out a deep breath, runs his hand through his hair, then turns around. I let out a sigh of relief.

When I turn around, Peter is watching with raised eyebrows. My cheeks flush and I turn my back to him to head to my seat.

But before I can sit down, he says, "I have never seen Warren get that mad over anything before—hell, I've barely seen him get mad at all." I close my eyes while he still can't see me. I guess that did give us away after all. "He really loves you."

My entire body goes cold. Slowly, I turn to face Peter and only find a smile on his face. *This wasn't a surprise to him.* I cock my head and my face twists. "You knew?"

His eyes soften. "If it wasn't obvious enough from how you two act around each other, Mac overheard a particularly interesting conversation at the hotel bar last week."

I drop into my chair, my body sagging, remembering what conversation that was and my face burning red that she heard that all. It wasn't our best moment.

"And . . ." Peter continues, and I look up as my stomach drops. *Oh, god.* What else could they have seen? All of the careless decisions we made this past week come flooding back. "Warren came to talk to me this morning."

I look down as a small smile forms on my lips. *That damn idiot.*

"What did he tell you exactly?" I ask, still looking at my lap.

"That you're considering turning down the job offer because of what happened at Triniti."

He pauses and I look up slowly.

"Listen," he adds, "I don't need to know the details of your personal life, that's between you and whoever you choose to share it with. And if you don't want to take the job because you don't want to move, or you're simply not interested, that's fine. That's your decision to make."

"But . . ." he continues as I'm just about to respond. "If you're not going to take the job because you're with Warren, and you're worried about how that will play out in the work environment, that's between you and me."

My eyes narrow in confusion. Is that not my personal life?

"I don't care who you spend your time with outside of work, unless it negatively affects the workplace. We're all adults. As long as we can remain professional at work, I don't care about anything else."

The corner of my mouth tugs down into a frown. "Everyone says they don't care—until they do. In my experience, it's not an issue, until it is. And by then, it's too late."

"Analise," he sighs and leans forward, placing his hands on his knees. "I respect that you have genuine fears about history repeating itself. But I don't think I'll come across talent like yours again, so I'm going to tell you something about *my* personal life. I'm married."

"Oh, congratulations," I say, slowly, closer to a question than a celebratory remark. What does this have to do with this conversation?

He laughs lightly, a smile growing on his face. "To Mac."

"Oh." It slips out on a breath as my face smooths out. "You know, I've thought a few times these weeks that if you two weren't together, you'd make a good couple."

He laughs, sitting back in the seat, and I let a smile creep onto my lips.

"The point is, you don't have to worry about any repercussions from dating a co-worker, because I did it first."

Now, *I* laugh. The weight I felt since the offer lifts—I feel lighter. "So, you're not one of those hypocritical bosses who'll punish someone for something they do too?" I tease, because I've had too many of those bosses and I already know he's not one of them from the past two weeks.

But his eyebrows shoot up. There's an amused smile on his face, and I blanche. *What did I just say?* He doesn't know me well enough to understand my humor or that sometimes I can't stop stupid things from coming out of my mouth.

"Sorry." My cheeks heat and I look down. "Sometimes I speak before thinking. I know you're not like that. I actually think you're a really good boss from what I've seen."

I press my lips together to stop rambling as he laughs. My cheeks get even redder.

"Does that mean you'll consider the offer?"

I look up and smile at the hopeful expression on his face. I say what I wanted to say when I got the offer—before my worry clouded my excitement. "I think it means I'll accept."

He stands and reaches his hand out towards me with a smile. I stand and shake it.

"I'll have someone send the documents over right away," he says. "Now, you probably should go make sure Warren didn't change his mind about going after Jason."

I cringe. I don't think he did—especially after I told him not to—but it was only last night that we were joking how the only time he'd kill someone would be if they hurt me. And this definitely qualifies. "Right."

"Peter," I say, just before he leaves the room. He looks back at me. "I know Matt is next in line on Jason's team if you're trying to promote from within, but whenever we want the work to be done right, we go to Victoria. I had to transfer her to my team because there were certain . . ." What's the correct term for a boss who withholds promotions because his subordinates won't go out with him? Jackass. Douchebag. Prick. All of the above. But I go with, "Barriers to promotion on her old team."

His eyes widen and he nods slowly. "I'll keep that in mind. Thanks."

Once he's gone, I take a few minutes to compose myself and process the day. Thankfully, it's Friday so I can leave now that it's lunchtime. I think I've had enough drama for one day and I want to celebrate this good news with Warren.

But when I get to the conference room, he's not there and all of his stuff is gone.

That fucking *idiot.*

I stop breathing, anger surging through me and seizing my ability to function. I'm going to kill him if he went after Jason.

I'm digging through my purse for my phone when footsteps approach me, but they're not heavy enough to be his so I ignore it.

"Analise?" A quiet voice that I recognize speaks, and after taking a deep breath, I look up with a smile.

"Hey, Jasmine. What are you still doing here? It's early Friday." Most of the office has cleared out by now.

"Mr. Mitchell stopped by my desk earlier and asked if I could give you this when you came looking for him." She holds out a small, unaddressed envelope.

A note. He left a damn note.

I try to hide my frustration in front of Jasmine, but I don't think I'm doing a good job. "Thank you, Jasmine. Enjoy your weekend."

"Thanks." She smiles. "You too."

I wait until she's gone and there's no one around to open the envelope.

I tilt it into my hand and a hotel key and small piece of paper fall out.

Room 305.

I know what you're thinking, and no, I didn't go after him . . . even though I really wanted to.

I let out a long sigh of relief. *Thank god.*

But if it's not about that then what *is* it about?

I double-check the room number against the note one more time. This is it, room 305. I take a deep breath and scan the room key. There's a soft click and the light turns green. Slowly, I turn the handle and open the door.

The light from the hallway floods into the room and reflects off the ground. Or rather what's on the ground. Blue tulips line the entryway and as I step further into the room, I see they cover every surface. My eyes flash around the room, taking in every detail—the trail of flowers leading me down the small corridor past the bathroom and into the open room, the dim lighting, and the flowers scattered atop the bed—and eventually land on Warren.

He's standing in front of the bed, in the same navy suit he was wearing earlier, but the jacket is now draped over the desk chair and the sleeves of his white button up are rolled up. In his hand are two blue tulips, and he's looking at me with a smile that has me gravitating towards him even before I've consciously told my legs to take me there.

"Looks like Lola's forgiven you," I say, with a raised brow that asks: *What is all this for?*

He laughs, but his face quickly turns serious as he looks me over. "Are you okay?"

I reach out and run my hand down his arm so he can feel that I'm truly here, that I'm okay, because it doesn't look like he quite believes it yet.

"I'm okay," I say, softly, letting his arms wrap around me and pull me as close as he can. I breathe his scent in and sigh in relief at the comfort it brings. "They got there before anything happened."

He goes rigid around me. His voice is rough when he says, "Why are you always so quick to brush things under the rug? None of what happened was okay. Not one second of it, and I'm sure I only know a small fraction of what actually occurred in that room."

"I know it wasn't okay." My voice squeaks, and my vision blurs with pooled tears I don't want to fall. My body starts to shake as the horrid feeling of being pinned against that wall comes flooding back. I pull myself tighter to Warren. "I'm not okay, but I will break if I keep thinking about it. If I let myself become a victim, he wins, and I won't let him leave any legacy behind. I *will* be okay, in time, but not by giving him power over me."

It might not make sense to most people, but I have my own ways of dealing with bad things. Warren leaving, my mom dying, my dad drinking, and now this. I'll survive—I always do.

Warren pulls back and looks at me, a frown on his face. "I will let you do this your way, for now, because I know how strong you are. But say the word, and we'll get you an appointment with my therapist."

I narrow my eyes back at him. "Your therapist is in D.C."

"That brings me to my next point." A smile grows on his face —a smile that melts my heart and makes me glow from the inside. "I made the biggest mistake of my life six years ago when I left you, and I don't want to make the same mistake again. Analise, you are my everything. Now that I have you in my arms again, I never want to live another day without you, without your love, without your touch. If you're not comfortable taking the job, then I'll quit and move back here. I don't care what city we end up in, I just want to be where you are."

My eyes widen—he loves that job, he loves that city.

"I love you, Analise. I never stopped loving you. It's like you said, there are thousands of jobs, but there's only one you. You are all I need to be happy in this life. I want to be wherever you are." He drops to both knees in front of me, holding the two tulips and now, my two hands. *What is he doing?* "Before you call me crazy, I'm not proposing." My heart drops slightly. "I don't even have the ring with me, and I think it's only fair that I earn your full trust back before actually asking you to marry me. What I am asking is for you to stay with me forever, by my side —not states away. I'm asking you what you want so we can make a decision, together, this time. A few days ago you asked me what the probability of this working was, and I didn't have time to answer. But to me, the probability of us *isn't* a probability at all—it's a certainty. It was always meant to be you and me."

I was wrong last week, because he loves me more.

"Warren." I gently tug his hands until he finally stands again. I put my hands on his cheeks and kiss him. Then I pull back just enough to be able to look in his eyes as I say, "I accepted the job —in D.C."

"What?" His eyes light up and his smile grows brighter and

brighter until it is blinding, and his shine is all I can see. It's all I can feel. "When?"

"Earlier, when Peter and I talked." I smile. "Apparently, *someone* told him about us this morning."

He smiles sheepishly at my raised eyebrow. "I didn't want this to be a secret—whether you accepted or not—and I would've needed a reason eventually regarding why I was asking to work from Hartford so often."

I laugh, but then my expression softens. "Thank you, for not letting me make the mistake this time."

"We have plenty of time to make many more mistakes," he whispers, leaning in until our lips are just touching.

"I'm looking forward to it," I say, then press my lips to his.

Thirty

AUGUST 5 YEARS AGO

I frown at the fully stocked pantry.

I've stopped by to check on my dad every day since mom died but I haven't seen any signs that he's eaten—only new, empty bottles of bourbon that join the ones already by the sink. I don't know where he keeps getting them from because he didn't drink much before, and I didn't buy them. I took his car keys when I noticed how much he was drinking too. So how the hell do they keep showing up?

Mom went so quick—she was seemingly healthy one minute, and the next she was being taken away in an ambulance after collapsing while we were all out at lunch. The next time I saw her she was being kept alive with machines.

It was so fast I didn't have time to process what happened. She was there, and then suddenly she was gone. I still feel like she'll walk through the front door at any moment.

It's been hard since she died, but I thought I'd at least have my dad. Someone who could support me, who could understand what I was going through. But instead, I'm watching him drink himself into a grave—I'm watching him kill himself slowly. And I can't stand to watch it anymore. My attempts to talk to him this week, to get him to stop drinking, ended with him yelling at me and me in tears. I've never heard my dad raise his voice like that before.

I want to talk to someone. I *need* to talk. I've tried talking to Ali, but I don't just need someone to listen—I need someone to help.

I want to talk to Warren.

I've missed him more this past week than the whole year and a half since he's been gone—and that's saying a lot because I miss him every damn day. He would know what to say, what to do, to help.

I pull out the loaf of bread from the pantry and make a ham and cheese sandwich, then bring that and a glass of water over to where my dad is sitting on the couch, watching the TV with a blank expression.

"You should eat something," I say as I set down the plate.

He doesn't move or give any indication that he heard me. He's lifeless, no spark left in his eyes, and I have to look away. That person is not the dad I knew.

I move to grab the half-full glass of liquor so I can dump it, and I almost spill it when an angry grunt sounds from behind me. I can't stand to look at him as a tear drops down my face.

"I'll be back tomorrow," I say, leaving the glass and grabbing my jacket and purse.

As I'm heading toward the door, I think I hear a low grumble say, "Don't bother," and I feel like my heart is giving out too. I get in the car and start driving. I don't have a destination in mind, I'm just aimlessly driving—wanting to be anywhere but here. It's not until I turn onto I-84 E that I realize I *do* have a destination in mind.

I can't talk to Warren, but this is the next best thing. I just hope it's okay that I'm showing up unannounced.

～

My hands shake as I walk up to the charming, brick house. I pause in front of the door. What if she's not home? What if she doesn't want to see me? I shouldn't have come here.

But my fist still knocks on the door, because if I don't, I'd have driven almost two hours for nothing. And this is my last resort.

My breathing gets heavier the longer I wait. Just as I think she's not going to answer at all, there's a soft click and the door opens. Her bright, cheery smile falls into confusion when she realizes it's me.

"Analise?"

My lower lip starts shaking and her confusion fades into concern.

"I'm sorry," I squeak, and all the tears that have been building up over the past week finally make their way to the surface. "I didn't know where else to go."

"Oh, honey." Her voice is calming like ocean waves. Her hands are on my shoulders leading me through the door and to the living room couch. As soon as we sit, she pulls me into her arms and holds me as I cry and cry and cry.

When I finally start to calm down, she pulls back to look at me. "Would you like some tea?"

I nod. While she's gone, I take deep breaths and try to stop my body from shaking. When she comes back with the tea, I take a sip and close my eyes as the warmth seeps through me from the inside out. My shaking slows and I take a normal breath.

"Thanks," I say, opening my eyes to find soft, kind eyes staring back at me.

"Is everything okay?"

I shake my head. "My mom died last week."

Her face drops and she reaches over to grab my hand that began shaking again. "I'm so sorry."

I chew on the inside of my cheek and look down. "And my dad has done nothing but drink since. I have no one to talk to about this—at least, no one that has any idea how to help. I just needed to go somewhere else, talk to someone, and this was the first place I thought of."

Her face softens. "You're welcome here anytime. Just because you're not with my son anymore doesn't mean you can't still be family to me."

My chest tightens at the reminder that he's gone too. My eyes close and I think of the first time he brought me here. When we sat on this couch, side-by-side, so in love we couldn't stop smiling. They told me story after story about his childhood as we went through all the photobooks—like I was the last person who'd ever hear them. Like I was his forever. I was so excited that she could be my mother-in-law; I was excited to be part of her family.

She squeezes my hand. "Well, I can promise to listen and do my best to help if I can—if you want to talk."

So, I tell her everything that's happened, and as I talk, I feel some of the weight lift off my chest. I also realize that there's nothing anyone can do to help me here. The only way to help the situation is to get my dad help, and right now, he doesn't want to help himself. But talking to an adult who has gone through their share of hardships does help.

"Are *you* okay?" she finally asks.

I shrug. "It's harder to watch him do this to himself than it was to be there when she passed. At least with her, it was quick, and I knew she didn't feel any pain at the end. But with him, he's hurting himself and I can't do anything to stop it. My attempts to talk to him haven't gone well. It's like he's a whole different person."

"It sounds like you're doing everything you can, you're trying. That's all we can do for the people we love—keep trying." She reaches out to take my hands in hers. "Maybe one day he'll realize you were trying to help him all along and finally be ready to help himself, or maybe he never will, but you'll know that you didn't give up. But always remember that this is not your fault. There's nothing you could've done to stop it, and it was never your issue to solve. Don't put that burden on yourself."

"This is not your fault."

Those five words are enough to bring tears back to my eyes. Deep inside I've been holding onto the fear that something I did or said caused this. That if I had done one thing differently, we could've avoided this outcome. That my mom would be angry with me for letting him get this bad.

I was mad at myself for it.

"Thank you," I whisper. I needed to hear that.

I check my phone and can't believe how much time has passed. I've already taken up too much of her time; I should be heading out. I glance at the door.

Just before I can speak, she says, "Analise?"

"Yeah?" I turn back, and my eyebrows pull together at her suddenly somber expression.

"Do you know why Todd and I got divorced?"

I blink blankly, where did that come from?

"No," I say. "Just that you were."

"Back in the day, I was an artist—a muralist more specifically," she starts with a smile. "People would hire me to paint murals for business, and even in homes. It didn't make us a lot of money, but I loved my work."

Now that she says it, I can see her as an artist clear as day. She's beautiful but in that carefree, haphazard way of someone who doesn't care about making a mess. I've always admired that about her.

"That was back when we used to live in Boston together," she continues. "But then Todd had the opportunity to take a job in New York. It was a decent promotion, and he was excited about it, so he accepted it. But he accepted it before talking to me. He came to me one day and just said "we're moving" and I had no say in it. He didn't care that my clients were all local and moving would mean I had to stop doing what I loved. I tried to find similar work there, but it was a lot harder, especially being unknown. But I went along with it because Warren was in middle school, and I wanted him to be around both parents."

My eyes grow wide as she speaks, my mouth slowly dropping open. I have a feeling I know where this story is going . . . and why she's telling me it.

"But the longer we stayed there, the more he started acting like his work was all that mattered, and that what I did was a silly hobby. I grew to resent him, for making me give up my work, and for acting like it didn't matter. Things got so bad that we eventually made an agreement that we would stay together until he moved out for college, and only then would we separate. Looking back, it wasn't the best decision, but we didn't want to uproot his whole life—we thought it'd be easier that way. But I don't think we ever stopped to consider how it felt from the other side. We acted like everything was fine for his sake, but I was counting the days until I could leave Todd.

"It must've been jarring to a kid, to have parents who seemed like they were in love for so long to seemingly overnight decide to split." She pauses, a sad smile on her face. "It affected him, and the way he viewed love for a long time. I could see it even if he didn't admit it. Maybe it *still* affects him."

It's a nice thought. That Warren didn't leave because he didn't love me, but because he didn't want to make the same mistake his parents did. But did he ever stop to think that maybe I could grow to resent him for *not* asking me to come with him too?

It's too much—the sliver of hope the story lodges in my heart. Hope only makes this hurt exponentially more. If that was the only reason he left, then why would he continue to stay away? If he felt how I felt, *how* could he continue to stay away?

I smile and stand. "I should get going."

"Of course." Her smile is sorrowful, and it pulls at the makeshift stitches holding my heart together. "Don't ever hesitate to come again."

I hug her, but make no promises, and spend the entire drive

back boarding up the sliver of hope in me—covering the light it cast until only darkness is left. Darkness where he once lived within me. Darkness in the space my mom once occupied. And a dark shadow over who my dad used to be.

When I enter my parents' house the next day, there's only darkness there too. I open the curtains and flick on some lights, freezing in front of a photo of my parents on their wedding day. They looked so happy, so in love.

Is my dad like this because his other half is gone? Is this all that's left of him? Looking at this photo I'm reminded of that polaroid of Warren and I, so in love. And now, in many ways, I feel as empty as my dad is.

When I look at it that way, how can I blame him for acting this way?

I clean up as much as I can, frowning when I find the sandwich and water untouched, but a full glass of liquor that wasn't there yesterday. There's another empty bourbon bottle with the others. I let them pile up—hoping he'll realize one day how excessive this is.

"Did you bring more bourbon?" A voice groans from the couch where he'd been asleep—not even bothering to make it back to his room. It's the first time he's spoken to me in days.

"No."

"Then why the fuck are you here?" He spits the words at me angrily.

I stumble back like I've been slapped or punched in the chest. Tears spring to my eyes. Who is this person?

I don't stick around long after that, but I pray that my dad will come back to me soon.

Thirty-One

I open all of the cupboards in my kitchen and groan at how much crap I've accumulated over the years. Surely, I don't need most of this. Then my eyes land on the shelves where I keep my baking dishes and utensils, and I smile—except those. I definitely need those.

Warren and I picked up some moving boxes last night and I'm starting to go through my stuff and sort it into keep, toss, and give away piles while he's gathering his last items from the hotel and checking out. I won't officially start in D.C. until September, but Warren cancelled his flight home—Peter gave him permission to work out of this office this week—so he can help me pack and move next weekend.

I frown as I turn and look at my furniture. I'm not sure what he has in his place now, so I don't know what else we can fit. I considered getting my own place in the beginning, but I know I wouldn't spend a single night there. It's more economical this way. I smile to myself and let out an actual chuckle at the thought. That's obviously just an excuse because really, I'm just excited to be back by his side again.

There's a knock at my door and my smile grows. Finally—it took him long enough to get back here. I can't do much else without his help anyways.

"You don't have to knoc—" I open the door and the words die in my chest. The brightness I just felt fades, because it's not Warren at the door . . . it's the last person I ever expected to be here.

He stares at me, shifting his weight from leg to leg. There are dark circles under his eyes, his skin looks so pale, and he's skinnier than he's ever been. Skinnier than he should ever be. But at least his hair looks washed and he's in clean clothes—and he doesn't reek of bourbon.

"Dad?" My voice is barely a whisper, barely a breath. I didn't think he knew where I lived. Even though I'd told him I moved, I didn't think he remembered. He never listened to me.

"Hi, Annie," he says, his voice croaking, like he hasn't spoken in years, and my lips start to tremble.

Annie.

He hasn't called me by his childhood nickname for me since my mom was alive. I'm unsteady—legs weak and a tear drops down my face. I just keep blinking. This isn't real, is it?

"Can I come in?" he asks, looking down, unable to meet my eyes.

I'm too shocked by the fact that he's out of his house, let alone here, to question whether it's a good idea or not. I step aside and let him in. He takes a few steps in then stops awkwardly, like he's afraid to intrude on my space. His head moves around as he takes in the space and the boxes strewn about.

"Redecorating?" he asks, his cheeks flushing slightly.

"I'm moving," I say after a moment, and his head whips over to look at me. "I'm going to Washington D.C."

His eyes turn glassy, and a tear drops down his cheek. He shakes his head as he whispers, "I'm so sorry, Analise."

I close my eyes as I rest my hands on the edge of the counter to try to stop the shaking. This is definitely a dream.

"I've done and said some horrible things to you over the past years," he says, and more tears drop down my cheek. I flinch as I remember the cut on my cheek that's healed now but could've been so much worse. "And that's only what I can remember. There's probably so much more I *can't* remember. There are so many holes in my memory, so much lost time. So many things I wish I could go back and change."

I look up at him as silent tears drop down my cheeks. Tears full of anger and resentment. Tears that question how long this version of my dad will last. Tears that want to hope but can't yet.

He takes a step around the island, to comfort me like my old dad would've done, but I move in the opposite direction, keeping us on opposite sides. I'm not ready for that yet.

His body deflates. He looks so tired, so worn down. It's hard to look at the damage he's done to himself—and to us—in the broad daylight.

I can't stand to see the hurt and regret in his eyes—and I feel guilty for thinking he deserves all of it—so I look away.

"I went to an AA meeting last weekend," he says. "I'm going to another one today."

I nod, still looking at a half-packed box of decorations across the room. "That's great."

The silence that descends over us is heavy and uncomfortable —like a cheap, wool blanket that scratches at your skin. The father-daughter bond we once had was severed, and one apology isn't going to be enough to fix it.

He clears his throat, and I slowly look over. He wrings his hands together, scratches his neck, and looks everywhere but at me. "So, when do you leave?"

"Next week."

"Would it—" He swallows and shifts his eyes to meet mine. "Would it be okay if I visited?"

I take a deep breath, looking up to try to stop the burning

sensation building behind my eyes again. "Why don't we see how your meetings go for a bit first?"

He looks down, his face turning red. "Of course."

I don't know what else to say. I hope he does stick with it. I hope he gets sober. I hope we get to a point where he does visit. But I'm not expecting anything. I need proof before I'll open space for him in my life again.

"Well." He tries to smile but the corner of his mouth twitches between a smile and frown. "I'll let you get back to it then."

I nod, and he turns to leave. There's defeat in the way he's holding himself as he slinks to the front door. My chest tightens. I was going to just let him leave, but when his hand grabs the handle, the words leave my mouth before I can stop them.

"Why—" I take a shaky breath, and he stops. "Why now?"

But what I really mean is: *Why not the hundreds of times I tried to help you?* I tried so hard, for so long, but it did nothing. He screamed and yelled and cursed at me. And just as I'm about to move away—and started to feel the smallest bit of relief that I won't be close enough to feel obligated to stop by anymore— that's when he decides to change.

"I'm not sure if any of this actually happened, or if it was just a hallucination, but last week Warren came to visit me." He doesn't turn to look at me, but my eyes immediately go wide.

Last Thursday he was late to work for *personal reasons*—the day after he found out my dad threw that glass at me. Of course, he went to see my dad. How did I not realize that sooner?

"He was furious with me," he continues. "He said something about how I hurt you. That I was lucky it wasn't a more serious injury. He told me that if I ever hurt you again, he wouldn't hesitate to call the cops and have me locked up."

Warren must've restrained himself a lot—to be there and not lay a single hand on him. To not say he'd kill him if he hurt me again. Because I know for a fact that's what he wanted to do.

"When he left, I figured one of two things had to be true. Either I actually hurt you and that was real, or I was dying, and it was just a hallucination." His voice cracks, and tears stream down both of our faces. "And in that moment, I prayed I *was* dying. Because having to deal with the reality that I might've truly done those things to you"—he shakes his head and the next words barely make it to my ears—"was too much to bear."

I expect him to keep talking, but he goes silent, his body rigid. and after a time, I realize he wants to know. He wants me to tell him if he truly hurt me—if he threw that glass. My stomach turns and I feel sick knowing he could do all these things to me and just simply forget them when the sight of him lifeless on the couch, the anger in his eyes when he yelled at me, and the sting of the cut are engraved in my memory. I'm the one who had to deal with this for five years, yet *he* gets to forget.

"It actually happened," I say, my voice shaking and barely more than a whisper, and it sends shockwaves through his body. I hear gasps of him trying to catch his breath, trying to breathe after getting hit by the truth.

"I'm sorry," he squeaks, and then he opens the door and is gone.

I drop to the floor where I stand, pulling my knees into my chest, and cry.

I don't know how long I stay like that before the door opens again.

"An—" Warren's words stop the moment he spots me. "What happened?"

He's beside me in a moment, arms wrapping around my shoulders and pulling me into his chest. I release my legs and wrap my arms around his waist. His hand runs through my hair and down my back in soothing strokes.

"You . . . went to . . . see my . . . dad," I eventually get out as my tears slow and I finally start to catch my breath.

His hand freezes its movement at my words but quickly continues. In a soothing, apologetic voice, he says, "I'm sorry. I should've told you. I—"

"Thank you," I whisper and squeeze him tight. His body relaxes with my words.

"What happened?" he asks again.

"He's trying to get sober," I say, a smile tugging at my lips. "I'm trying to keep my expectations low, but it's the first attempt he's made since she died. He's trying; he's *finally* trying."

He lets out a breath of relief and kisses the top of my head. "I'm so glad to hear that. I want your life to be full of nothing but sunshine."

"You're still my sun." I pull back and smile at him.

"And you're still my summer." He lifts his hand to my cheek, and I lean into the touch.

"Summer is nothing without her sun," I say, leaning closer to him.

Just before our lips touch, he says, "It's *me* who's nothing without *you*, Analise," then presses his lips against mine. And I feel it this time—in the way he kisses me, in the way he pulls me close, in the way he looks at me—the unwavering promise of forever.

Thirty-Two

SEPTEMBER CURRENT DAY (MONDAY)

I look out of the wall of windows behind my desk and gulp. I grip the arms of my chair tight to keep them from shaking but my breathing picks up. Instead of the incredible view, I see my body falling through the glass and plummeting towards the ground. Why did we have to be on such a high floor in this building?

My eyes close and I turn my chair around. Slowly, I open them and try to convince my body that this office is actually on the ground floor. But the height is quickly forgotten when the man leaning against the doorframe comes into focus.

I take in all six feet of him. His suit jacket is off and the muscles in his arms ripple against the thin button up shirt. His honey-colored hair is perfectly in place—I want to run my hands through it and mess it up. His freckles aren't as prominent because of how much sun his face has gotten lately, but up close they're still there, in all their perfect chaos. His butterscotch eyes shine bright, with more love than I thought was possible—it steals the breath from my lungs.

"Come here often?" he says, his lips pulling up into a smirk.

I smile, fighting a laugh and say, with a shrug, "I'm new to town and this place came highly recommended so I thought I'd check it out."

"And what do you think so far?" He steps into my office, and my heart pounds in time with each step he takes.

"It's a little too far off the ground for my tastes, but the people are great so far." I smile when he chuckles; the sound still coats me like liquid sunshine—warm and bright. "But ask me again in a few weeks, my mind might change by then."

"About the height, or the people?" He's only a few steps away now, and I stand, ignoring the question.

"What about you, is this a favorite spot of yours?"

"It is now," he says, stopping right in front of me and holding out his hand. "Warren Mitchell."

"Analise Summers." I smile as I take his hand. "Looks like I'll be your new neighbor."

He tugs me closer and wraps an arm around my waist. In a voice that sends a shiver down my back, he says, "And what if I want to be more than just your neighbor?"

"Oh no." I push against his chest and take a step away. "We said we could be professional at work. It's day one and you're already suggesting office sex."

His eyes light up and his smile turns wicked. "Oh, Analise." My eyes close at the way he says my name. "*I* didn't say anything about office sex. Once again it's *you* who can't stop thinking about it."

My eyes fly open. *Damn him.* How does he always do this to me?

"I hate you," I grumble.

"You love me." He grins and the corners of my frown twitch up.

"I love you *and* I hate you."

"That I can deal with," he says, moving closer and leaning in until his lips are at my ear. "Hate sex is hot."

"Keep this up and you're sleeping on the couch tonight." It comes out shaky and I feel his smile grow.

"You don't want to do that." His voice is pure sin. We're playing with fire here, but as much as I love it, I won't let us mess up on the first day. No matter how tempting he is.

"And why's that?"

"Because I think you're going to enjoy what I have planned for you tonight." He runs his hand down my back as he says it and I suck in a breath.

"You better leave before you get me in trouble on my first day." My voice is nothing but a breathy whisper.

"I think your boss would be forgiving this once . . ." His lips press against my jawline, and I laugh.

"*My* boss isn't the one I'm worried about, I've heard he can be bribed easily," I tease. "But I promised my boss's boss."

He groans, but when he pulls back there's a smile on his face. "How about a kiss to get me through the day?"

"Now *that's* something I will gladly agree to." His lips press against mine and I sigh. "I'll see you later."

As he's walking towards the door, Peter enters and presses his lips together as he looks between us. Warren smiles at him then leaves so fast you'd think he was late for something. Peter watches him go then turns to me with an expression that says he's trying to be tough, but there's amusement in his eyes and a smile pulling at his lips.

"I'm going to regret this decision, aren't I?" he teases, a full smile growing on his face.

"Oh, absolutely," I say, and we both laugh.

It wasn't until I moved here last week that I realized how close Warren and Peter actually are. Outside of work, they're best friends. It didn't take long for me to realize Peter was the one who suggested Warren start going to therapy. Even though he didn't know everything prior to coming to Hartford, he knew enough to piece together what was happening and who I was to

Warren. And he felt no shame stepping in at times to push us together.

In the past week, we've seen him and Mac many times. I'm not worried about him misinterpreting my humor anymore, and I understand his better now—he's even more relaxed here than he was in Hartford. It's nice to have real friends from the start.

"You guys still good for dinner tonight?" he asks. As much as we can pretend it's a dinner to celebrate my first day of work here, it's really just another double-date night.

I smile and nod. "We'll be there."

At the end of the day, Warren stops by my office, and we head home together.

"I hope my boss thinks I did a good job on my first day." I bump my shoulder into his on the walk.

He grins at me. "You know, he actually asked if I could tell you to tone it down a bit. If you were that impressive on day one, soon he'll be reporting to you."

I laugh. "I've heard he has quite the fetish for bossy women, he might like it if that happened."

He grabs my arm and pulls me off to the edge of the sidewalk, kissing me the way he can't at work—long, slow, and deep.

"You might be onto something," he whispers against my lips. "Do you think there's time for me to take you home before dinner?"

I check the time and even though there's not a lot of it, I say, "If we run."

His face lights up like the sun—*my sun*—and I almost can't believe the last month was real. That he came back to Hartford, that we mended this relationship, that we're both still so in love with each other, that I now live with him in D.C. Everything finally feels exactly how it's supposed to be.

Ali, Trent, Sterling, and Will are all coming to visit at the end of the month and we're obviously still planning to go back to Hartford for Sterling and Will's wedding in November.

For the first time, I don't feel like I have to give up anything —Warren, my friends, my career, or even my dad. So far, he's kept up with his meetings and is getting close to one month sober. That relationship is slowly re-building, but I'm trying to give him a chance. When we go back to Hartford we plan to see him, but I haven't invited him out here just yet. Maybe for the holidays if all goes well up to then.

Warren grabs my hand and starts running back to our place, even picking me up and carrying me when I can't keep up in my heels. We laugh and smile as we maneuver through the streets of our new city, our new home.

He's still carrying me as we step through the door of our place. "Welcome home, Miss Summers."

"Keep this up and you might get promoted to Mr. Summers." I pull his lips to mine.

"What am I now?" he asks between kisses.

"The sun, obviously," I say against his lips, and smile at the laugh it pulls from him.

"No." He pulls back, shaking his head. "I'm *your* sun."

"Summer and her sun." I point between us with a bright smile on my face and the love that washes over his features steals the breath from my lungs.

"Exactly," he whispers. Then his lips crash into mine and there are no more words shared between us other than *"I love you."*

Acknowledgments

There's no other place to start this than with my family. The way you all so fiercely and continuously support me in this adventure reminds me daily how lucky I am. Whether it's my immediate family, extended family, or found family (friends), I see you all show up for me time and time again and I could fill pages and pages just trying to thank you. I'm a big believer that the people we surround ourselves with are reflections of our own selves and I sure hope that's true because I'm surrounded by some incredible people.

But as grateful as I am that my parents always want to be the first to read my books (even when said books contain spicy scenes that no child wants their parents to read), I would like to humbly request of my entire family that any sex scenes in my books be considered banned topics at any family events. Please and thank you.

This book was easier for me to write than You Light Me Up in some ways, and much harder in others. While it wasn't as emotionally personal to me as You Light Me Up was, Analise works in the same field I do, and even in a niche topic within that field that I've spent a lot of my career in (my mantra at work has become *"What would Analise do?"*). I really wanted to write a strong female character in a male-dominated STEM field but with that comes the challenge of addressing some of the discrimination that still unfortunately happens. I've been blessed enough to have bosses and colleagues that are more like Peter and Warren than like Jason or some of Analise's previous coworkers but adding in Jason's blatant sexism as well as some of the less obvious acts of discrimination was important to me. As was showing Warren as a supportive partner who encouraged Analise to never let their words lessen her strength. Every strong woman deserves a secure partner boosting her up and cheering her on.

To the author and reader community who have embraced me and my books with open arms, I'm always inspired by the love, support, and friendship you've shown not only me but everyone in this genre. I'm so grateful that we can all look around and see friends instead of competition. I will forever cherish the connections I've made because of writing and the readers who surprise me daily by picking up my books. Every purchase, page read, message, or post about my book makes me feel like the luckiest person on the planet. Success was never about the numbers for me, I only hope I can make people feel as seen with my words as my favorite authors have made me feel.

To my wonderful editor Caitlin, you are still one of the sweetest humans I know and I'm so grateful I got to work with you again on this project. Your comments, voice memos, and overall love for this story were exactly what I needed to make this book everything it could be. I can't wait to work together again!

And of course, to MiblArt who designed another stunning cover. How they took the stick figure drawing of my idea and turned it into this masterpiece is beyond me, but I'm so grateful for their collaboration!

Thank you. For reading. For supporting me. For allowing me the opportunity to live out my dreams.

This is still only the beginning, so I hope you're ready for a lot more to come.

About the Author

Brooke Noel is a romance and fantasy writer by night and an actuary by day. She is a proud woman in STEM, which is why it's a common trope in her writing. After growing up in Central Florida, she moved cross-country to Southern California, where she currently resides. You Light Me Up was her debut novel. You can find her on Instagram @brookenoelauthor or at her website brooke-noel.com.

Also by Brooke Noel

You Light Me Up